I0614890

THREE BODY PROBLEMS

STAR CITY STORIES
FEATURING FRANK SLADEK, P.I.

BY GREG FOWLKES

Includes previews from the book

The Blood Red Sands of Mars:
Book One from the Murder on Mars Series

THREE BODY PROBLEMS

© 2020 The Fictional Press
www.TheFictionalPress.com

All rights reserved. No part of this book may be used or reproduced in any manner without written permission except for brief quotations for review purposes.

The Fictional Press is a small, independent press specializing in the publication of fictional works by emerging authors. If you are interested in bringing your fictional works to life in print as well as electronically, contact us! We can help!

www.TheFictionalPress.com

ISBN 13: 978-1-943403-50-9

Printed in the United States of America

BOOKS BY GREG FOWLKES

From the Wizard at Law Series:
The Laws of Magic
Trial by Magic

From the Murder on Mars Series:
Blood Red Sands of Mars
A Death at Station Alpha
A Corpse in Hut Town
Murder at the Mars Club

From the Fictional Detective Series:
The Fictional Detective
A Fictional Detective Trifecta

Star City Stories: Space Opera Noir Featuring Frank Sladek

The Uncorrupted Corpse

Tequila Visions

Cargo From Paradise

Ice Viking

TABLE OF
CONTENTS

PROLOGUE..1

THE BODY WITH FOUR ARMS......................3

THE BODY THAT WASN'T...........................79

THE BODY OF AN OLD FRIEND..............131

AUTHOR'S AFTERWORD............................203

THE BLOOD RED SANDS OF MARS.......205

PROLOGUE

In celestial mechanics there is no exact solution to the problem of calculating the orbits of three bodies circling each other. I have another sort of problem that also involves three bodies, which is how to deal with them without in the process joining them, i.e. ending up dead.

My name is Frank Sladek. I'm a private investigator on Star City, a hollowed out asteroid orbiting a brown dwarf, or, as we locals like to say, a failed planet circling a star that never made it to the big time. It's in the middle of nowhere, but being in the middle of nowhere is the same thing as being in the middle of everywhere. This makes Star City the major transit hub for that irregular patch of space known as the sphere of human influence, the perfect place for passengers to make connections between the great starliners. Sooner or later, everyone traveling beyond the confines of their own star system must pass through Star City to do so.

There are some two million people, along with fifty thousand or so aliens, that live on the inside of a rock cylinder fifteen kilometers long and three kilometers across. Star City is a busy place with all sorts of attractions to keep the travelers amused. But along with these travelers come those who prey on them, the low-lifes, the pickpockets, the two-bit grifters and other criminal types working to part the honest people, and some of the not so honest, from their hard earned money. Sometimes, in the process, things get messy and people end up dead.

That's where I come in. I'm the guy that gets called in to clean up the messes. One way or another.

THE BODY WITH FOUR ARMS

THE BODY WITH FOUR ARMS

I was in the Blue Moon trying to decide whether to have another drink when the call came in. It was late at night long after the after work crowd had gone home and there were only a few people left in the bar.

Normally I don't do my late night drinking in bars, preferring the peace and quiet of my apartment, but I'd been working and felt the need. I'd been hired by the wife of the manager of one of the big hotels to find out why he'd been spending nights out and withdrawing money from their accounts.

I had tracked the husband to an uptown bar of the sort the tourists and travelers go to when they want to say they've seen the wild side of Star City. It wasn't what you'd call rough, just noisy and crowded. My target and a half-dozen other business types had sequestered themselves in a back room, and I'd spent four hours sitting at the bar drinking seltzer water on the rocks, waiting for them to come out.

The bartender had given me dirty looks until I'd slipped him a Crockett sawbuck. After that he started getting creative by sticking little umbrellas and fruit into my seltzer and serving it in various fancy glasses. I think he found that amusing. I didn't care because I was able to milk him for the information that the boys in the back room had a standing game of eight card Crockett Holdup going once a week. The game was friendly and closed and the stakes were modest. The only woman in the room was Mavis, the dealer, who was in her fifties and had a face that looked like it had been used to launch a starliner.

The game had broken up around midnight, and I had followed my mark as he went straight home. It had been an easy night's work, but boring, which was why I was in the Blue Moon at that hour having a drink. I felt that I had earned it.

The call, when it came in on my comm was from Vel Lindol, who ran a catering and event staging business. I'd done work for him off and on in the past, vetting employees and investigating when supplies had gone missing. We weren't really friends, but we had a cordial business relationship, which was why I answered the call when I saw who it was from.

Vel sounded rattled, which for him was unusual. In his line of work, maintaining your composure was a necessity.

"Frank, I need your help."

"It's late, Vel. Can this wait until morning?"

"No, it really can't. Can you come over to the office?"

"Now? I was about to go to bed. What's this about, Vel?"

"I can't explain over the comm. I need to talk to you in person."

This also was unlike Vel. Normally, he was pretty open about things. I had a feeling that whatever was bugging him must be serious.

"Okay. I'll be there in half an hour or so."

"Thanks, Frank. I appreciate it. I'll leave the side door open."

Vel's catering office was in a converted warehouse down city on the fringe of the industrial zone. I took the down West tram and walked the rest of the way. It was a nice night, but then, living on the inside of a hollowed out asteroid circling a brown dwarf, every night is pretty much the same, except once a week when they turn the sprinklers on to wash down the streets. Then it rains for half an hour between two and two-thirty.

The side door was open, just as Vel had said, so I let myself in. Inside, I called out "Hello," but didn't get an answer. I'd been there enough time before so that I knew my way around. I figured that Vel would be in his office which was on the second floor. I was almost right. When I found him, he was standing just outside his office looking like he'd seen a ghost.

"What's up?" I said.

"Thank goodness you're here, Frank."

"Okay, I get that. What is so important that I'm not getting my beauty sleep."

"It's in there," Vel said, pointing to his office. Vel isn't usually mysterious, either.

I pushed past him into the office. He'd turned on the overhead lights, so I had no trouble seeing. What I saw was a pair of feet projecting out from behind his desk. They were unusually large feet. Star City gets people from all over, so one gets used to odd fashions, but the "shoes" on the feet were decidedly odd.

From the fact that the feet hadn't moved I assumed that the body they were attached to was either unconscious or dead.

"Who is it?" I asked. Maybe not particularly original or brilliant, but to the point.

"I haven't got a clue. I've never seen it before in my life."

"It?"

"Take a closer look, Frank," Vel said. He was a little calmer now.

I went around so that I could see behind the desk. I saw what Vel meant. The corpse wasn't human. Oh, it was vaguely humanoid in shape if you discounted the four arms, but it was definitely not human. It was definitely a corpse, though. There was a big chef's knife sticking out of the chest and quite a bit of something blue was pooling underneath the body.

"Did you kill him, Vel?"

Vel seemed startled by the question. "No, why would I do that? I've got no idea who or what he is. I just found him like that." He was starting to get worked up again.

"Calm down. Look, why don't you start from the beginning?"

"There's not much to tell, Frank. I was catering an event at the Museum tonight. Some fund raiser. That got done around eleven. We packed up and brought the equipment and left over food and booze here. After everything was unloaded, I sent everyone home and came up here to check up on a couple of invoices. That's when I found the body."

"Had anyone been here during the event?"

"No. Everybody was working at the museum."

"And there wasn't any sign of a break in?"

"If there was, I didn't notice. We came in by the big doors in the front."

"I didn't see anything by the side door, but I can check that later. And you don't have any idea who our friend is?"

"No. I was hoping you might."

I took another look at the corpse. It looked to be just under two meters tall, thin, and bilateral, by which I mean the legs and arms were paired, one and each side, just like a human, except this guy had two pairs of arms, a longer, upper pair coming out of the shoulder area and a shorter pair sprouting maybe halfway between the shoulders and the waist. Each hand had three fingers and an opposable thumb, though the thumbs were on the outside rather than the inside of the hands.

It's always hard to read alien expressions, but the face was frozen in what looked like horror, probably because the owner realized that his blue stuff was bleeding out of him. The face wasn't that odd. There was a mouth, two eyes, and something that wasn't quite a nose. There was an ear on each side of the head. They were placed a little higher than on a human and the flaps looked like they had been more mobile in life, but they were recognizably ears. The head, and for that matter what I could see of the body, was hairless. The skin was a mottled mixture of blues and green, not unattractive, but not like a human's, not even a blue-skin.

In addition to the "shoes" the corpse was wearing a kilt like skirt that reached just below the knees and a loose sleeveless shirt in a bright yellow that had a slit on each side running from the upper to the lower arm.

"You ever seen anything like him, Frank?"

"Can't say that I have. There's a bartender at Vik's that has four arms. He can make some interesting cocktails, but he doesn't look to be the same species at all."

Most of the two million or so inhabitants of Star City are humans, but there are a few aliens, maybe fifty thousand or so, plus some genetically modified humans like the blue-skins. Most of the aliens come from a few species whose territories abut human space like the like lizard men, but sometimes the odd member of a lesser known species does make it to the city, either as a transient or as a permanent resident. The corpse on the floor was definitely not of a species I'd seen before.

"What am I going to do, Frank?" Vel pleaded.

"As I see it, you got two choices. You can call the police and try and explain the situation, or you can try to get rid of the body in a way that won't be traced back to you."

"Isn't there anything else?"

"Well, I suppose you could just leave it lying there, but I have a feeling that sooner or later someone would notice."

"This is no time to be joking around, Frank. This is serious. I can't go to the police. My reputation would be ruined. Besides, they'd tie me up with questioning, maybe seal up the place as a crime scene for who knows how long. I've got a dozen events scheduled in the next two weeks worth over two hundred thousand credits. I've already ordered food and supplies. I can't afford to lose that business."

"So we get rid of the body, and just hope we don't get caught doing it," I said. I wasn't convinced that that was the best solution, but I was willing to let Vel make the choice.

"I knew I could count on you, Frank," Vel said. "So how do we do it."

"Well, one thing is clear, we can't just pick it up and dump it in the street somewhere. There are too many security cameras scattered around. Let me think for a minute."

How does one get rid of a body, human or otherwise, anyway? Cutting it up and dumping it down the sewer sounded both messy and time consuming. It would be far better to stash the body someplace where it wouldn't be found for a long time, but on Star City that would be hard to do.

"You keep supplies in cold storage don't you? I mean off-site?"

"Sure," Vel replied. "Meat and things like that. Stuff that is brought in by starliner. Sometimes we get a big shipment in and break it down here into smaller lots just big enough for one event. Then we store it in one of the specialty warehouses until we need it."

"You wouldn't happen to have one of those containers laying around, would you. One big enough for our friend here?"

"I don't know. I'd have to check."

"Well, do it. Now."

Vel went around the desk, stepping gingerly over the corpse so he could get at the comp. on his desk. He played around looking at his inventory for a couple of minutes.

"Yeah, I think I've got one down in the kitchen. It held some steaks from Nebraska. We used most of them for the dinner at the Museum tonight. It's about a meter square. Will that do?"

"Depends on if this fellow folds nicely, but it's worth a shot. You've got an elevator, don't you? I don't fancy carrying our friend here down the stairs."

"Yeah."

"On second thought, maybe it would be better if we brought the container up here. We don't want to spread any more of that blue blood around than necessary."

It took us ten minutes to empty the container of what was left of its contents and maneuver it up to the office. Fortunately, Vel had one of those little levitation sleds which made moving the container a lot easier. Along the way, he grabbed a couple of bunny suits, too. No sense getting blue gunk on our clothes.

It took a lot longer to stuff the corpse in the container. It bent, alright, but not always at convenient points. The container opened from the front, and as we tried to get the body in one or more of the six limbs kept flopping out. It took us three tries before we managed to get it all in so that we could shut the door. We both had worked up a sweat by the time we were done and despite our best efforts, some of the blue stuff had gotten on us. Fortunately, the bunny suits were disposable.

The container had been designed for use in deep space and was insulated and air-tight. I didn't know how quickly the alien would decompose, but if the box was in cold storage, it might be a long time before anyone noticed. I helped Vel move it back downstairs and into the freezer.

"Frank, we can't leave it there. Sooner or later one of the kitchen staff is going to notice and wonder what's inside."

"Leave that to me, Vel. I'm going home, take a shower, and then sleep for a dozen hours."

"What about my office? There's still that blue blood on the floor."

We ended up spending another half hour cleaning up the mess upstairs. It was a good thing that Vel had never splurged for carpeting. It was nearly four by the time we finished. I was bone tired, but hungry, too. So was Vel. He whipped up a couple of omelets down in the kitchen. Vel's a pretty good cook, which was how he got into the catering business in the first place.

By the time I got home to my apartment across from the Blue Moon they were just turning up the glow tubes on the central spine that runs down the center of Star City to mark the dawn of a new day.

I slept past noon. When I woke up, I called my client, the woman whose husband I'd been tailing, and informed her of what I'd found. She seemed vaguely disappointed and decided not to continue the surveillance. After she had transferred the agreed upon number of credits to my account, I was unemployed and hungry.

On the corner of the block where my apartment building sits there's a little corner diner. It serves typical Star City food, the kind I'd grown up on and not what the tourists eat at the better hotels, which means that it's vat grown at the down end of the city and comes in a variety of colors, mostly brown, beige, and faintly pink. I admit that it's nothing like the omelet that Vel had made me, but for me it's comfort food, just like I got when I was a kid, that is when we had enough money to eat. I ordered a slab of brown "meat" covered with gravy and mashed starch.

As I ate, I wondered what I was going to do with the crate sitting in Vel's freezer. It couldn't stay there forever, but we couldn't just take it and drop it somewhere and hope no one would find it. Every crate, box, and barrel coming into Star City has an ID number printed on its side along with a matching ID chip for the convenience of the robots that do most of the shuffling around of cargo. It's all part of a system where every item of cargo is registered with central data to prevent loss or rerouting errors. The chips can't be altered, and a container where the chip and ID number didn't match would raise a red flag with the authorities, which was the last thing we wanted. What we needed to do was create a fake data trail for the container with the four armed corpse, one that couldn't be traced back to Vel.

I'm okay with a comp, and I've been known to poke my nose into databases where I shouldn't, but this was beyond my skill set. I needed to find an expert. Fortunately, I knew just the guy.

I'm pretty sure that Larry Bit Basher isn't his real name, but that's what everyone calls him, at least those that make use of his professional services. He probably has a real life somewhere on Star City, but I'm sure there is nothing tying it to "Larry."

He doesn't have an office, but then, I don't either. Mostly I conduct business out of a booth in the Blue Moon. Larry prefers to work from outdoor cafes where he drinks endless cups of Joe and subsists on sweet pastries. He shifts location according to some algorithm that appears to be random but probably isn't. It makes him a little hard to find, which is the whole idea. It took me an hour and four tram rides to find Larry, but then I'm a trained detective.

Larry is kind of nondescript. He's closer to forty than thirty, medium height and slightly pudgy which isn't surprising considering his diet. His hair is that color that some people call sandy but which is really just light brown. He tends to favor the kind of clothes that you imagine accountants wearing on their days off. How much of that is just a front and how much reflects the inner Larry I don't know.

He spotted me as I approached his table and gave me a faint smile. "Sladek, have a seat."

I took the offered chair and tried to get the waiter's attention. He came over and I ordered a cup of Joe, and for good measure, one of the pastries that Larry had sitting on a plate next to his tablet. As far as any bystanders might observe, we were two accountants on our day off who happen to have run into each other by chance. It was done according to the rules of the game Larry played. I didn't object; I didn't want to attract attention any more than Larry did.

He waited a suitable interval after my Joe had arrived before getting down to business.

"So, what do you need, Sladek?"

"I've got a container I want to bury."

If he was surprised, he didn't show it. Larry never looks surprised.

"What's in the box?" he asked.

"Meat," I answered.

"Meat?"

"Bad meat," I replied.

"Like that, is it?"

"Pretty much," I said with a shrug. Larry just blinked. He was used to requests like mine. That was his business. The less he knew about the details, the better he liked it.

"And what exactly do you want done with this container of meat?"

"I'd like it to go someplace where no one is going to come looking for it. Preferably for a really long time. And I need to eliminate any links to the current owner."

"Off Star City?"

"No, I'd like to keep this local. Fewer problems that way." I'd thought about sending the crate off on some starliner, but the problem with that was that there was a chance that customs at the far end might open the container up on arrival which would be embarrassing. It would be a lot better to just bury it in the back of some warehouse on Star City.

"Anything else?"

"The meat is frozen at the moment. It would probably be best if it stayed that way."

"That's a little trickier, Sladek. There aren't that many cold storage facilities on Star City."

"I have faith in you, Larry."

"And how much is it worth to you, Sladek?"

"My client is willing to pay a reasonable rerouting fee."

"Five hundred? Crockett?"

"That sounds reasonable."

"In advance?"

"I'm sitting right here, Larry. I'll transfer the money as soon as your done. Or you can do it yourself. You probably know my account."

Larry laughed. "That's what I like about you, Sladek. You understand how the game is played. No bullshit. No nickel and dime stuff."

"We're both professionals, Larry. Just different professions."

"So what's the box number?"

I pulled out my comm and showed him an image I'd taken of the side of the container with the ID number.

"You could have had better lighting, Frank."

"You can read it, can't you? I didn't know esthetics mattered."

"You should take pride in your work. That's all I'm saying. Give me a few minutes."

I sat there drinking my Joe and eating the pastry while Larry did his thing with his comp tablet. The Joe was passable and the pastry wasn't bad. A steady stream of young women tramped by on the sidewalk out front. There were worse ways to spend an afternoon. After ten or so minutes Larry looked up to get my attention.

"Okay, here's the deal. This evening a robot carrier will pick up the crate at Lindol's Catering and take it to Star City Cold Storage. That's the company that they always use. Two hours later, another robot will pick it up and transfer it to Interspace's freezer warehouse. En route, the record of it belonging to Lindol will disappear and be replaced by one indicating that it belongs to the Rigel Royal." The Rigel Royal was one of the larger hotels. "Their inventory will be adjusted to reflect this."

"Won't that trigger suspicion?"

"The Rigel Royal has hundreds of containers at the warehouse. The accounting department doesn't keep track of how many carrots the kitchen orders. All they care about is that the numbers balance. As for the kitchen, if no one ordered the container, no one is going to check on it. It's possible that an audit might find it, but probably not, if all the invoices are in order. Which they are."

"You're a genius, Larry."

"You're probably right."

"Go ahead and transfer the credits."

"I already have, Frank."

I finished my Joe and said good-bye to Larry.

After that I gave Vel a call. He seemed relieved that the crate would be off his hands. He hadn't balked when I said that it would cost him six hundred dollars Crockett. I figured that he owed me at least a hundred for my services and lost sleep.

A robot came and picked up the crate right on schedule, and a few hours later it was out of Vel's hair forever. Mine, too. Or so I thought.

A few days later I got a text message on my comm. It was just after eleven in the morning. It was from someone named Grot Fender. I didn't recognize the name, but that wasn't unusual. Many of my clients are referred to me by word of mouth by former clients. I don't advertise much. It's safer that way.

The message asked if I would be available to meet for lunch to discuss the possibility of hiring me. I did a quick search on the name Grot Fender which came up blank except for the fact that Fender had arrived on a starliner from Crockett two days earlier. That didn't mean much. Crockett was the second most populous planet in human space and lots of the liners coming from that general direction made stops there on the way to Star City.

I wasn't working on anything else, so I sent an acknowledgement. At the least I'd get a free lunch out of the meeting.

The meeting was at the Grill Room of the Rigel Royal. There wasn't anything unusual about that. It was one of the biggest hotels, one favored by businessmen arriving on starliners, especially those with expense accounts. I spruced myself up and caught a tram headed uptown.

The Grill room at the Rigel Royal isn't as pricey as the roof top restaurant at the Casino, but it's not a corner diner, either. It's dark, quiet, and discrete. The wait staff are professional rather than obsequious, the food good rather than flashy or ostentatious.   It's just the type of place business men go to to conduct business.

The maitre d' gave me a look that indicated he thought that I'd be happier at the coffee shop in the lower level, but when I mentioned Grot Fender's name he smiled and said "Come this way, Mr. Sladek."

Fender rose as I approached the table and gave me the kind of smile that only someone in the diplomatic corps uses.

"It's so good of you to come, Mr. Sladek."

"My pleasure, Ms. Fender."

I hadn't been expecting a woman, but then I had had only the name to go on, and it's always hard to tell gender from names which have evolved so many local variations. It wasn't hard to place where Ms. Fender came from, though, and it wasn't one of the backwater systems. She was wearing the kind of dress you just can't by off the rack on a place like Nebraska. It was conservative in cut and color, but perfectly fit her figure like the proverbial glove, just the sort of thing a professional woman from Crockett or Terra would wear to a business meeting. She had one of those sophisticated hairstyles that trend in and out quicker than most governments, long, almost shoulder length on one side and cut short to the chin on the other, shading smoothly across a spectrum from auburn to blonde. It looked good on her, too, but then almost anything would. She was at that age, I judged her to be in her early thirties, when beauty came naturally rather than from artifice.

"Why don't we order, then we can discuss our business while we wait to be served."

"That suits me."

As I looked over the menu, I was glad that Fender would be picking up the check. At least I assumed he would. When the waiter came, I ordered a small beef steak and a green salad. The menu assured me that the beef was corn fed and came only from the planet Nebraska, which is known for its beef and not much else. Fender ordered some sort of fish, from Montego I think. I have to admit the thought of enough water that creatures could swim around in it gives me the willies, but then the thought of looking up and seeing sky rather than the other side of Star City I find just as disconcerting.

After the waiter left, I said, "Okay, Ms. Fender. Having lunch is great and all, but just who are you?"

"Do you always ask such pointed questions of potential clients, Mr. Sladek?"

"I find it saves me a lot of grief in the long run. I like to know who I'm working for and why."

"Fair enough. You've probably guessed that I'm from Terra, at least if you're half as good as your reputation."

"I am, or you wouldn't have asked me to lunch."

"I work for the government there, the Department of Exorelations."

That surprised me a little, not so much that she worked for a government agency, but that she had been sent as far as Star City on an assignment. Usually that would be reserved for someone with more seniority.

"You've come a long way, then, Ms. Fender."

She seemed to have read my mind. "You mean for someone so young, don't you, Mr. Sladek? Well, to be honest, my mission was supposed to be a very simple one. I was to be an escort from here to Terra. The matter is of a sensitive nature and it was felt that a more junior person would attract less attention."

"You said 'suppose to be.' I take it you've lost something, Ms. Fender?"

"Yes, or rather a person. More or less."

"More or less?"

"Well, technically, the person isn't human." Fender looked to see how I reacted. I'm not one of those people who will say "some of my best friends are aliens" but I don't have a problem with them, either. Mostly.

"Just what kind of non-human."

"That's a bit difficult to say. You wouldn't recognize the species name even if I could pronounce it. They've actually only come in contact with humans very recently. The individual in question is coming as an emissary. I was supposed to meet him at Star City and escort him to Crockett and then on to Terra. Unfortunately, my ship was delayed. When I arrived I discovered the individual had vanished."

"But he had arrived? On Star City, I mean?"

"Oh, yes. That much has been established."

"But you can't find him? Or it? Or whatever?"

"No. I've consulted with the authorities, but they have been unable to help. A Lieutenant Latimer has been assigned to the case, if you know him."

"Oh, I know him alright." Ms. Fender raised an eyebrow, but didn't press for details. I didn't offer any, but stuck to business. "Could you describe this individual to me?"

"I can do better than that, Mr. Sladek, I can show you an image."

She reached into her jacket pocket and brought out a comm unit. At least I think it was a comm. It wasn't local technology. It had a screen, though, a very good one. I could see the image of an alien, one with four arms and mottled blue-green skin.

"You looked disconcerted, Mr. Sladek. Perhaps you recognize the individual?"

"No. It's just the four arms. You don't see that much around here. There's a bartender at one of the local clubs with four arms, but he doesn't look much like this guy. The bartender has got three eyes."

I'm not sure, but it's possible she thought I was joking. I wasn't in a joking mood. I didn't have any doubts that the image was that of the alien Vel had found in his office, the one I'd put in cold storage.

"Just what is it you want me to do, Ms. Fender? Do you want me to find this alien, or do you just want me to find out what happened to him?"

"The former, preferably, but the latter, in any case. I'll be frank, Mr. Sladek, I'm in something of a bind. This is my first official assignment off of Terra, and if I fail it will be the end of my career. I've worked very hard to get where I am and I don't want to risk that."

This is the point where most young women would be breaking down in tears looking for sympathy. Ms. Fender didn't show any signs of breaking down. I admired her for that.

"I guess I could say that I'll be Frank, because that happens to be my name, but that's kind of a corny joke. It might make it easier, though, if we're going to be working together if you called me Frank, rather than Mr. Sladek, and I call you Grot."

"Grot." She pronounced the "o" has sort of halfway between an "o" and a "u."

"Grot," I corrected myself. She smiled.

"Why don't you start at the beginning?"

"What do you mean?"

"Like where this alien was coming from and how he got here. By the way, does he have a name? It seems a little impersonal to keep calling him 'the alien'."

"Mr. Smith. John Smith."

"Excuse me?"

"I'm afraid you might have some difficulty pronouncing his name. I know I did. He was traveling under the name 'John Smith.' My department had issued him travel documents under that name."

That wasn't that unusual an occurrence. Many of the aliens humans had run into spoke languages that were hard for humans to handle, when they had languages at all. It worked the other way, as well. They often assumed human names to use in their interactions with humans. John Smith did show a certain lack of creativity, though.

"And where was this John Smith coming from?"

"His species' home system is some fifty light-years beyond the boundary of human space roughly in the direction of the Lizardmen. They've only become aware of the existence of humanity in the last few years. They appear to want to use us as a counterbalance against their neighbors."

"Which include the Lizardmen?"

"Among others, yes. Why do you ask?"

Lizardmen had been traveling between stars back when humans were still pounding rocks together to make fire. They were expansionist, but because they had a low birthrate they tended to view things in longer timeframes than humans. They weren't a military threat, war between star systems had proved largely impractical, but there were the occasional frictions with humanity. There was also a reasonable amount of trade between the two species, especially where they overlapped.

"If something has happened to Mr. Smith, I need to know who the possible players are."

"This isn't a game, Frank."

"That's where you have it wrong, Grot. These things are always a game. You just have to figure out what the rules are and how to score."

At that point our discussion was interrupted by the waiter bringing our lunches. I wasn't about to spoil a chance to eat food that hadn't come out of a vat by discussing business, so it wasn't until after we had finished eating that I asked, "What ship did Mr. Smith come in on?"

"The Unicorn Queen. Is that important?"

"Probably not, except that I need to know when Mr. Smith docked and it may be of interest to find out who else was on that ship. Do you know what hotel he was staying at? I presume the Hotel Galactic?"

"Yes. How did you guess?"

"Because it's the one most used by non-human travelers. It has the capability to adjust the atmosphere in the rooms to match the conditions on various home worlds. The gravity, too, to some extent. It also is set up to accommodate dietary requirements. Did Mr. Smith check in?"

"Yes. I've established that much."

"And did he check out?"

"No. The room is still being held for him. It's being paid for by my department."

"You might want to rethink that."

"What do you mean, Frank?"

"I mean he might be dead. It's pretty hard for a four armed alien to go missing on Star City, at least for any length of time. There aren't that many of them that they aren't noticed. Now it is possible that he's been kidnapped or something like that, but then you'd expect a request for ransom. You haven't received anything like that, have you?"

"No. Oh, this is awful," Grot exclaimed. For a moment, I thought I really might see tears, but then she pulled herself together. "Do you really think he's dead?"

"I'm just saying that you should be prepared for the possibility, that's all."

"Yes, I can see that."

"I wouldn't expect too much help from the local police, either."

"Why is that?"

"Star City likes to maintain its neutrality. It's all we've got going for us. That means avoiding getting involved in interstellar politics."

"That's kind of short sighted, isn't it?"

"The way we see it, its survival. We tend to avoid dealings with all governments impartially."

"Do you mean to say the government here won't help at all?"

"Oh, Latimer will pursue it if it does prove that Mr. Smith was killed or kidnapped. He's as honest as a policeman can afford to be, and protecting travelers on Star City is good for business, which is all that really matters to the powers that be, but I wouldn't look for him to do much if the culprits are some other government."

"I didn't realize that Star City was—so unique."

"That's a nice way of phrasing it, Grot. Look, I've got enough to go on, I think. Are you still sure you want to hire me? My rates are a hundred and twenty dollars Crockett a day plus expenses. I'm not sure what the exchange rate is with Terrans, but I'm sure we can work that out. I usually ask for a few days in advance. I've had clients try to skip out on me. No offence."

"I doesn't seem I have any other choice, Frank. I can give you five hundred now. I'll have to make arrangements for any more than that."

"Oh, that will do nicely. I assume I can get in touch with you at the hotel here?"

"Yes."

"Good. Then I'd better get to work. Thanks again for the lunch."

I got up, leaving her sitting at the table. I admit that I had qualms about taking her money when I already knew what had happened to Mr. Smith, but then, business is business. It also put me on the inside if things got too close to Vel and I. The question was, was I going to "discover" the body or not.

If I was going to take Ms. Fender's money, the least I could do was try and figure out why Mr. Smith had been killed and who had been responsible. It wasn't just a case of trying to be honest; the best way to prevent repercussions from the murder affecting Vel and myself would be to find the real killer. I knew how the story ended, but the logical place to begin the investigation was where it began.

Despite its reputation, and prices, the Hotel Galactic wasn't at the top end of the city where the other first class hotels like the Casino and the Rigel Regal were located. Instead, it was about a kilometer down city in the heart of the commercial district. This makes a lot of sense, as few aliens travel to the heart of human space for pleasure, they are either there for business or politics, and the location is convenient for both. From the Rigel I took a down tram to the nearest stop and walked the rest.

The Hotel Galactic won't win any prizes for its architecture. It's basically a ten story cube occupying an entire block. The façade is a featureless grey except for the entrances. There are no windows. Many of the residents come from worlds where the lighting conditions are far different than the home world of humanity, and the rooms are equipped to match the illumination to each occupants requirements. The lack of a view is made up for by wall sized displays that can provide views to suit the needs and whims of the guests. The clientele of the Galactic is exclusively alien. It is possible for a human to book a room, but as far as I know, it has never been done.

Considering this, the lobby of the Galactic is surprisingly ordinary. It's a large space, two stories in height, designed to look impressive, if you don't look too close. There are even potted palms scattered around, or at least some sort of foliage. I'm no expert on such matters. About where you'd expect to find it is the registration desk. The clerk behind the counter looked a lot like the clerks behind similar counters in any hotel, except this one had bright green skin and purple—well it was kind of a cross between hair and feathers. Like most aliens, he had bilateral symmetry with two arms, two eyes and one mouth. The clerk was dressed in a shirt, tie and blazer, I couldn't see if he had pants on because of the counter. It was obviously a hotel uniform, and there was a name tag pinned to the blazer that declared the owner was "BOB" and something else in a script that I didn't recognize.

"Yess? How may I help you."

"How much for a room in this joint?"

That got his attention. He looked at me as if wondering if he was missing something. His training showed, though, because his next question was, "Is that for single occupancy or double, and are there any particular environmental requirements?"

"I was just kidding, Bob. I don't really want a room. I'm just looking for some information about one of your guests."

"I'm afraid that is against hotel policy to divulge that kind of information, Mr.—"

"Sladek. Frank Sladek. I think you've got me wrong, Bob. You see, I'm a private investigator, and I've been retained by an associate of this guest. It seems he's gone missing, and they want me to find him. They thought it would be more efficient than bringing in the local authorities." I showed him my license. Bob examined it closely before returning it. For all I know, he'd actually been able to read it.

"And the name of this guest?"

"Mr. Smith."

Bob consulted a comp terminal behind the counter.

"We have seven Smith's currently staying with us. Also a Smythe."

"John Smith is the one I'm interested in."

"Five of the Smiths are named John. There is also a Johanna and a William."

"Maybe if I described him to you, you'd recognize which one he is. He's about so high, mottled greenish blue skin, no hair or feathers. Oh, and he's got four arms, too."

That seemed to strike a chord with Bob because his skin turned a slightly paler shade of green. Obviously, the absence of Mr. Smith had been noticed.

"Perhaps it would be best if you talked to Security, Mr. Sladek. They may be able to answer any of your questions."

"Suits me, Bob."

Bob picked up a comm. and muttered something into it.

"Someone from Security will be with you shortly, Mr. Sladek. If you'll just take a seat over there—"

I had no objections. I'd been in the Galactic a few times before. It's quite a sight if you aren't used to it. Like I said, the lobby is like most hotel lobbies, people bustling back and forth, except most of these people weren't human. I must have counted more than a dozen species before I gave up, all the colors of the rainbow. Some were dressed in more or less standard business attire and some were wearing—well it's hard to describe.

It was all very educational, and I was almost sad when the someone from Security showed up.

If you know what to look for, you can always spot a hotel dick for what he is. Despite the fact that this one was a Thessarine, better known as a lizardman, I knew him for what he was as soon as I laid eyes on him. Maybe it's the weary eyes or the developing paunch, or just the sense of having given in, but I could tell.

"You S-sladek?" he asked. His speech was slightly sibilant, but his accent was good.

"Yeah, that's me."

"S-sam Johnson. Why don't we go to my office where we can talk in private?" At least he wasn't Mr. Smith.

I followed him down a corridor to his office. It was really more of a closet, but there were two chairs and a desk, so I guess you couldn't complain. There was also a wall of display screens showing various views of the hotel. I'd been in similar rooms in a dozen hotels.

"So, what you want to know, Sladek?"

"The usual. When was Mr. Smith last seen. Did he have any visitors? Any calls? Any messages. Had anyone come looking for him before or after his disappearance? That kind of thing."

"You know I give all this to Lt. Latimer?"

"Sure. But Latimer and I don't always talk. You know how it is?"

"Yeah. Sure. No visitors, no calls. One message from Grot Fender saying she had been delayed but would arrive soon. You know this Grot Fender?"

"She's the one who hired me. She works for some agency on Terra."

"Yeah. That's what she say. No way to verify, though."

That was always the problem. The fastest way to send a message between planets was by starliner, which would take nearly three weeks to get to Terra and as long to get back. Radio, traveling at the speed of light would take over a century each way. For the moment we'd both have to take Ms. Fender at her word.

"When was Smith seen last?"

"Six days ago. About two in the afternoon. He asked the concierge for map of Star City." That was the day that Vel had found the corpse in his office.

"Did he say where he was going?"

"No."

"Not a big help, is it?"

"That's what Latimer said."

"I don't suppose there is any chance that I could look at Mr. Smith's room. I understand that it is still being kept for him."

"It's pretty irregular, Sladek. Against policy."

I had tucked a Crockett double sawbuck in my pocket for just such an eventuality. I pulled it out and laid it on the table. I suspect that one of the reasons we were talking in Johnson's office was it was the one place in the hotel without a security camera.

The lizardman picked up the bill and stuffed it in an inside pocket of his shirt. Like I said, hotel dicks are all cut from the same mold.

"We'll take the freight elevator. Don't want to upset the guests." I'm pretty sure he was referring to me.

We rode up the elevator to the fourth floor, sharing it with a cart from the kitchen. Whatever was under the dome covering the plate was still alive and kicking.

Mr. Smith had been staying in room 417. Johnson had a keycard that let us into the room. It wasn't much different than a room in the Rigel, but then Mr. Smith had been able to breathe oxygen and didn't sleep in water. The bed looked like it hadn't been slept in, but housekeeping had had six days to tidy up.

"You need me for anything else, Sladek? It's busy time and I should be down in the lobby keeping eyes on things."

"You can run along. And thanks for the help, Sam. I'll remember that."

"You do that, Sladek." He left, closing the door behind him.

The room was furnished about the way you'd expect. There was a bed up against one wall and a dresser opposite. The display on the wall where there'd normally be a window was showing some sort of jungle scene with colorful flowers and blue and green leaves. It might have been Mr. Smith's home world, but then it might not. He might have just thought it attractive. A round table that could be adjusted in height was in front of the display flanked by two chairs, also adjustable. In the corner was a sort of armchair that appeared to be adjustable in more ways than I could imagine to suit the anatomy of the occupant. None of this was particularly interesting.

The closet had two suits of clothes similar in cut and pattern to the one the corpse in Vel's office had been wearing. Both looked clean and pressed. Probably room service. Two traveling bags had been stowed in the closet as well. Both were empty.

The drawers of the dresser held about the amount of clothing as would have fit in the bags in the closet. It looked like someone had been through the drawers before me. It had probably been Rossetti, Latimer's partner. Latimer would have been neater about it. It didn't look as if they'd found anything.

A quick check of the bathroom didn't reveal much, either, except that Mr. Smith seemed to brush and floss his teeth. There were some small tubes and bottles, but I couldn't tell if they had been Smith's or supplied by the hotel.

The only thing that I hadn't checked were the nightstands on either side of the bed. The one on the left held a bible provided by the Reconstituted Catholic Church. It struck me they must be desperate for converts if they're putting bibles in a hotel for aliens.

The stand on the other side had one of those books that hotels provide listing local restaurants and attractions. There was another book that, judging from the cover, the hotel had not provided. The cover showed two characters, both with four arms, glaring at each other. One was armed with a laser pistol, the other with a wicked looking knife. If the cover was an indication, Mr. Smith had had low-brow tastes in literature. Out of curiosity I picked it up, but when I thumbed through it, I couldn't read the script it had been printed in. I was about to toss it back into the drawer when a slip of paper fell out. This I could read.

Dear Mr. Smith,

I regret that circumstances prevented me from meeting your starliner yesterday when it docked. If it is convenient, could you meet me at Tracewood Square at three o'clock this afternoon?

Grot Fender

Ms. Fender hadn't mentioned any note, but then, according to her, her own starliner hadn't docked until three days ago, two days after Vel had found the corpse. Either she was lying, or the note had been a plant meant to lure Smith to his death. The latter seemed most likely, as Tracewood Square wasn't exactly the place one would choose to meet an alien emissary. Or anyone else, for that matter.

I pocketed the note. As an afterthought, I slipped the book I had found it in into my pocket as well. There didn't seem to be anything else in the room that was a clue to what had happened to Mr. Smith, so there was no point in my hanging around. I shut the door behind me. Down in the lobby I gave a little wave to Sam Johnson and made for the exit of the Hotel Galactic.

It was mid-afternoon. It was probably too late to complete a canvas of the shops around Tracewood Square to see if anyone had seen Mr. Smith. I wasn't particularly in the mood for leg work, either. I know it's part of being a detective, but it's boring and hard on the feet. There was, however, one more thing for me to follow up on. I didn't think it would lead anywhere, but at least I'd get a drink out of it.

Viktor's isn't the biggest casino on Star City, nor is it the most fashionable, but it does have a certain reputation. Perhaps that's because it is the only gambling establishment that caters to non-humans, or perhaps it's because the previous owner, the one it was named after, died in a gunfight on the gaming floor. The place hasn't been quite the same since, but it still does a good enough business with those looking to walk a short distance on the wild side. After Viktor's death, ownership passed to the head bartender, Glzz. Glzz is one hell of a bartender. He also has four arms.

The bouncer working the front door knew me, but he still patted me down. Maybe that was why he patted me down. It didn't matter, because I wasn't carrying. I try not to unless I have a good reason. When he didn't find anything except the book in my pocket he waved me through.

Glzz was behind the bar. I don't think I've ever seen him anywhere else. He might own the joint now, but he still mixes drinks just like he did when Viktor ran the place.

Glzz and I get along pretty well. Maybe that's because I'm at least partly responsible for the fact that he's the owner. Or maybe it's just because I'm a good tipper.

Glzz can't talk except to say the word "Glzz," but he can use a synthesizer gizmo strapped to his belt to make speech when he wants to. It sounds kind of flat and buzzy, but it is understandable.

"What it be, Sladek? Brown on ice?" Glzz doesn't think much of my taste in booze, and I could hear the disdain despite the synthesizer.

"I'm getting paid expenses, Glzz. Why don't you surprise me, just—"

"Nothing glow, nothing green. Glzz remember." He probably did. As far as I can tell, he can remember every drink he's ever made and who he's served it to.

He grabbed three bottles with three different hands and poured them into the shaker that he held with the fourth. There was no measuring, just expert flicks of each appendage. The top went on the shaker which did an intricate little dance guided by the two arms on his right side. With the arms on the left he grabbed a glass, added some ice and some sort of fruit as a garnish. He finished with this just as the shaking was done. He removed the top of the shaker and poured the contents over the ice. Satisfied with the results, he slid it across the bar towards me.

By some magic of chemistry or density, the liquid in the glass had stratified into three distinct layers, brown, clear and amber. It was also faintly effervescent though I hadn't seen Glzz add any soda or seltzer. I took a sip. It wasn't bad. Not what I'd expected, but not bad at all.

"Pretty good, Glzz. You should think about becoming a professional."

"Always with the joke, Sladek. So why you here?"

"I'm working a case. I thought you might be able to help me."

"Why else? What you want?"

"I was just wondering if you'd ever run across anyone else on Star City with four arms?"

"Glzz only one of his kind here."

"Oh, I don't think this guy is your kind, Glzz. I just has four arms."

"Why would Glzz care?"

"I just thought you might have taken note, that's all. Out of curiosity, if nothing else."

"Does Sladek note every being that pass through Star City with two eyes?"

"Well, when you put it like that—Glzz, I guess not. Forget I asked. But as long as I'm here, take a look at this." I pulled the book from Mr. Smith's room out of my pocket and laid it on the bar."

"Glzz got no time for books. Just booze."

"But do you recognize the language it's written in?"

He picked up the book and looked the cover over before riffling through the pages.

"Sorry, Sladek. Never seen that kind of writing before in my life. Not language written from where Glzz come from."

"Yeah, I didn't think so, Glzz. I just wanted to make sure. Thanks for the drink. How much do I owe you?"

"On the house, Sladek. Maybe next time."

I didn't want to insult Glzz, so I finished the drink. It really wasn't bad.

I hadn't gotten any useful information from Glzz, but at least I had gotten a free drink, so Viktor's hadn't been a total waste of time. It was only late afternoon, so I still had time to do some investigating.

The inside of the cylinder which is Star City might have a surface area of roughly a hundred and fifty square kilometers, but there are only one or two of those where an non-human, four armed or not, doesn't stick out like a sore thumb. If Mr. Smith had left an obvious trail, the police would have picked it up without any difficulty. The only place where he might have been able to lose himself in the crowd was the Souk, the district where most of Star City's non-humans live, so that was where I headed next.

The Souk, or at least part of it, is on the path from my apartment to the nearest tram stop, so my face isn't unknown to those who live there. I won't say that I have any friends there, but my relations with some of the shop keepers are at least cordial and my reputation is ok with most of the others. At a minimum, I had a better chance of getting answers to my questions than the cops did.

I spent a couple of hours stopping in at the places I knew and asking if anyone could remember seeing a tall guy with four arms. Mostly I got blank stares or whatever the equivalent alien expression was. A few mentioned that Viktor's had a four armed bartender. No one could provide a clue as to what had happened to Mr. Smith.

After two hours my feet were getting sore and I was getting hungry. I decided to remedy both problems by having dinner.

There's a corner café near the middle of the Souk that I eat at often enough so as not to need the menu, which is just as well, as I couldn't have read it anyway. There's a sign over the door in the same alien script. I'm told it read's something like "The Pickled Passion Pod." I'll have to take that on trust. It has outdoor seating, which I've found is as good a spot as any to observe the universe passing by.

As non-humans go, the couple that own the place are less non-human than most. Dress them up in the right clothing and put them in bad lighting and you'd have to be within a meter or two to realize their ancestors didn't come from Terra. Of course, their café is under a street lamp and they both wear something that is similar to a long caftan in loud floral prints, which spoils the illusion, but then they've never tried to hide who they are.

The cuisine, so I've been told, consists mainly of stews and soups made from vegetables imported from their home world. From past experience, that seems quite possible, though you couldn't prove it by me. I admit to having the Star City prejudice against any food that doesn't come from a vat. The thought of eating something that was grown in dirt with all sorts of bugs and critters stomping all over it seems kind of unnatural if not downright unwholesome, but over the years I've learned to overlook that or at least not think about it too much. In any case, some of the stuff tastes pretty good and none of it has actually killed me, though I have had to make several emergency stops at the nearest autodoc when some dish turned out to be poisonous to the human system.

Like many of the non-humans on Star City, the owners use adopted human names when interacting with humans, in their case "Bill" and "Beverly" though somehow they manage to pronounce Bill as if it had an "R" and Beverly as if it didn't. When he saw me come up, Bill came out of the interior to greet me.

"Sladek, helro. Table?"

"Sure, Bill. One outside where I can watch the crowd."

"Take your pick, Sladek. Plenty tables."

Bill was right. It was still early by Souk standards and no one was sitting yet at the outside tables. I picked one that gave me a good view while allowing me to put my back against the wall of the building. I wasn't expecting any trouble, but some things just become habits.

"You want usual, Sladek?" Bill asked once I was seated.

"Sure, that sounds good." I hadn't been aware that I had a usual, but it saved me the trouble of ordering. Bill disappeared inside and came back a few moments later with a cup of some sort of beverage. It wasn't joe and it wasn't tea, but it seemed to serve that function.

"Food be up soon, Sladek."

"Good. Say, Bill, you didn't see a tall, skinny guy around here maybe five six days ago? With bluish green skin, no hair. Oh, and he had four arms, too."

"Four arms? Bartender at Viktor's has four arms—"

"Yeah, Glzz. This guy isn't the same kind as him. He's taller and only has two eyes."

"Sorry, Sladek. Bill no see such guy. Four arms pretty unusual. I remember if see."

"Well, thanks, anyway. But if you hear about a guy like that, let me know, OK?"

"Sure thing, Sladek," Bill agreed, and then disappeared back into the café.

He came back a couple of minutes later with a large bowl and placed it in front of me. It contained a lot of red, orange, and yellow chunks of what I assume were vegetables floating in a thick greenish broth. Despite it being my "usual" I couldn't remember ever having had it before, but then communications is always hit and miss at places like the Pickled Pod. I took a tentative spoonful of the stew. It was spicy, salty, and had just a hint of vinegar to it, but it was actually pretty good.

I'd nearly finished when I heard a familiar voice hailing me from the street. It was Jack Feldman.

"Sladek, I haven't seen you in ages," he said as he approached the table.

"Jack. Have a seat." I thought it only good manners to make the offer seeing as he had already pulled out a chair and sat himself across from me.

Jack Feldman wrote one book some twenty years back which was the talk of human space for about three months. He hasn't written a thing since. Instead, he landed on Star City and became the unofficial mayor of the local artist colony, an office whose duties seem to consist of attending every party he can, getting drunk, and sleeping with any woman that's willing. What he survives on, I've never been able to discover. It certainly isn't off sales of his book which is so turgid that it has become a by-word for bad fiction. I don't think a copy has sold in years, and Jack has been reduced to foisting off free copies on anyone who will take one.

"What looks good, Frank?" Jack asked when he had gotten himself comfortable.

"This stuff isn't bad," I replied.

Bill came out and Jack and he had a long conversation in a language I couldn't understand. Along with the non-humans, the Souk is where most of the artsy types on Star City live, mostly because the rents are cheap and so is the food. Jack surprises me sometimes. I hadn't been aware that he had a facility with alien languages.

It appeared that Feldman was joining me for dinner, because Bill brought out a plate of something and set it in front of the writer. It definitely wasn't the same thing that I'd had, the broth being browner and the vegetables whiter. Neither of these facts seemed to bother him, as he dug into the dish with gusto.

I waited until he slowed down before picking up the conversation. Feldman might be a has been as a writer, but he was pretty good as an observer, and there wasn't much that went on in the Souk that he didn't know about.

"You haven't seen an alien with four arms around, have you?"

"Not intentionally, my dear boy, but now and then when under the influence of you more potent pharmaceuticals I may have."

"This would have been say five or six days ago. Tall, skinny guy. Bluish-green. No hair."

"Can't say that it rings a bell, Frank. But then my sense of time isn't what it was. One day just seems to run into another, you know. I take it your interest is of a professional nature?"

"More or less. This four armed guy has gone missing. I'm trying to find out what happened to him."

"I note that you said 'what happened to him' and not 'where he is.' I assume that's because you believe he is deceased?"

"Let's just say I think that's a good possibility."

"Doesn't that make it a matter for the local constabulary?"

"It would, if they thought he was dead, but so far they don't seem to care much one way or the other. In the meantime, I'm being paid to track him down."

"Well, rest assured I'll keep my eyes and ears open and let you know if anything should turn up regarding the unfortunate creature." Feldman may be a sot and a reprobate, but he does have his uses. He's provided me information more than once in the past.

"Thanks, I'd appreciate that, Jack."

"Think nothing of it, old boy. I must be off now. Hansen is throwing a party, I mean giving a showing, and I don't want to be late."

Feldman got up and left, leaving me to pick up the check. It wasn't the first time, and I was sure it wouldn't be the last, but then that's just part of the price of doing business. At least in this case I could expense it.

I spent another hour walking the streets of the Souk asking questions, all with no results. I decided to pack it in and head back to the apartment. As I crossed the street that marked the boundary of the Souk I had the feeling that I was being followed. I tried to use the reflection in a shop window to spot them, but either there was no one there or they were on to me. The glow tubes a kilometer and a half overhead had dimmed for twilight, providing plenty of shadows to conceal someone.

More out of interest than caution, I took a left rather than heading straight planning to double back on my track. If I had been paying attention rather than worrying about who was following, I might have been okay, but when I had made a second left I found myself facing two guys that had the look of hired muscle. They looked like they had been expecting me.

As far as I could tell, neither one of them was armed. At least neither one had a weapon in their hand and I couldn't spot the tell tale bulge of a holster under either of their jackets. Of course, I wasn't packing, either. Both of them had about ten kilos on me and the one on the left was about ten centimeters taller. The one on the right was about my height, but with two of them, that wouldn't make much difference.

They didn't look like they were planning to step aside. I thought about turning around, but I didn't want to risk turning my back on them. Instead I asked, "What's this about, boys?"

That seemed to confuse them for a moment. It crossed my mind that they were just a pair of muggers, and it was possible. We were only a few blocks from New Minglewood, and the neighborhood isn't the safest. That turned out not to be the case, though, because the shorter one asked, "You're Sladek, aren't you?"

I didn't have time to reply. The taller one swung at me with a left aimed at my head. I ducked underneath and hit him one where it hurts, but the other one came at me from behind with a clubbed fist. That left the taller one to plant one on my chin. I was about to go down when there was a spatter of brick chips raining down on us. Someone had fired a laser pistol at the wall just behind us. The two toughs looked around and then took off running.

I struggled to my feet to lean against the wall while I tried to shake the cobwebs from my head.

"Are you alright, Mr. Sladek?"

It was Grot Fender. There was a small laser pistol in her hand. I recognized the type, low power but a short cycle time. It was the kind of weapon favored by professionals. I've got a similar one myself.

"You missed," I responded. It's hard to miss with a laser pistol at less than twenty meters.

"I wasn't aiming at them, Mr. Sladek. I just wanted to scare them off."

"It appears that you've succeeded, Ms. Grot."

"You didn't answer my question. Are you alright?"

"I should be. A couple of pills from the nearest autodoc should fix me up. There's one just a few blocks from here."

"You seem certain of that."

"I've used it before." The fact was me and that particular autodoc were old friends.

"Can you make it there by yourself?"

"I can get there under my own power, but you can tag along if it will make you feel better."

I tried to stand up without the help of the wall. I wavered a little, but managed to stay upright. Ms. Fender reached out her left hand to help. She still had the pistol in her right. I took a step and then another. My legs seemed to be working more or less as intended.

"Were you the one following me?" I asked.

"I was." Her response was flat, as if she was telling me the time.

"Mind if I ask why?"

"I was interested to see what you were doing."

"Did you find out?"

"You went to the Hotel Galactic which made sense, but then you stopped in a bar. After that you spent several hours asking questions of shop keepers, seemingly at random. Then you had dinner with an old drunk."

"Jack would be offended at that. It's true, but he'd still be offended. That old drunk probably knows more about what goes on in the Souk than anyone else. And for your information, the bartender at Viktor's is the only other four armed non-human on Star City."

"I wasn't criticizing, Mr. Sladek, just observing. I'm sure that there is a method to your actions. What have you found out?"

"Well, I've found out that someone is trying to stop me from finding out any more. That's something."

"You mean those two men?"

"Yes. That's exactly what I mean."

"But who are they working for?"

"I don't know that. If you had wounded one of them or let me subdue them—"

"It didn't look like that was going to happen, Mr. Sladek."

"Maybe not. No point arguing about it now. The autodoc is just around the corner."

She helped me into the booth, and then stepped out while the diagnostic ran. Nothing was permanently damaged. The autodoc injected something into my chin and then dispensed a vial of pills. I took a couple on the spot as recommended and my head started to clear. The autodoc read out the bill and after I had stuck the appropriate amount of currency into the payment slot the door to the booth opened. When I stepped outside, Grot Fender was gone. I shrugged and walked the two blocks to my apartment.

I live in a place called the Aldeberon Arms across the street from the Blue Moon which is convenient, maybe a little too convenient at times. It had been constructed as a semi-luxury apartment building back in the days when New Minglewood, which starts only a block over, was going to be a park. That didn't happen. New Minglewood became a notorious slum and the area never became as fashionable as intended. That left the

Aldeberon with apartments that were too big and rents that were too low which suited me just fine.

It did mean that some of the niceties such as maintenance and security were a bit lax, but that's the price you have to pay. When I reached there, the elevator wasn't working again, which was to be expected. I walked up the three flights to my floor, something that keeps me in shape.

To make up for the deficiencies in the building's security I had augmented it with my own touches, a moderately sophisticated system. The door to my apartment was locked, but the telltale informed me that someone had entered while I had been out.

I regretted the fact that I wasn't armed, but I was hoping that whoever was inside wouldn't know that. I entered the apartment trying to make as much noise as possible just to make the intruder think that I wasn't afraid of him. If I had hoped to spook them, I had failed.

As I turned the corner from the entryway into the living room I saw a familiar figure sitting in my favorite chair. He had a drink in his hand. I hoped it was just brown and not from the bottle of good stuff I kept for special occasions.

"You know I should call the police," I stated. It didn't get a reaction from the intruder, but then I hadn't expected that it would.

"Oh, wait. You are the police, aren't you? What are you doing here Latimer?"

The person sitting in my chair drinking my booze was Lt. Latimer, lead detective of the Homicide and Major Crimes unit. It wasn't the first time he'd made an unexpected visit, but usually I didn't find him waiting for me. I took it as a good sign though that he was alone and that his shadow, Sgt. Rossetti wasn't with him. That meant that the visit wasn't official.

"I just thought you and I should have a talk, Frank. Pour yourself a drink and have a seat."

I thought about saying something, but then decided that I really could use a drink. Latimer had gotten some ice out so I put a few of cubes in a glass and poured a couple of fingers of brown over them. I didn't bother with water or soda.

"So what's this about, Latimer? It's late and I've had a rough night."

"I can see that, Frank. What happened?"

"I got mugged by a couple of rent-a-thugs that were waiting for me."

"You should be more careful. Any idea who they were working for?"

"Not a clue. It might have something to do with a case I'm working on, but it could just be someone trying to settle an old score. They didn't stick around to let me ask them."

"Oh?"

"My client showed up unexpectedly and they made a dash for it. I wasn't in any shape to chase after them at the time."

"About your client, Frank. How much do you really know about her?"

"Is that was this is about? My client?"

"You didn't answer my question."

"I know she's from Earth. She's young, attractive, and she paid in cash up front. I didn't think that I needed to know much more than that."

"Did you ever wonder why she got in touch with you? A sweet young thing, fresh off of a starliner? It's not like you advertise, Frank."

"What's your point, Latimer?"

"What I'm saying, Frank, is that this Grot Fender, if that actually is her name, might be more than she appears. You say that she showed up unexpectedly just in time to save your bacon. Have you asked yourself why?"

In point of fact, I'd been asking myself that question ever since I'd emerged from the autodoc. Grot had been tailing me and doing a damned good job of it too. She'd taken a shot that would scare off the muscle but not leave any mess to be cleaned up afterwards. It did have all the hallmarks of a professional, and not the sort of thing they teach in junior diplomat school.

"I could ask what concern is it of yours, Latimer?"

"You could, Frank."

"Look, Latimer, this banter is all very amusing, but why don't you quit wasting both of our times and get to the point?"

"Okay, if you put it that way, here it is. You know as well as I do that Star City is vulnerable. We don't have an army and we don't have a navy. All we've got is a few unarmed patrol craft that are used for search and rescue. The only thing that protects Star City is its neutrality, the fact that we don't take sides in interstellar politics. Hell, we don't even participate in politics."

"Yeah, I heard all that in school. When I went."

"But you still believe it, don't you?"

"Sure, but what has that got to do with me and Ms. Fender?"

"What's this case you're working on, Frank?"

"That's confidential."

"Confidential my eye. You're looking for a non-human with four arms that's gone missing. What did Fender tell you about him?"

"Just that he's a representative of some newly contacted species."

"That was on his way to Terra. Not Crockett, not Novya Magnetogorsk, not some other world, Earth. You know that Terra has been trying to reassert its primacy over the other human worlds for over a century, and that the other systems have all been resisting those efforts."

"Yeah. That's all old news, Latimer."

"Not to me it isn't. Terra was trying to do an end around with this four armed alien, and it looks like someone has gummed up the works."

"You're mixing your metaphors, Latimer," I commented just to interrupt Latimer's tirade.

"Maybe I am, but the last thing Star City needs is to get caught in the middle of a turf war between Crockett and Terra. We get involved, and the first thing that is going to happen is there's going to be pressure to pick sides, and if we do that, we're done for as an independent entity."

"And if we don't pick sides, both sides will be mad at us. I get that, Latimer. But what has that got to do with me?"

"What I'm saying, Frank, is that you've got to tread lightly on this one. There's a lot more at stake than a few credits and your worthless hide. I want to make sure that if things start getting to dicey that you let me know before it blows up in our face."

"What will you do, if that does happen?"

"I'll see that all the parties involved are kicked off of Star City forever. You know, that by the treaties that established Star City, it's supposed to be off limits to the espionage services of all the planets that signed them. That includes Terra, Crockett, and every other planet, because if any planet didn't sign they couldn't use Star City and half the transport in human space goes through here."

"You can't tell me their aren't agents from half the human planets on Star City? And groups like the Reconstituted Catholic Church and aliens like the lizardmen?"

"Yeah, and we let them as long as they don't cause trouble. But someone has crossed the line on this one, Frank."

I looked at Latimer's glass and it was empty. So was mine. Talking will do that to you.

"Have another one, Latimer?"

He looked at his glass.

"Sure, why not."

I poured two more glasses of brown over fresh ice and handed one over to Latimer.

"So let me ask you this, Latimer. What do you think happened to this guy with the four arms?"

"I think he got himself killed. I'm surprised that we haven't found his body yet. What do you think happened to him?"

"Me? How should I know? All I've been able to find out so far is that he had a note asking him to meet Ms. Fender in Tracewood Square at three in the afternoon the day he went missing. The only thing is, it was written a couple of days before she says she landed here. You've checked when she arrived, haven't you?"

"Yeah. She was on that ship. That was the first thing I checked when she filed the missing person report."

"So it looks like this Mr. Smith was lured to Tracewood. I haven't had a chance to follow up on that yet. I'm not holding my breath, though. You know that part of the city; no one sees anything, no one hears anything."

"Yeah. Tell me about it."

Latimer took a long slug of his drink, then looked me in the eye. "You aren't holding out on me, are you Frank? You don't know something about this business that I don't?"

"How could I? I'm just a dumb two-bit shamus."

"You better be telling me the truth, Frank."

"Is that any way to talk to me after I've given you a couple of drinks?"

"Yeah. It's getting late. I'd better go. But remember what I've said. If anything looks like it's going to go bad, let me know pronto."

"Sure thing, Latimer," I said as I showed him to the door. "And give my regards to Rossetti."

He laughed at that as he walked through the door into the hallway, the first laugh of the night. I shut and locked the door behind him and reset the security.

The next morning I decided that it was time to check out Tracewood Square to see if there were any witnesses to what had happened to Mr. Smith. I don't usually carry a weapon for something like that, but given the previous night's incident I strapped on a shoulder holster for a laser pistol. The pistol itself is only a 25 kJoule model, but it's been retrofitted with a fast cycling capacitor from a much heavier weapon so that it can fire every couple of seconds. The modifications throw off the balance a little and it can only be fired maybe fifty times before the battery has to be recharged, but I think the improved rate of fire is worth it. For good measure, I slipped a needle gun into my belt in the small of my back.

Tracewood Square was originally supposed to be part of a park complex as a complement to New Minglewood, but like the latter, the plans were never carried through when space on the inner surface of Star City filled up quicker than anticipated. The square itself was built, but it became surrounded with low-rent housing and lower rent business catering to the needs of the neighborhood's residents. It wasn't as lawless as New Minglewood, but it wasn't exactly friendly to outsiders either.

I spent the morning asking questions of shopkeepers, shoe shine boys, and food cart vendors. The results were about what I had expected; no one had seen anything, no one had heard anything, and no one knew anything. I thought about checking security camera imaging, but looking around me it looked like most of the cameras had been stolen. Besides, I figured that the police would have already done that.

Around eleven I gave up in disgust and bought a tube steak sandwich from one of the food carts, hoping that it, at least, was vat grown. I found a bench to eat my lunch and ponder what my next move was going to be.

I'd pretty much run into a dead end trying to track down what had happened to Mr. Smith starting from the hotel end. The only other clue that I had was that the body had ended up at Vel's catering business. It was always possible that Vel's had been chosen at random, but that didn't seem likely. His business was a couple of kilometers down city and halfway around the cylinder which was a long way to drag a conspicuous non-human. It was much more likely that Vel's had been chosen because someone had a grudge against him.

I finished off the tube steak, and after licking the sauce off my fingers I tossed the wrapping paper it had come in into the refuse bin. The latter action drew several looks of disbelief from passers-by. The denizens of Tracewood aren't known for their neatness.

At Vel's I was greeted by Rhonda. Rhonda is a woman in her late fifties maybe, who has been working for Vel for at least twenty of those years. She probably knows as much about the business as he does, and everyone who works for him tries to keep on her good side. She didn't seem surprised to see me.

"It's been a while, Frank."

"Yeah. Business has been slow. Is Vel in?" We both knew that he was. The catering business is as much about preparation as the events themselves, and work on that evening's bookings had probably started before six that morning.

"I'll check. Is this about anything in particular?"

"Just tell him it's about the meat in the freezer. He'll understand."

Rhonda looked at me curiously, but picked up the comm on her desk and spoke into it.

"He's in his office. He says to go right on up."

"Thanks, Rhonda."

I went up the stairs to Vel's office. I noticed that there was new flooring under his desk. Vel didn't look exactly pleased to see me.

"What's this about, Frank? I'm a busy man. I've got four cocktail parties and three dinners tonight."

"I'll be quick. It's about that meat we stuffed in the freezer. It turns out someone is looking for it, or at least wants to know what happened to it. They hired me to find out."

"But you already know—"

"Yeah, I know how things ended up. But I don't know the how or who or why. That's what I'm trying to find out. It turns out there may be repercussions if things aren't resolved."

"What kind of repercussions?" Vel asked, suddenly very worried looking.

"I'm not sure you want to know, Vel. Let's just say that it may involve Terra, Crockett, and who know who else. Latimer has already approached me privately about how this business has to be handled discretely."

"Jesus, Frank. What have we gotten ourselves into?"

"That's what I'm trying to find out, Vel. That's why I'm here."

"I don't understand, Frank. I never saw the guy before in my life. I've got no idea who he is or how he ended up in my office."

"I don't think it was a random act, Vel. They picked your office to kill the alien in for a reason. Someone must have it in for you. Some enemy or competitor.

"I'm just a caterer, Frank. I don't have enemies. Sure, I might have some competitors, but I can't think any of them would be responsible for something like this. We've all got enough on our plates as it is. And it's not like there's not plenty of business for everyone."

"There must be someone with a grudge. Some supplier or someone that feels you didn't treat them right."

"I swear, Frank. There's no one. I've been in business a long time. I've always tried to treat people fairly. Ask anyone."

Vel was getting a little hysterical which wasn't going to help. I tried to calm him down. "Look, I'm not saying they've got an honest beef against you. I'm just saying that maybe they think they've got a reason to cause you problems."

"Honest, I can't think of anyone—" Vel paused as if something had just occurred to him.

"You've thought of something."

"Yeah, but it was a while back. I don't think it can be him."

"Who?" I said, getting a little frustrated with Vel.

"You know how hard it is to get staff, particularly temporaries. I got a bunch of people that I hire regular like, waiters, bartenders, busboys, those kind of people, but sometimes, particularly if I've got a lot of events going on at once, that's not enough, so I've got to hire extra. Usually, I go through one of the agencies, but sometimes even that isn't enough if lots of things are going on at the same time."

"Yeah, I can understand that. So what do you do?"

"I do what I have to. Sometimes it means dealing with people that I'd rather not. There was this guy, Lester Kornflus. He called himself a labor contractor. He'd get you as many warm bodies as you needed for a cut of their wages. Not necessarily the best people, but, let's face it, it doesn't take much to stand around in a white jacket with a tray of canapés."

"Ok. So you did business with this Lester Kornflus—"

"Yeah. Like I said, I was real busy. A couple of weddings, a big reception at the Casino, some parties, and a big dinner, also at the Casino. They were booked solid, so they couldn't handle it themselves, which shows you how crazy it was."

I kept wanting Vel to get to the point, but I realized the best thing to do was just let him tell it in his own way.

"Anyway, he sent me a bunch of people, maybe a dozen or so. Along with them were these two big guys. All muscle. I couldn't use them as waiters, they'd scare the guests, but I figured I could use them in the back to move things around, arrange tables, that kind of thing."

"I take it things didn't work out."

"I discovered after the reception when we were prepping for the dinner that a crate was missing. Not one of mine, but one of the Casino's. It was the meat for the entree for the dinner. Two hundred and fifty kilos of prime beef filets. A thousand of them. Do you have any idea how much they cost? Even wholesale?"

"A lot, I bet."

"Over ten thousand dollars Crockett, that's how much. But that wasn't the worst of it. The dinner was less than six hours away and I had to get a replacement. You can't just go to a butcher and buy that much. You got to special order it. I couldn't get enough to matter. Fortunately, it turned out I had some prime rib that I'd been stockpiling, so we served that instead."

"I take it you think these two musclemen that Kornflus supplied boosted the filets?"

"It couldn't have been anyone else. It had obviously been planned from the beginning by Kornflus."

"So what did you do about it?"

"It wasn't me, Frank. That's what I'm trying to tell you. Well the guests didn't complain about the prime rib. It was actually a big hit. But somebody noticed the switch and they told Mr. Anthony."

I could see why Vel was blanching as he related this part. Mr. Anthony runs the Casino. And a lot of other things. Star City doesn't have organized crime. It doesn't need it, the people who run the place, the hotel and casino owners are essentially the government, and when you're the government what you do isn't crime. Mostly, Mr. Anthony's organization was legitimate. They could make more than enough money that way. But their methods of dealing with obstacles could be unorthodox at times. I let Vel continue.

"Well, I get called to Mr. Anthony's office. I explained the situation to him. I said that I'd make up the cost of the filet and that the prime rib was on me. I must say he was very understanding. He said I should bill him for the prime rib and that he would take care of the filets himself."

"And that's it?"

"Yeah. As far as I was concerned. Except that shortly after that Lester Kornflus disappeared. Permanently. There was a rumor that he had been stuffed into a shipping container and sent off to Nebraska by slow freight. I don't know if that's true or not. All I know is that he hasn't been seen on Star City since and his labor business doesn't exist anymore."

"And the two guys who lifted the beef? What happened to them?"

"I don't know, Frank. I don't care and I certainly wasn't going to ask. Maybe they ended up in the same shipping container. Maybe not."

I knew what Vel meant. There were a lot of ways for people who crossed Mr. Anthony to disappear on Star City.

"Just out of curiosity, what did these two muscle guys look like?"

"I don't know. I only saw them for a couple of hours when I was busy with other things. They were big and strong. One was maybe your height, the other maybe ten centimeters taller. Does it matter?"

"Probably not. It's just that two guys that fit that description tried to pound me into the pavement last night."

"What have we got ourselves into, Frank?" Vel said, the panic back in his voice.

"Let me handle things, Vel. The best thing for you to do for all concerned is to go about your business as if nothing has happened."

It took me another fifteen minutes to get Vel settled down to the point where he could function, but when I left the catering business, I felt reasonably comfortable that he wouldn't do anything too stupid.

Vel hadn't given me much to work with. He had the names the two thugs had been hired under, but chances were good that they weren't their real names. Even if they had been, they certainly wouldn't be the ones they were using now. I passed them on to Latimer anyhow, working on the theory that it would make it look like I was trying to be helpful. When he asked the embarrassing question of how I'd come by the names, I explained that I'd picked up a "rumor" on the street that they might have been the same guys that had attacked me. I couldn't tell if Latimer bought it, but at least it gave us both some cover.

After I had talked to Latimer, I gave Grot Fender a call. She had paid me enough in advance for three or four days plus expenses, so technically, she was still my client, and was due periodic reports. My real reason for calling her was that I had some questions that I wanted to ask her. I suggested that we meet for dinner. Somewhat to my surprise, she agreed and left it up to me to pick the place. I gave her an address and said we should meet there around seven.

I spent the remainder of the afternoon trying to get a line on the two thugs that had ambushed me. This wasn't as much of a fool's errand as you might think. The bosses who run Star City, the Mr. Anthonys and the like, don't approve of things that might put off their customers. The hotels and casinos bring in much more money legitimately than they could ever realize through crime. For that reason if for no other, freelance thuggery is discouraged. Sure, they'll allow the occasional spacehand to be rolled and they turn a blind eye to what goes on in New Minglewood, but anything that adversely effects the first, second, and even third class passengers on the starliners gets quashed pretty effectively, and not by the police.

That meant that the pool of hired muscle that wasn't employed by one of the organizations was relatively small. Add in the fact that this pair had run afoul of Mr. Anthony which would have made them pretty toxic, and it wasn't too hard for me to track them down. By the time I had headed back to my apartment to get cleaned up for dinner, I had an address and the names they were currently using. I was feeling pretty smug with myself as I took my shower.

The place I had chosen for dinner was called The Montego Café. It was run by a chef who had come from the planet of the same name, a world that is mostly water and islands. The cuisine is spicy and mostly features chicken, which is a kind of flightless bird, pork, which is some kind of four legged animal that is not a cow, and fish, which are animals that live in the water, which I've always thought was pretty bizarre. Nothing is vat grown and all of the ingredients are imported from Montego. The various dishes are served with rice, vegetables and lots of herbs and spices that I can't name. The portions are generous, the prices moderate, and the clientele is split between travelers and locals well off enough to afford something that doesn't come out of a vat.

The Montego Café is located just down city from the commercial district a block off of the West tram line which makes it pretty easy to get to. From the outside, it looks much like any other corner restaurant, but the interior has been done up in what is supposed to be "authentic" style. Maybe it is. I wouldn't know, never having been off of Star City in my life. Montego is a well known vacation destination, though, so at least some of the patrons probably would know from having been there.

I arrived about fifteen minutes early so as to be there before Grot. I explained to the maitre d' that I was expecting a young lady to join me. He flashed a big white smile in his dark face and sat me at a table off in a secluded corner.

Ms. Fender arrived exactly on time. She had ditched the conservative clothes for a sleeveless dress that had as many colors as her hair, mostly reds, oranges, and yellows, which fit in perfectly with the décor. I could tell from the look on the maitre d' face that he approved, and that his estimation of me had risen several notches.

"What a charming place, Mr. Sladek," Grot said after she was seated.

"I thought we had agreed that we were on a first name basis."

"If you like, Frank."

"I'd like."

I was saved from further awkwardness by a waiter asking if the lady would care for a drink. She chose a tropical punch which when it arrived, proved to be a tall glass with fruit floating in it and stratified layers matching the colors of Grot's dress. We both laughed at that. I was drinking a beer called "Olde Fisherman," which may have been a pretty accurate description.

The waiter gave us time to drink our drinks before returning to take our orders. Grot ordered some sort of fish. Out of curiosity, I ordered something called "blackened pork," which I figured had to be more appetizing than it sounded.

"Have you been to Montego, Frank?"

"Me? No, I've never been off of Star City. I don't believe in all this space travel stuff. It strikes me as dangerous."

She looked at me as if trying to decide whether I was joking. "That's an odd response for someone in your line of work, Frank."

"I guess it depends on what you're used to. Me, I grew up on the inside of a hollowed out rock. Anything else strikes me as unnatural."

"That's an odd way of looking at things, Frank."

"I am what I am. I take it, though, that you have been to Montego?"

"Yes. Once when I was younger. My parents took me. I thought it wonderful at the time."

"And now?"

"Oh, don't get me wrong, Frank. I'm sure Montego is much as I remember it. It's just that I've got a different perspective on things now. That's why I went into Exorelations."

I was about to ask more, such as why she was so good with a laser, when the food came. Grot's fish looked as though several steps had been left out of the preparation, steps like removing the bones and skin. She gave me a bite to try which was interesting. The blackened pork wasn't so much black as a little charred around the edges, but it was spicy. I found myself flagging down the waiter for another bottle of "Olde Fisherman." Grot ordered a glass of white wine.

After we had finished eating, Grot said, "You didn't ask me to dinner just for the food. You've found out something about Mr. Smith, haven't you?"

"Let's go someplace for a drink."

Grot raised an eyebrow.

"Trust me, it's relevant. I think I've got a line on the two men who attacked me the other night."

We settled up the bill and left.

I had gotten an address for the two toughs that had tried to put me out of commission. It was for an apartment in a lower middle class residential district, not exactly luxurious, but not a slum, either. That in itself was a sign that they had some money behind them. I was familiar with the neighborhood, and knew that there was a bar across the street and a couple of buildings down that had a few outdoor seats. That's where we were headed.

Grot hadn't asked any questions on the tram ride there, but I could tell that she was wondering what I was up to. I didn't bother to enlighten her.

As I had hoped, one of the tables was vacant. In a show of manners, I pulled out one of the chairs for Grot. What I really wanted was to make sure that I could sit in the other one which faced the entrance of the apartment building.

"Not quite what I was expecting," Grot said with a half smile. "what do you recommend?"

"I'm having a brown and soda, which is usually safe. You might prefer clear because it has less taste. I'd avoid having them add lemon, though, because it's not really lemon." The alcohol in brown and clear comes out of the same yeast vat and still. The difference between them comes in the artificial flavoring and coloring that gets added afterwards. "Lemon" is some chemical additive that is supposed to taste just like the real thing. I've had the real thing. It doesn't.

"Does everything on Star City come out of a vat?"

"It does if you're a working stiff. Everything else has to be imported and costs too much. It's not that bad, though. If you were born here you get used to it."

"You were born here, then, Frank?"

"About a kilometer that way," I said, pointing down city.

A bored looking waiter came out. He looked surprised when he saw Grot and tried to straighten up and look professional. I ordered a brown and soda on the rocks. Grot said that she'd have the same, maybe to impress me as to how tough she was.

After the waiter had brought our drinks and left us alone, Grot said, "You didn't ask me here just to show a girl a nice time. What are we really doing, Frank?"

"Fair enough. But first I've got a few questions of my own."

"Such as?"

"Such as, who are you really?"

"I told you, Frank. My name is Grot Fender and I work for the Department of Exorelations."

"Oh, I'm willing to believe that part, Grot. It's just that I don't really think you are some junior gofer who was sent to escort the gentleman with four arms because no one else wanted the job."

"What makes you think that?"

"For one thing, the way you shoot."

"That's simple. My father taught me to shoot when I was a little girl."

"Don't get me wrong. It's not that you can hit something with a laser pistol. That's not all that hard. It's that you knew what to hit—and what not to hit. You could have hit either of the thugs that were roughing me up, but you didn't. Instead, you shot just to scare them off."

"What's your point, Frank?"

"You did what a professional would have done. You defused the situation without making a mess that you'd have to explain to the authorities."

"You make it sound like I'm some kind of spy."

"Well, aren't you?"

She took her time, as if trying to decide how much to reveal, all the time looking me straight in the eye.

"OK, Frank. I do work for Exorelations, but I am more than just an errand girl. I'm more of a security trouble shooter."

"In other words, a bodyguard," I interrupted.

"That's one way of putting it. My department received some back channel information that there might be an attempt to stop Mr. Smith from reaching Earth. It was too late to make alternate arrangement for transport, and it's not clear whether Mr. Smith would have agreed. I was sent because it was believed that my presence would be least likely to cause diplomatic problems. Does that satisfy you, Frank?"

"For the moment."

"Does this change our working arrangement?"

"Not as long as I keep getting paid."

"Fair enough. So what are we doing here?"

"See that apartment building across the street, the one with the green awning?" She looked over her shoulder casually as if looking farther down the street. "Well that's where the two guys that attacked me live. By the way, there a names, or at least the ones they are using now, are Edgar and Terrence, which shows more imagination than I would have expected."

"And we're here to confront them?"

"Not just yet. Now I'm pretty sure that these two were sent to stop me sticking my nose into things, and I wouldn't be surprised if they had a hand in the disappearance of our four-armed friend, but neither of these guys is smart enough or connected enough to be behind it all. I came here tonight on the off chance that I might find out who that is. You wouldn't have any ideas along those lines, would you?"

"No. The intel was pretty vague."

"But you don't think it was someone working for Crockett, do you?"

"It's not their style. They might have tried to hijack Mr. Smith, but they would have been more subtle about it. And they would have made a point of letting us know what they'd done."

There'd been bad blood between Earth and Crockett ever since the latter had won its independence from Earth some seven hundred years earlier. Crockett took every opportunity to show

Earth, and every other human planet, that they were now the wealthier and more powerful world.

"So, if not Crockett, who?"

"I don't know. I wish I did."

After that exchange we sat in silence for a while sipping our drinks. It was a perfect night, but then, Star City doesn't really have weather and every night is the same. People keep telling me that weather is something I'm missing, but it seems to me just unreliable and inconvenient.

I was debating whether to give it up or order another round when I spotted two men walking down the street.

"There are two men coming this way. One's got on a green shirt, the other a brown jacket. You got a better look at them the other night than I did. Are these guys the two that jumped me?"

Grot glanced behind her making it look as if she was just stretching. When she turned back, she nodded.

I kept my eye on the two of them. One was carrying a bag. It looked like it might be groceries. The other had a brown paper bag, probably a bottle of brown. So the two of them had been out shopping. They entered the building, and a few minutes later a light came on in a third floor window.

"At least we know their home. Feel like sitting here for awhile?"

"Why not," Grot answered. "I've got nothing better to do."

I caught the waiter's eye and ordered another round. We were half way through the drinks when I saw Grot stiffen slightly.

"There's a lizardman coming this way," Grot said softly.

That was an anomaly. It wasn't a neighborhood where lizardmen lived. Mostly, they stayed in the Souk. It would be pretty unusual for one to have business locally this late at night.

Thessarines are called lizardmen for a reason. Their skin is covered in greenish scales in a mottled pattern that helped their ancestors blend into the jungles of their home world. They are bipedal, usually just under two meters in height, with two large eyes perched above something that isn't quite a nose, and wide, toothy mouths. Someone once told me that they resemble what might have evolved on Earth if an asteroid hadn't wiped out the dinosaurs. It's a pretty fair description.

"Recognize him?" I asked.

"Maybe. It's always hard to tell with lizardmen."

I knew what Grot meant. The pattern of mottling on the scales is supposed to be distinctive, but the reality is that to humans they all pretty much look alike.

As I said, a lizardman in that neighborhood at that time of night was suspicious, but confirmation came a few moments later when he entered the apartment building. If we needed any further proof, a little while later I caught a glimpse of the lizardman through the window of Edgar and Terry's apartment.

He didn't stay long, though, and five minutes later he was back out on the sidewalk.

"How do you want to play this, Frank?" Grot asked.

"I think we should take a walk."

I dropped enough on the table to cover the drinks and provide the waiter with a decent tip, then we got up. I grabbed Grot's hand in mine. She took the hint, and a moment later we were just two lovers going for an evening stroll.

We followed after the lizardman, leaving a block or more between us. Fortunately, there wasn't much chance of our losing him in the crowd. He was the only lizardman, or for that matter non-human, in sight.

I had expected our quarry to head towards the tram line that would take him down city towards the Souk, but instead, he headed spinward. After a dozen blocks he turned up city. The area was becoming less residential and more commercial. There were fewer people out on the street, which meant that there were fewer people for us to blend in with. We dropped back a little farther.

I could sense that the lizardman realized he was being followed. He started glancing back more often, and he picked up his pace. He reached a corner and turned around just as we were caught in the glare of a street light. I pulled Grot close to me as if we were embracing. I could smell the perfume of her multicolored hair. She must have figured what I was up to, because she didn't resist. Instead, she kissed me. Maybe it fooled the lizardman, and maybe it didn't, but I didn't care.

There was an excitement between the two of us, two hunters on the chase. I could see the widening in Grot's eyes, the alertness in her lithe body. The lizardman had turned the corner and was out of sight. We hurried towards the spot, but as we approached I held up my hand to slow us.

It was a perfect setup for an ambush. The lizardman would have plenty of time to find cover in a doorway or alley opening. There was no one else in view. I reached into the small of my back for the needle gun that rested there. A glance at Grot showed that she was holding the tiny laser pistol she had used earlier. She must have been carrying it in her purse, because there would have been nowhere else to hide it.

I couldn't look around the corner, but I could see across the street where there was an entryway to a storefront that would provide cover if I could reach it. I motioned for Grot to stay where she was and cover me, then I dashed across the street to the waiting shelter.

Nothing happened. As I looked down the street the lizardman had vanished. Grot stepped out into the street, her pistol held in the two handed grip they teach security services. I came out of the entryway, the needlegun at the ready.

Slowly we walked down the street, one of us on each side so that we could cover the other. If there had been anyone watching, it would have been like something out of a espionage video, the beautiful young woman in the colorful dress holding a laser, the handsome man, okay, it was dark, with his own weapon drawn. The only problem was that the lizardman had given us the slip. After a few moments we both realized we looked a little foolish and put our weapons away.

"What now?" Grot asked after I had crossed the street to rejoin her.

"I think we need to talk. But not here. Someplace private."

"Where? At my hotel?"

"My apartment is closer. We can be there in ten minutes."

For a second I thought she was going to demur, but then she just nodded.

We walked to the nearest tram stop and rode it down city to the stop closest to my apartment. The quickest way from there involves cutting through the Souk. I've done it so many times that I never think about it, but I could see that Grot was on edge at the sight of so many non-humans. Even at that hour the streets were full of beings, human and non-human, and most of the shops were still open. I felt Grot's hand in mine. She was, for the moment, a young woman in a strange place.

It's only a few blocks from the edge of the Souk to my apartment. The sign for the Blue Moon was still lit across the street, but then, like most places on Star City, it never closes.

For once, the elevator was working, and it shuddered upward as it carried us to the fourth floor. The security telltale showed that no one had been in since I had left for dinner. It would have been embarrassing if Latimer had been waiting.

I unlocked the door and ushered Grot inside. When I turned on the light there was a little gasp. There is a painting hanging in the hallway facing the door as you enter. It's an unusual piece, not really a portrait, but the image of some inner reality.

"If I didn't know better," Grot said, "I'd say that was a Lucinda. But she never does portraits."

"She made an exception for this one. You can check the signature if you don't believe me. There's a title on the back. It reads 'Portrait of Frank Sladek.'"

"She must have—" but then she realized the real meaning of the portrait. "No, she didn't hate you, did she?"

"No, she didn't. But she also realized that she couldn't live with what I was. It was fun while it lasted, though."

I led her into the living room, and went over to the sideboard to mix us both a drink leaving Grot to look around. As I said earlier, it's larger than most places. I've furnished it with older pieces salvaged from the street, good stuff mostly that's just gone out of fashion. Nothing matches, but that doesn't seem to matter. There's also a small balcony out front with a great view of the Blue Moon's sign and New Minglewood beyond. Another

Lucinda hangs on the wall, this one a more conventional landscape of someplace that may or may not exist in reality. Lucinda was always good at that.

"It's not quite what I was expecting," Grot remarked as I handed her a drink.

"The rent is cheap because of the neighborhood. And having a bar across the street is convenient."

"Still, it's not what I had pictured—"

"For the apartment of a two-bit private shamus—"

"I guess that's one way of putting it. I see you have a collection of real books. Have you read them."

"Yeah, some of them. Being I private dick there are times when I've got time on my hands. People give me things sometimes. I've got a copy of Jack Feldman's book, for example. I gave it away, but he found out and gave me another."

"I see you've got a number of Marcus Fitzroys' books. Do you know him, too?"

"Yeah. We met in the bar across the street one afternoon."

Grot pulled out the copy of A Farewell to Holm, and read the inscription, "To Frank, Who made me what I am, Alive."

"That's was kind of a joke on his part, I think. I helped him get out of jam he was in. He keeps sending me copies of each of his new books as they're published. I liked The Old Man's Fish. I thought that was pretty good."

"I've read The Sun Never Rises. That's supposed to be based on his time on Star City, isn't it? Oh, my god. You're Deke Slater."

"Well, people say he based that character on me. Personally, I've never seen the resemblance, myself."

She put the book back on the shelf and gave me a look like she was wondering who I was. I thought it best to change the subject.

"Getting down to business, do you think it's likely the lizardmen are behind Mr. Smith's disappearance?"

"Who knows? With the Thessarines anything is possible. There are so many factions. But yes, it's possible. Mr. Smith's species occupy a system close to some of the Thessarine worlds.

There may be a faction that would prefer that they not open relations with Terra or any of the human systems."

"And if something were to happen to Mr. Smith?"

"There very well might not be another emissary sent to replace him," Grot replied.

"It's pretty clear that Terry and Edgar are on the payroll of the lizardman we followed tonight. Those two have been involved in some shady business in the past."

"How do you know that?"

"They lifted ten thousand dollars Crockett of prime meat from a caterer I know. He told me about it. That's how I got a line on those two." I wasn't exactly lying, I was just scrambling the order of things a bit.

"So what are we going to do about it, Frank?"

"I should be able to track down this lizardman. There aren't all that many of them on Star City. Give me a day or so."

"That sounds good," Grot responded, and drained her drink. "It's getting late, Frank."

"Yeah, I guess you're right. We had a busy night. Did you want me to see you back to your hotel?"

"That wasn't exactly what I had in mind."

A look into her eyes made it clear what she did have in mind.

"In that case, there's another painting by Lucinda in the bedroom if you'd care to check it out."

In the morning, I offered to make breakfast, but Grot said that she had to get back to her hotel to write a report so that it could be aboard a starliner that was heading to Earth later that day. It is one of the big contradictions of space travel that the quickest way to communicate across interstellar distances is to put a message aboard a ship, either in electronic or physical form.

I was still hungry, so after she had left I scrambled myself a plate of vat grown egg along with some vat grown bacon and vat grown orange juice. Maybe it's my upbringing, but it all tasted fine to me.

As I ate, I pondered the situation. After last night's disappearing act, I was convinced more than ever that the lizardman was behind the death of Mr. Smith. That the corpse had ended up in Vel's office, had probably been Edgar and Terry deciding to settle an old score rather than part of the bigger plan.

I wasn't deluding myself. Sooner or later, the corpse in cold storage would be discovered. It might take a year, maybe even much longer, but sooner or later someone was bound to ask questions about a crate that had been sitting there for years, and when they did, there was a better than even chance that the crate would eventually be traced back to Vel, and, by association, to me. But that would only happen if the authorities bothered to make the effort.

A serious crime had been committed, the murder of Mr. Smith. There was no way that that could be covered up, not with the interspecies ramifications. The police would demand a solution to the mystery, but it wouldn't necessarily have to be the right solution. All the solution had to be was plausible enough to satisfy the bureaucratic machinery so that the case could be closed. Ideally, it would also satisfy Grot and her bosses, or at least her bosses, but there was a good chance that Terra would go along with the local ruling if the solution presented to them was good enough.

To pull this off, I would have to link Edgar and Terry to the corpse of Mr. Smith. I didn't think that that would prove to be too difficult. Neither one had struck me as the intellectual type and they wouldn't be hard to manipulate. The lizardman would have to be tied in, as well, which might prove to be harder. The important thing was, that in the end, none of them could be in a position to dispute the facts. That meant one thing. It wasn't pleasant, but I didn't see any way out of it.

First, though, before I could do anything, I had to identify the lizardman. That might not be as hard as it might seem. At any one time, fortunately, there are only a few hundred lizardmen on Star City. My guess was that the lizardman in question wasn't one of the long term residents, which would eliminate many of those. He would also have had to have arrived long enough before Mr. Smith had disappeared to make contact with Edgar, Terry, and whatever other henchmen he had on his payroll. The lizardman was also still around, at least as of the previous evening.

Star City is a closed system. The only way on or off of it is through one of the two docking rings, the one used by starliners at the upper end of the city and the one used by freighters at the ass end. There is no way to conceal the arrival or departure of a spaceship, and every passenger and crew member that enters or leaves the city is recorded.

Passenger manifests are open records. Anyone can access them and find out the names, times, and ships of every departure and arrival. The information on crew members is a little more restricted, but a friend in the records department had long ago given me a password granting access to that database in exchange for a good dinner and a night on the town.

This is the part of detecting that doesn't get shown in videos or mentioned in books, the patient sifting and sorting of information to winnow down a list of possible suspects to a few, and ideally to one. It took the better part of the morning, but I finally came up with a name. I won't bother to give it here. Neither one of us would be able to pronounce it. For the purposes of this account, let's just call him Mr. Green. As a bonus, Mr. Green gave as his address a location that was only a few blocks from where we had lost him.

By lunch time, I was feeling pretty proud of myself. I treated myself to a hot meat sandwich at the corner diner and then stopped into the Blue Moon for something to wash the taste out of my mouth. I had the information that I needed, now all I had to do was set the trap.

The first step was to turn up the heat on Edgar and Terry. That wasn't too hard. I made a call to Latimer and told him that those two might be the same toughs that had roughed me up. It wasn't anything definite enough for Latimer to bring them in, but it would be enough for him to pay them a visit and ask some pointed questions. The last thing I wanted was for that pair to be arrested, but I did want to make them nervous.

Mr. Green would be a tougher nut to crack, but I had an idea of how to put pressure on him, too. I paid a visit to the Landfal Hotel. The Landfal is best described as a mid-level commercial hotel mostly favored by business travelers with modest expense budgets. The reason I went there is that I know the house dick well enough to ask a favor, and he knows me well enough to do it.

After I had made my call to Latimer, I went to the lobby of the Landfal, found a nice seat in view of the reception desk, and parked my butt in it. I didn't have long to wait. Within five minutes, Rik Lane, the house detective, was standing in front of me looking nervous.

"I haven't seen you in awhile, Frank. Is something going down that I should know about?"

"Nothing like that, Rik. Take a load off your feet, so we can chat."

Lane did as I asked. He's not the brightest bulb in the universe, but he's not stupid, either. He knew that the best way to avoid trouble was to follow my lead.

"How'd you like to make fifty bucks Crockett?"

"Doing what, Frank? You know I don't do anything illegal."

"I wouldn't think about asking you to, Rik. I just thought you might feel like doing me a favor and make yourself some scratch at the same time."

I knew that the Landfal didn't pay Lane much, and Rik had a weakness for fancy clothes that took up much of what he did get. Like most hotel dicks, he wasn't above doing a little freelance work on the side.

"So what are we talking about?"

"I've got a little surveillance job that I can't do myself, because I'd be recognized. Can you get free for a few hours this evening, say from five to around eight."

Rik thought about it for a moment. I'd picked those hours because that's always a slack time for trouble in a hotel, it's too early for people to be drunk and too busy for guests to be mugged.

"Yeah, I should be able to manage that. What do you want me to do?"

"I want you to go park yourself across the street from this address," I gave him the address I had found for Mr. Green. "I want you to go there and keep a note of anyone entering or leaving."

"You want me to follow them if they do?"

"No, that won't be necessary." The fact was, I really didn't care about the comings and goings at that address, but I had to give Lane some kind of explanation as to why he was there. I continued, "Now here's the important part, Rik. I don't want you to try to hide the fact that you're watching the place. I want you to be seen."

"I don't get it, Frank. You want me to be seen."

"Yeah. See, the thing is that I'm trying to put pressure on the guy that lives there so that he'll panic and be flushed out into the open."

"Oh, I get you."

"Good. Think you can do it?"

"Sure thing, Frank."

"OK. Here's the fifty," I slipped him a couple of twenties and a sawbuck. "If you see anything, give me a call. If nothing happens, you don't have to bother."

Rik slipped the cash into the side pocket of his jacket.

"Thanks, Frank."

"Oh, one other thing. I don't think that there will be any rough stuff, but just in case, be on your toes."

I really wasn't expecting any problems, but I'd picked early evening as a time when people would be around to insure Lane's safety.

There was one more step in my plan, but that would have to wait until the targets had been softened up a little. I thought about giving Grot a call and see if she wanted to have dinner, but I decided to spend a quiet evening at home. If things went as planned, I'd be very busy the next night.

I had a quick one across the street at the Blue Moon, and then left before the after work crowd filtered in. They get noisy and spoil the gloomy atmosphere of the joint. After a meal at the diner on the corner and I went back to my apartment to read and listen to some music.

I had some jive samba playing on the sound system and a glass of brown over ice in my hand when Rik Lane called just after nine.

"How'd it go, Rik?"

"It went fine. The only one in or out was a big ugly lizardman who went in about seven and came out about half an hour later." To Rik, every lizardman is big and ugly, but then, if you think about it, that's a pretty fair description.

"Did he spot you?"

"Yeah. I was standing across the street just like you said, leaning against a lamp post. He noticed me for sure when he came out, because he was looking right at me. That's okay, isn't it Frank? That's what you wanted?"

"Yeah, Rik. You did just fine. Perfect."

"Is there anything else you need me for?"

"Not at the moment. I'll let you know. And, thanks again."

As I hung up the comm there was a grin on my face as big as a lizardman's. I finished my drink and went to bed.

I slept in the next morning. I had a long night ahead of me. I took my time making breakfast, too. A little after noon I sent a message to Edgar and Terry's apartment. It read:

The package of meat you left at Vel's is waiting for you at Interspace Cold Storage. You might want to pick it up before Latimer does.

I included the image I had taken of the ID markings on the container. All I had to do now was wait and see if they would take the bait.

I left a message for Grot as well, asking for her to meet me later that evening. I said she should wear something warm.

In the message to Grot, I had told her to take the west down tram at eight o'clock, and that I would join her along the way. I was waiting at the tram stop, and unlike some women, she was right on time. The tram wasn't particularly crowded, and I was able to take the seat next to her after I had boarded.

She had taken my advice about clothing, as well as she had on a pair of black pants and a dark, high necked sweater. The heavy, ankle length boots she was wearing showed signs of use, as well.

She raised an eyebrow when I took my seat, but all I said was, "I'll explain later."

Passengers on the tram got off at each stop, and by the time we were far enough down city to be out of the residential districts we had the tram to ourselves.

"Okay, Frank. We're alone now. Would you mind explaining what we're doing."

"I've got a line on our lizardman. I left him a message that I'm hoping will cause him to tip his hand. We're going to be waiting for him."

"And the warm clothing?"

"You'll understand when we get there."

I was kind of enjoying myself being mysterious, but Grot didn't rise to the bait and ask more questions. Either it was discipline on her part, or she just didn't want to give me any satisfaction.

"There's a chance things might get a bit serious. Did you bring a weapon?"

Grot didn't say anything, but she turned and lifted her sweater. Tucked into the waistband in the small of her back was a laser pistol. It wasn't the one that she had carried in her purse earlier, but a heavier Kunstler 65. I opened my jacket to show her the modified little number that I had tucked into the shoulder holster I was wearing. It wasn't as heavy duty, but it had a quicker recycle time.

"Are you expecting trouble?"

"I'm hoping for it, but if we're lucky, not for us."

The stop where we got off was in the heart of the warehouse district. Except for the two of us there wasn't a soul around. The only movement came from the occasional robot shuffling cargo around. We walked four blocks spinward and then a couple of blocks down city. Grot was alert, but not nervous, confirming my notion that she was more than some minor diplomatic functionary.

I stopped us at a small doorway marked only with a ID number. The warehouse district isn't big on signage. The robots all know where they are going and any human with legitimate business should know where they're going as well.

I punched a code sequence into the keypad next to the door, and it unlocked, allowing us to enter. The door locked itself after us. We found ourselves in a small, dimly lit vestibule facing another door. This one wasn't locked. I opened it and ushered Grot through.

It was cold on the other side, freezing cold, maybe colder than I'd ever been before. I had worn a sweater over a shirt underneath my jacket and I was still feeling the cold as soon as we had stepped inside.

"Just where are we, Frank?" Grot asked.

"This is Interspace's Cold Storage Unit. I have reason to believe that the lizardman is going to try and retrieve something tonight. We're going to catch him in the act."

"And then?"

"Then we see what it is he's trying to retrieve."

We'd only been inside less than a minute, but my fingers were already going numb. I'd thought ahead and brought along a pair of gloves. I pulled them out of my pocket and put them on. They helped a little, but not much. I'd brought another pair for Grot, but before I could get them out she'd produced a pair of her own from her purse. She had a little knit cap in there, too, which she put on, pushing her hair up under it. I hadn't thought about that. Hats aren't a big deal on Star City where it never rains, except for the weekly shower when they wash down the streets, and that happens in the middle of the night.

"According to my information, the item of interest should be over in this direction," I said pointing along one of the aisles. On either side of us, shipping containers had been stacked two or three high with enough space between the rows to allow the cargo robots to maneuver. Glow strips on the ceiling provided enough light to see by, but there were still plenty of shadows, enough to hide an army of lizardmen.

I had a pretty good idea of where the container with the corpse had been stashed, and it only took a couple of minutes to find it. I checked the ID code on the door to make sure.

"Okay. This is the one. Now we need to find a hiding place where we can keep it under observation. Over there looks like a good place."

I pointed out a stack of crates that was about a meter and a half tall. It was high enough to provide cover, but low enough that someone standing behind it could look over the boxes at the container without revealing too much of themselves. There was a little alley next to the boxes so that we could get behind them without a lot of trouble.

"Make yourself comfortable, Grot. There's something I've got to attend to."

"What?"

"The door we came in through records every access. I've got an access code because I'm supposed to be checking up on some crates for a client. It knows I came in, now I have to make it think that I've left. I'll only be gone a few minutes."

I retraced my steps back to where we had come in. There was a keypad on the inside that matched the one on the exterior. I punched in my code and heard the door unlatch. I opened it and then shut it again without going through. It wasn't the most sophisticated security system, but then most of the items stored in the warehouse weighed hundreds of kilos and were too big to fit through the access door.

When I got back to our hiding place Grot looked cold, but not as cold as I felt. She seemed to be dealing with it a lot better than I was, probably because being from Earth she was used to there being weather. On Star City, the temperature never varies by more than a few degrees.

"Just how cold is it in here, Frank?"

"It's supposed to be kept at minus five degrees Celsius."

"And how long are we supposed to wait?"

"Until they show up. It might be a few hours."

"I don't suppose you thought to bring some hot coffee, did you?"

"Coffee? No. This is Star City. But I take your point. A container of hot joe would have been a good idea."

I was getting colder by the minute, and starting to grow envious of the little hat Grot was wearing. I'd never had to do a stakeout in condition like that and I was starting to wonder if my plan had been such a good idea.

"Don't think about the cold, Frank. That will only make it worse."

"You think?"

I checked the time on my comm. It was after eleven. I wasn't sure how much more of the cold I could take. I was starting to shiver. I looked over at Grot. She looked pretty miserable, but not as bad off as I was.

I was almost ready to call it quits when I heard a sound coming from the direction of the entry. I flexed my fingers to make sure that I'd be able to handle my pistol if I needed to. Grot had stripped the glove off of her right hand and was doing the same.

There were two sets of footsteps echoing through the warehouse. From their pacing, they sounded like humans. I thought about taking a peek over the boxes but decided against it. That was probably wise, because a moment later the footsteps stopped right in front of the boxes we were hiding behind.

"So where is he, Edgar?"

"How should I know. All I know is that Mr. Green said that he'd meet us here at a quarter after eleven."

"It's almost that now," Terry complained.

"You got a problem with it, you tell Mr. Green he's late."

"Not me. I just didn't know it would be so damn cold."

"Quit your complaining. We'll be out of here soon enough."

"You are correct," boomed a voice. It wasn't a human voice.

"Mr. Green. I didn't hear you. So what are we doing here?"

"There is a container I want to examine. It should be around this location." He rattled off the ID code of the container with the corpse and the three of them started searching for it.

"Here it is," Terry shouted.

I chanced a peak over the boxes. The three of them were standing in front of the container.

"Yes-ss. This is the one," the lizardman said. "Open it."

Edgar seemed to know his business. He produced a small gizmo and held it next to the lock on the door. A few seconds later there was a beep. He reached out for the handle and the door of the container swung open.

"Hey! It's the guy with four arms. The one you had us snuff. What's he doing here?"

"Yes-ss. What is he doing here? I told you to dispose of the body."

"We did," Edgar protested.

"Obviously not permanently. What did you do with body?"

"It ain't so easy getting rid of a body. Particularly an alien one. We left it in the office of a guy that caused problems for us in the past. We thought that if he couldn't deal with it, they'd pin the murder on him."

"It seems he was more clever than you were."

"What do you mean by that? And how did you know the body was here, anyway?" Terry asked.

"Because I received a message informing me of that fact," the lizardman answered.

"Who from?"

"That is a proper question," Mr. Green replied. "Someone who knows of my involvement. I see that I must clean up this mess as best I can."

The lizardman had a pistol out and was pointing it at the two human henchmen. He'd been fast, but not fast enough, because Edgar had a weapon of his own out. A second later, the other human also had a pistol pointing at the lizardman.

It was a standoff. The lizardman could get one of the two, but he would be shot by the other one before his laser could cycle for another shot. Neither of the humans was willing to risk the possibility that they would be the one that the lizardman shot.

Grot had poked her head up next to mine, taking in the scene.

"What are we going to do, Frank?"

"Help things along, I think."

I had my laser out. I'm not sure why I did what I did, but it seemed the right thing to do. Taking aim at a spot between the lizardman and the humans I fired. The results were what you'd expect. All three of them fired in reaction to my shot. Edgar went down. The lizardman had been hit, but he had just enough left in him to reach in and pull out his second gun. He fired it before Terry's own pistol could cycle for the second shot. He fell just as the lizardman slumped to the ground.

We were out of our hiding place. A quick check showed that the two humans were dead. I didn't think the lizardman would last more than a few seconds.

"Looks like we've found Mr. Smith," I said pointing at the container.

Grot pulled a little flashlight from her purse and illuminated the face of the corpse. "He's been dead for some time."

"Since before the container was sent to the warehouse, probably," I agreed. "There's nothing we can do for him now. I found out what happened to him for you, so you can report back to Earth."

"Yes," Grot said woodenly. "I can make my report."

"Look. It's not your fault. He was dead before you ever arrived on Star City."

"I know that, Frank," she responded with a shrug. "That doesn't mean I have to like it."

"I suggest we get out of here. Depending on how this place is wired, an alarm has probably gone out already."

She looked at the corpse with the four arms. There was nothing more to be done. "You're right. Let's go."

The door we had come in had been jimmied, either by the lizardman or the two humans. It didn't matter. We didn't have to use a code to get out, so there'd be no record of our having left the second time.

We walked to the north up tram. It was a little farther, but any police would probably be coming from the opposite direction.

I offered to buy a drink for Grot, but she refused. She said she just wanted to get back to her hotel. I didn't argue. Instead, I got off at the closest stop to my apartment and walked home.

I woke to the sound of pounding on the door of my apartment. Throwing on a pair of pants I went out to the entry hall. When I turned on the screen of the corridor security camera I saw a swarthy face that I recognized. It was Detective Rossetti, Latimer's partner. I opened the door and stepped back to let him burst in.

"Rossetti, do you know what time it is?"

"It's eleven, Sladek. Latimer wants to see you. Now."

"Can I get dressed first?" I was standing there with nothing on but my pants.

The question seemed to take Rossetti by surprise. I think that he was hoping I'd put up a fight.

"Okay. But make it quick."

"Sure thing. It will only take a minute. Make yourself at home."

I retired to the bedroom and proceeded to dress, taking my time about it. I didn't bother with the shoulder holster. One way or another, I wouldn't be needing it. As a finishing touch, I carefully combed my hair.

"You took your sweet time, Sladek," Rossetti commented when I finally appeared in the living room.

"I wanted to look presentable for the lieutenant."

"Can it, Sladek. Those wisecracks might play with Latimer, but they won't work with me."

"Have it your way, Rossetti. Should we get going? I wouldn't want to keep the lieutenant waiting." I waved Rossetti towards the door.

Down on the street there was an unmarked prowler parked at the curb. I've never understood the logic of unmarked police cars on Star City. With almost no private transport, police cars stick out like a sore thumb, marked or unmarked.

"You want me to get in back, Rossetti, or can I sit up front with you and work the siren?" I was enjoying myself. Both Rossetti and I knew that Latimer wanted me unharmed, so there wasn't anything the detective could do but take my wisecracks.

"Get in back, Sladek."

I got in back. The locks on the doors slid into place. It wasn't the first time I'd ridden in the backseat of a police car, and it probably wouldn't be my last.

Rossetti got in front and we headed down city.

I wasn't surprised when we pulled up in front of the Interspace cold storage warehouse. The meat wagon from the medical examiner was parked there as well as the crime lab truck.

"Hey, Rossetti. Something happen here last night?"

The detective turned around in the driver's seat and retorted, "As if you didn't already know," but the locks on the doors popped open.

"I take it we're going inside?" I asked. Rossetti didn't answer, but the cop stationed on the door opened it. We went inside.

I didn't need to pretend that I didn't know my way. The crime lab boys had set up some bright lights on poles down at the back. They lit Latimer up as if he were an actor on a stage.

"What took you so long?" Latimer asked, aiming at Rossetti, not me. He gets along with his partner about as well as I do.

"Sladek wanted to make himself pretty for you," Rossetti joked. It fell flat with Latimer.

"Why don't you get a statement from the warehouse foreman or something."

Rossetti looked like he was going to say something, but then thought better of it and walked away.

"So what's this about, Latimer?" I asked when Rossetti was out of earshot.

"Look around you, Frank. This has all the hallmarks of one of your last act of Hamlet scenes. I've got two dead humans, a dead lizardman, and a corpse with four arms. Unless I miss my guess, the latter is the one you've been looking for."

"Probably. Not many non-humans with four arms on Star City, and that doesn't look like Glzz."

"Glzz?" Latimer said, puzzled.

"The bartender at Viktor's."

"Yeah. It ain't him."

"Looks like you've got quite a mess on your hands, lieutenant. I'm not sure why you wanted me here, though."

"We checked the log on the door. It says that someone using your code entered about ten last night."

"It should also say that I left about fifteen minutes later. These guys weren't here at that time. At least not that I saw."

"Yeah. It says that, too. So what were you doing here, Frank?"

"A client of mine asked me to check up on some containers that he's got stored here. He was worried that they might have been stolen or broken into."

"Mind if I ask who your client is?"

"Not particularly. It was Vel Lindol."

"The caterer?"

"Yeah. He's got some containers with frozen Nebraska beef."

"That wouldn't happen to be one of them, would it?"

He was pointing to the container with Mr. Smith. The alien was still folded up inside, though one of his four arms had flopped out.

"No. That's not one of his. I can give you the ID numbers for the ones that are his." I pulled out my comm and read off the numbers of half a dozen containers that belonged to Vel.

"So you checked the containers and left?"

"Yeah. Everything seemed to be in order. The containers were where they should be and the seals were intact."

"And you didn't see anything out of the ordinary?"

"Like dead bodies? No. When I logged out, everything was quiet as a graveyard."

"You should watch you remarks, Frank. Some people might take them the wrong way."

"I'll keep that in mind."

"The two dead humans match the descriptions that you gave me of the guys who attacked you. Don't you think that's kind of a coincidence?"

"Maybe, maybe not. Those two were obviously criminals. It's not surprising that they came to a bad end."

"Yeah," Latimer said. We both knew I was playing games, but so far Latimer hadn't seemed ready to call me on it.

"So what happened?"

"It appears that there was quite a bit of gunplay. As far as the M.E. has been able to determine, the two humans and the lizardman all died of shots fired from laser pistols. By the way, you don't happen to recognize the lizardman, do you?"

"No, but then to me they all look pretty much alike. Big, green, and ugly."

"Yeah."

"What about the guy with the four arms?"

"He was knifed. Some sort of long, thin blade." Latimer made motions with his hands to indicate the size of the presumed weapon. It was about the size of a chef's knife.

"Did you find the weapon?"

"No. Apparently it had been removed before he was stuffed into the box."

"How long has he been sitting there?"

"The records show the container arrived in the warehouse seven days ago. Of course, it also looks like the records have been tampered with, so who knows. Why all the interest, Frank? If everything was alright when you left."

"I'll need to make a report to my client. Ms. Fender, not Lindol. After all, it does look like this is the alien she was trying locate."

"Yeah. So what do you think happened here, Frank?"

"I'm just guessing, but it looks to me like a case of thieves falling out. I'd say that the lizardman had hired the other two to do some dirty work for him. Probably it involved the guy with the four arms. They probably stashed the body here after they killed him. Maybe they got nervous and broke in to retrieve the body so that they could dispose of it in a more permanent way.

Anyway, either the lizardman had decided that the two henchmen were a liability and was trying to get rid of him, or the two humans were trying to double-cross the lizardman. Take your pick. Whichever you think will look better in your report. They came here, the shooting started, and when it was over, they were all dead."

"Kind of improbable, don't you think, Frank?"

"I don't know. The way I figure it, the humans got in the first shot, wounding the lizardman. He fired back killing both of them before dying. Those lizardmen are tough sons-of-bitches, Latimer. They can stay upright a long time even with a mortal wound."

"Yeah. I suppose it could have happened that way. Not that I believe it."

"Does it fit the evidence, Latimer?"

"More or less."

"Does it matter then?"

"What's your point, Frank?"

"Look at it this way, lieutenant. The lizardman takes the fall for killing the guy with four arms. That keeps Crockett and Earth out of it. If four arms' people come asking around about what happen, things all get blamed on lizardmen, not humans. It looks to me like a prescription for avoiding a diplomatic incident."

"And the two dead humans?"

"Do you really think anyone is going to morn them. From something Vel told me, I think they both were on Mr. Anthony's shit list. I wouldn't be surprised if he hadn't had something to do with this business."

"That's all I need," Latimer said. It might not be official, but Mr. Anthony was a much Latimer's boss as anyone was.

I knew what he was thinking. The story I had just spun him would allow him to tie the whole think up in a big red bow. He could write his report and file it away and everyone would be happy. Did it really matter that some of it was a tissue of lies?

"Sometimes, Frank, I think you stage these things just so you can concoct some wild yarn to explain it all away."

"Would I do that, Latimer?"

Latimer looked like he was going to say something in response, but then thought better of it. "Unless you got something to add, why don't you get out of here, Frank. Before I decide that this mess is all your doing."

"Sure thing."

On the way out, I waved at Rossetti. He just scowled in return.

Grot left for Earth the next day on the Arcturus. She asked me to see her off. I figured I owed her that much.

As we were standing on the boarding concourse waiting for the gate for her starliner to open she asked, "You knew the body was in the warehouse all the time, didn't you, Frank?"

I looked into her eyes. There was fire in them, but they looked years older than the face they stared out of.

"Yeah."

"Even before I arrived?"

"Yeah. I was the one that put it there." I went on to explain how the corpse had been planted in Vel's office, and how we had gotten it out of there.

"So you knew this and still you took my money?"

"It was Earth's money, not yours. If you remember, you paid me to find our four-armed friend or find out what had happened to him. Well, I knew he was dead, but I didn't know how he had ended up that way. Neither did you. I found out, and took care of the messy business of cleaning up, afterwards. The way I see it, it was money well spent."

Despite the look in her eye, we both knew that what I had said was true. Her bosses back on Terra would see it that way, too.

"You're a real bastard, Frank."

"That's what my mother told me. When I was five. She meant it, too."

"Frank—" but she didn't say anything more. We stood around until the purser opened up the gate and boarding started.

"Now I know why Lucinda painted that portrait of you, Frank." She reached up and kissed me, then turned and walked through the gate.

After that, I went up to the Promenade and stared out at the distant stars. Sometime later the Arcturus began its ponderous separation from Star City, slowly pulling away until it was far enough away that it could initiate the tachyon drive. I watched as long as there was something to see and then I went home.

THE
BODY THAT
WASN'T

THE BODY THAT WASN'T

It all started when I got a call from Rik Lane. Rik Lane is the house detective at the Landfal Hotel, a second class place that mostly caters to commercial travelers. Rik isn't exactly what I'd call a friend, but our relationship is amiable enough; he's let me park myself in the Landfal's lobby without asking questions, and he's tipped me off when someone I've been interested in was staying at the hotel. In return, I'll slip him a Crockett fin or sawbuck as the occasion warrants. Rik is okay as a house dick but maybe not the brightest bulb in a socket; he can handle the drunks alright or spot someone trying to hustle one of the hotel's guests, but he's out of his depth when it comes to the more sophisticated cons, and he knows it. Being the hotel dick at the Landfal doesn't pay the best, and occasionally Rik will pick up freelance work on the side; I've hired him myself a few times when I've needed an extra set of eyes.

I was surprised when I saw it was him calling. I didn't have any ongoing jobs that involved the Landfal or anyone staying there. In fact, at that exact moment, I didn't have any jobs going at all. Things had been slow and I'd been living off my cash reserves, so I answered in the hopes that the call might turn into something that paid.

"What's up, Rik?" Not the wittiest line, but then it was only 0900 and I'd been drowning my sorrows at the Blue Moon the night before.

"Hi, Frank. Thanks for picking up. I've got kind of a situation here at the hotel, and I was wondering if you could give me a hand with it."

Lane sounded rattled, not that that meant much. Despite being a house dick, he isn't a particularly physical guy, and it didn't take much to put him out of his comfort zone.

"What kind of a situation?" I asked, trying not to sound too suspicious.

"I'd rather not say over the comm."

I suppose that should have alerted me that something was up, but then handling "situations" is just part of the business I'm in.

"Okay. What do you want me to do?"

"Could you meet me in the lobby? Right away?"

"I'll be there as soon as I can."

"Thanks, Frank." Even over the comm, I could sense the relief in Lane's voice.

When I walked into the lobby of the Landfal twenty minutes later, Rik was pacing nervously back and forth threatening to wear a hole in the carpeting. He looked up with a start when he saw me. I gave a nod towards a secluded corner and headed in that direction. When he had caught up with me I asked, "Alright, Rik, what's up?"

"I don't know what to do, Frank. I need some advice."

"About what?" I asked, still unclear as to what his problem was.

"A body was found this morning in one of the rooms. Dead. What should I do?"

"Well, for a start, you could call Latimer. Bodies are sort of his line."

Latimer was the lead homicide detective for Star City. He and I had had frequent dealings in the past, enough so that I would have earned a volume discount if there were such a thing.

"That's just it, Frank. I'd really rather not involve the police."

"That's going to be kind of hard, isn't it. I mean with the dead body and all."

Rik looked nervous, but embarrassed, too.

"It's like this, Frank. I kind of have this arrangement with some of the working girls here in the hotel."

"Let me guess, you let them operate and they slip you some cash under the table."

"Something like that, Frank. Let's put it this way, I'm providing a service. I vet the girls, make sure that they don't roll any of their clients and make sure there isn't any rough stuff. In return, the girls show me their appreciation, if you get what I mean."

Prostitution isn't exactly legal on Star City, but then it isn't exactly not, either. Of course most of the whore houses are run by the same people that run the big hotels, and just about everything else, for that matter. That doesn't mean there aren't a certain number of freelance sex workers, though, trying to get by without the overhead of working for one of the operations.

"Like I said, they slip you a few bucks to conduct business."

"Well, yes, if you want to put it that way."

"But things didn't work out so well, and one of the guests ended up dead."

"Actually, it was the other way around, Frank. The body is one of the girls."

"And the guest?"

"He checked out early this morning. That was before housekeeping found the body."

"I still don't see why you don't just call Latimer, Rik."

"Look, Frank, management doesn't know what's going on, officially, at least. If the cops get involved I could lose my job. Good jobs like this aren't easy to come by these days for someone like me."

"I sympathize with your plight, Rik, but what do you expect me to do about it?"

"Well—I was kind of hoping you'd help me get rid of the body," Rik said sounding like what I imagined a young puppy would sound like.

"My line is more in finding things, Rik. Disposal is another department altogether."

"But you must have some idea of how to deal with something like this. After all, you have kind of a reputation for—"

That's my problem. I have a reputation. Sure, I know how to shoot a laser or a needle gun, and there have been a few incidents where the body count may have gotten out of hand, but I'm really not as hard-boiled as some people might think.

"Tell you what, Rik. Why don't we go up to the room where this—person is and I'll see if there is anything I can suggest."

"Would you, Frank?"

"I'm here. I might as well," I said with a shrug. Though I've seen more than a few bodies in my time, I don't relish the prospect, but I don't faint, either. I'm not sure that I could have said the same of Rik, the state he was in.

We rode the elevator up to the eighth floor and got off. At room 817 Rik used his key card and let us in, quickly shutting the door behind us. I looked around, but all I saw was a hotel room. I'd been in the Landfal a number of times before, and this room didn't look any different than any of the others. There was a bed that looked like it had been freshly made, an entertainment unit on the wall, a dresser, a table and a few chairs, etc. What there wasn't was a body.

I turned to Rik and asked, "Okay, where is she?   The bathroom?" Rik's jaw had dropped.

"She's gone, Frank."

"Well, it looks like your problem has been solved. Can I go home and back to bed now?"

"I tell you, Frank, she was right there on the bed. I saw her with my own eyes."

"Well, she's not there now. Are you sure she was as dead as you thought she was?"

"Geez, Frank. I'm no big shot shamus like you, but I know a dead body when I see one."

"Uh-huh. Look, you say the dead broad was laying on the bed. Had it been made?"

"What?" Rik asked unsteadily.

"Had the bed been made when you saw the body?"

"No. The covers had been thrown back and the pillows mussed up."

"And I don't suppose there's any chance that housekeeping came in and tidied things up after you left?"

"No. I left instructions to leave the room alone. I know the woman in housekeeping who works this floor. She wouldn't get rid of a dead body." Rik was right, there were probably union rules against it.

I thought things over for a minute. Then I opened the door to the bathroom and took a look inside. No body. I did notice that there was a dirty towel lying on the floor. Whoever had made the bed hadn't bothered with the rest of the housekeeping services. I went back into the main room. There wasn't anything in the closet. The drawers of the dresser and the nightstand were empty, too, except for one of those bibles you find in hotels.

"Well, Rik, it's like this. Either the girl wasn't as dead as you thought she was or someone came in here and cleaned things up a bit after you were here. Either way, I think it solves your problem. I'd call housekeeping, have them finish up in the bathroom and then forget about it."

"But I tell you, Frank, she was dead. No pulse, no breathing. I checked."

"Okay. Were there any signs as to how she died? Any blood? Marks on the body? Was she dressed?"

"There wasn't any blood. No bruises or anything that I could see. She wasn't wearing anything except her underwear."

"What about the rest of her clothes?"

"They were draped on that chair over there by the window."

"Well, that's good. At least you don't have to worry about a half-naked corpse wandering around the hotel," I quipped. I admit, I was finding the whole business amusing.

"How can you joke about something like this, Frank?" Rik complained.

"Oh, I can joke about almost anything, Rik. Especially when it doesn't affect me. Look, take my advice. Forget about it. The girl, or the body, or whatever, is gone. There's really nothing for you to worry about, is there? Just chalk it up to experience and move on."

"You really think that's what I should do, Frank?"

"It's what I'd do, Rik. Now let's get out of here before someone starts to wonder what we're doing."

We went out into the hall. As Rik was locking the door I glanced down the hall towards the elevator where a blonde in a bright orange sleeveless dress was waiting for the car.

I was admiring the view when Rik called out, "That's her! That's the girl!" just as the elevator doors closed behind her.

By the time we had reacted, the elevator was gone. The indicator above the door showed that it was headed down towards the lobby. Rik frantically pressed the down button for the second elevator. Fortunately, the car must have been on an adjacent floor and within moments we were descending.

Arriving at the lobby, Lane jumped out of the car and looked around. There were only a few people in the lobby, none of them in an orange dress. Rik got a few odd looks with these antics while I hung back in the elevator.

Grabbing Lane by the arm, I pulled him over to the reception desk.

I asked the desk clerk, "You didn't happen to see a woman in an orange dress get off the elevator just now?"

The clerk gave me an odd look. "No, there was just you and Mr. Lane."

"I mean the other elevator."

"No, it was empty. It does that sometimes. People call the car and then change their mind I guess."

"You're sure?" Rik chimed in.

"Quite sure, Mr. Lane," the desk clerk responded before making a point of busying himself with something. It was clear that he wanted the two of us to know he had better things to do than answer silly questions. Another time, I might have enjoyed Rik's discomfort, but I was worried he was going to lose it.

"Look, Rik," I said, drawing him away from the counter, "the dead dame must have gotten off on another floor. I don't suppose you have any way to track what stops that elevator made."

I knew, of course, that the elevators were controlled by a central computer and that records could be accessed by security, Rik being security, but I wanted to give him a chance to recover his composure and maybe save a little face in the process. He pulled out his comm, and after a few moments announced, "It stopped at the third floor. She must have gotten out there."

We hopped back on the elevator and rode it up to the third floor, but neither one of us was surprised when there wasn't any sign of a woman in an orange dress. Despite that, Rik insisted on checking out the floor. We looked in the alcove with the ice machine and the couple of closets used by housekeeping that weren't locked. He used his pass key to look into the rooms that weren't occupied, but they were all empty. The register had images from check-in for all the rooms that were occupied, and none of the guests looked remotely like the dead woman Rik had seen.

Lane suggested that we search the second and fourth floors, but I had a better idea. I took him down to the small bar off the lobby and ordered a pair of browns and soda. Brown is what passes for whiskey on Star City if you're on a budget. I wasn't going to waste good money on real imported booze, but I thought Rik needed something to calm him down.

"Look, Rik," I said, after I have put a glass in his hand, "are you sure that you want to bother with this? After all, you don't have a body to worry about any more, do you?"

"But she was dead, Frank. I'm sure about it."

"She didn't look dead to me when she got on that elevator," I objected.

"Maybe I don't have as much experience in such things as you do, Frank, but I know a dead body when I see one."

As I said earlier, over the years, I've acquired a reputation for being on the scene when the body count has mounted up. It's not really fair, as I haven't been personally responsible for more than half of those, but still I have the reputation.

"Okay. Are you sure that the woman that got on the elevator was the one from the room? After all, we only got a quick look at her, and that was from the back."

"I'm sure it was the same woman, Frank. She had the same hair color and style and she was wearing the same dress that I saw in the room. You have to admit, there aren't many women running around in bright orange dresses like she was wearing."

I took a sip of my drink. Rik was right about at least one thing, there weren't many women around who could pull off wearing a dress like that.

"Alright, let's say for the sake of argument that the woman we saw get on the elevator was the one in the room, and that somehow she managed to convince you that she was dead. It's quite apparent that she isn't dead, which brings me back to my original question. Do you really want to bother pursuing the matter?"

"I can't have people going around pretending to be dead in the hotel, Frank. It would be bad for business. I could lose my job."

"You've got no evidence that she's going to make a habit of it, Rik. Why would she. It was probably a one time thing. And who else saw the body?"

"There was the maid from housekeeping."

"You ought to be able to make up a story that will keep her happy. Tell her the woman was drunk or on some kind of recreational pharmaceutical. Slip her a couple of credits and she'll keep things quiet."

Rik thought about it for a minute. "There was the guy who was checked into that room. He must have seen her. That's why he checked out early."

"Look, Rik, chances are that he won't bring the subject up, either. After all, having a dead girl in your bed isn't the kind of thing you'd brag about. But maybe we should have a talk with him, just in case. Do you know where he is now?"

Rik shook his head. "No. Like I said, he checked out this morning. He didn't leave a forwarding address."

"But you do know his name, don't you? And where he's from?"

"I've got what he put down when he registered." Rik played some games with his comm. A moment later he said brightly, "His name is Jak Pringely. Home address is Alamo, Crockett. He's some kind of saleman."

I wasn't surprised. The Landfal was that sort of hotel.

"Okay. He's either taken a starliner somewhere, in which case he's no longer a problem, or he's still on Star City, which means he's got to be staying someplace."

I got out my own comm and did some checking. Passenger manifests were a matter of public record. It didn't take me long to discover that Jak Pringely was booked on a liner to New Albion in three days, which meant he was still on Star City. He'd probably checked into another hotel. Hotel records were a little less accessible, but fortunately I had a friend in Records who had slipped me a password in exchange for dinner and a couple of drinks. It didn't take me long to find that Pringely was staying at the Commodore, another second tier hotel, though maybe a step up from the Landfal. Maybe Pringely wanted to make sure he didn't end up with another corpse in his bed.

"Pringely is in room 514 at the Commodore. We could go over and have a talk with him."

"Gee, Frank," Rik said with a hangdog expression on his face. "I've got to stay here at the Landfal. Could you maybe go have a talk with this guy and square things?"

My first reaction was to ask myself why should I get myself anymore involved. It wasn't as if Lane and I were really good buddies. But I wasn't doing anything else at the moment and frankly, I was becoming interested in finding out more about this woman who could fake death.

"Sure, I'll take care of it, Rik. You wouldn't happen to have any scratch on you in case I have to grease Pringely to keep quiet?" Like I said, I was interested, but I didn't see any reason to spend my own money.

Rik looked pained at the thought, but he dug out his wallet and came up with a couple of well worn Crockett double saw bucks.

"I'll give it back to you if I don't need it," I said cheerily as I stuffed the bills in my own pocket.

As I said, the Commodore is a step up from the Landfal, but not one of the top notch hotels like the Casino or even the Rigel Royal. It caters to business travelers and tourists, is clean and respectable, and it has a bar where a decent keyboard player entertains in the evening. I used one of the lobby phones to call up to room 514.

"Hello?" The voice that answered was kind of a squeaky tenor.

"Is this Jak Pringely speaking?" I asked, trying not to sound threatening.

"Who is this?"

"My name is Frank Sladek, Mr. Pringely. I'd like to discuss something that happened at the Landfal Hotel earlier today. Can I come up?"

"I don't know anything about the Landfal Hotel, Mr. –"

"Sladek. Now we both know that isn't true, don't we, Mr. Pringely?"

"What is it you want?"

"Like I said, I just want to discuss the matter. However, if you'd rather not, I could pass the word to Sgt. Latimer in Homicide–."

"No, that won't be necessary," Pringely squeeked. "Come on up."

I headed up to the fifth floor. I'd caught the attention of the Commodore's house dick crossing the lobby, but I gave him a wave to tell him he didn't need to worry. He shrugged and turned back to the business of standing around with his eyes open.

When I knocked on the door of 514, it was opened by Pringely. Jak Pringely proved to be a pudgy, balding guy of just under average height. He looked to be around fifty if you were counting in Earth years, or maybe forty-five on Crockett. His pasty complexion was even whiter than mine which meant that he didn't get out anyplace where he'd be exposed to ultraviolet rays. He was wearing a light blue shirt with a frayed collar unbuttoned at the top and brown pants. He wasn't wearing any shoes.

As he shut the door behind me, I took a quick look around. There wasn't much to see except an open suitcase on a stand next to the dresser and a bottle of Old Star City sitting on the dresser itself. The bottle had been opened and there were about four fingers worth missing. An empty glass with a couple of half melted ice cubes was next to the bottle.

"Can I offer you a drink?" Pringely asked. I took that as a good sign.

"Sure, why not."

"Ice and soda?"

"Ice is fine. You can skip the soda if you want."

Pringely busied himself with the drinks. There was a bucket of ice on the dresser top along with another glass and one of those little bottles of soda that come from the mini fridge. I noticed that the bottle shook as he poured the brown.

"Just exactly what did you want to discuss, Mr. Sladek?" he said, handing me a glass.

"Thanks for the drink, Mr. Pringely. What I want to discuss is the dead woman that was found in your room at the Landfal this morning."

"I don't know what you're talking about," Pringley protested.

"Oh, I'm pretty sure that you do, Mr. Pringely. There was a dead woman in your bed when you checked out. A blonde in an orange dress, except that she wasn't wearing the dress when housekeeping found her."

"Is this some kind of shakedown, Sladek? If it is, I have to tell you I don't have much money—"

"This isn't a shakedown, Pringely. All I' interested in is a little information. Between you and me, I'd just as soon keep the whole business quiet. It might embarrass my client."

Okay, Rik Lane wasn't exactly a client, but Pringely didn't need to know that.

"Just who are you, Mr. Sladek?"

"I've got a license as a private investigator, Mr. Pringely, but let's just say that I'm looking after a friend and leave it at that."

Pringely looked as if he was going to object, but then he wilted and slumped down onto the bed.

"What do you want to know, Mr. Sladek?"

"Well let's start with who the dame was?"

"I don't know. She said her name was Peli."

"That's all? Just Peli?"

"I didn't ask."

"Look, Mr. Pringely, why don't you start at the beginning. Where did you meet this Peli?"

"I'm a salesman, Mr. Sladek. I checked into the Landfal yesterday. I've got a connecting passage to New Albion on the Thurston III in three days. I went down to the bar for a drink after I had dinner. I was just sitting by myself when she sat next to me. She ordered a drink, something blue that glowed. I must have stared at it. She saw me and smiled. We got to talking."

"What about?" I asked. "The weather?" That's kind of an old joke on Star City. Living on the inside of a hollowed out asteroid we don't really have any of what you'd call weather.

"Oh, just things. She asked what I did. I told her about the places I've been. You've got to understand, I get kind of lonely sometimes. If you've seen her, even dead, you know she was quite a looker."

I was starting to feel sorry for the poor sap. Living out of a suitcase, hopping from star system to star system, why shouldn't he react to a beautiful woman. I didn't see the need to mention that I'd only seen her from the back as she got onto an elevator.

"So what happened next?"

"We had a drink, and then another, I guess. Then she suggested we go up to my room. I agreed. You understand why, don't you, Mr. Sladek."

"Oh, I understand why, alright, Mr. Pringely. In your shoes I might have even done the same. What I don't understand is how she ended up dead in your bed."

"I didn't do anything. You've got to believe me." Pringely was sounding a little panicky.

"Take it easy, Mr. Pringely. Just tell me what happened next."

"Well, like I said, we went up to my room. We had another drink. I had a bottle in the room. She was being real nice to me. She kissed me and let me put my hand on her leg."

I could see that Pringely was getting excited in the retelling. I was getting excited, too.

"She asked me to unzip her dress. I did so. She slipped out of it and then laid down on the bed. I took my clothes off and laid down next to her. And then—"

"And then what, Mr. Pringely?"

"And then she began to get on top of me. That's when I found out she—"

"She what, Mr. Pringely?"

"She wasn't human."

"She wasn't human, Mr. Pringely? What do you mean? Do you mean she was a blueskin?" Blueskins are genetically modified humans who are adapted to live in oxygen rich atmospheres. They're different, but they are still human. I didn't think Pringely would have had a problem with that.

"No. She wasn't human. Down there. We weren't—compatible." I swear he blushed when he said that.

"What did you do when you found that out, Mr. Pringely?"

"I panicked. I guess I might have screamed."

"Did you hit her?"

"No. How could you think—No, when I screamed, she just went limp. At first I thought she had fainted, but then when I felt her, she didn't have a pulse and she was cold to the touch. I knew she was dead."

I found Pringely's story a little hard to believe, but I had to admit it fit the facts.

"What did you do then?"

"I pulled up her panties so I wouldn't have to look. Then I had a drink. I needed one. Then I took a shower. To think that I had touched that—thing."

Somehow that made me feel less sympathy for Mr. Pringely.

"What happened next?"

"I packed my bags and checked out."

"Just leaving the body in the bed? You didn't think to contact anyone?"

"I didn't want to get involved. After all, I hadn't really hurt her. I had just screamed. It's not my fault that she died."

I didn't see any point in arguing with him, especially as it looked like the woman wasn't really dead.

"Okay, Mr. Pringely. I want to thank you for being honest with me. Now, you can understand that the hotel wants to keep this matter quiet. If you don't mention it and just get on the Thurston III in a few days, we'll keep you out of it. You just have to promise me not to tell anyone, and I mean anyone. If you do, I'll have to tell what I know to the police. Do you understand?"

"I understand, Mr. Sladek. And thank you."

I stood up then. I thought about finishing my drink, but I decided I didn't want to drink any more of Pringely's booze, so I left.

If I believed Pringely's story, and I didn't see him as a particularly creative liar, this put a new twist on Rik's walking corpse. Now there are plenty of non-humans on Star City, the official figure is around fifty thousand, but most of them are, well, alien. A few of them might be able to pass as human—if the light were bad and you weren't too close. Most of them, though, were like lizardmen or Glzz, the four armed bartender at Viktor's; not only not human, but not even vaguely mammalian. Yet the woman, if that was even the appropriate gender, that had been in Pringely's room at the Landfal had been able to fool not only the salesman but Rik. Her true nature had only been revealed to Pringely when he had seen her in the altogether. Rik, who, to his credit, had not seen her naked, had been convinced that the alien was not only human but a damned attractive one at that.

I wasn't aware of any alien species that fit the bill, but it's a great big galaxy out there, most of it beyond the boundaries of that irregular blob known as the sphere of human influence. Contacts outside the boundaries are limited, but that hasn't kept the odd individual from making their way to Star City with the emphasis usually on odd. How or why this Peli or whatever her name was came to be on Star City was anyone's guess, but when it came down to it, I wasn't that surprised. As I headed back to the Landfal, I wondered how Rik would take the revelation.

Rik spotted me as I entered the lobby. Usually when that happens, he tries to be discrete. We go off to some corner of the lobby and have our conversation while pretending we don't know each other. This time, however, he came right up to me and blurted out, "Well?"

"Maybe we should go someplace where we can talk in private," I said as an answer.

Rik can be quick on the uptake when the situation arises. "Sure, Frank." He lead the way back to a service elevator at the back of the hotel, where a biosensor recognized him and gave us access.

Once inside, Rik said, "Subbasement." Deciding that we were authorized, the elevator descended.

I'd never had occasion to be down there before, but it turned out that Rik had a tiny office next to that of the head housekeeper's. There was a sign that read "Security" on the door. Inside, there were two chairs, a small desk and not much else. The wall behind the desk had a screen displaying multiple video feeds of the lobby and exits.

Rik didn't bother to offer me a seat, but I took one, anyway.

"So what did Pringely have to say?" Rik said anxiously.

"How good a look did you get at the corpse?"

"Geez, Frank. Stop saying that. She's not dead."

"Okay, she's not dead, but how good a look at her did you get when she was?"

"What are you getting at, Frank? I looked her over, felt for a pulse, that kind of thing. When I couldn't find a pulse, well, I guess I might have panicked a little."

"But did you notice if she was wearing a wig or if her breasts were real?"

"They looked real enough to me. Why are you so interested?"

"Because Pringely said she wasn't human."

"She looked human enough to me, Frank. Except for being dead I thought she looked pretty damned good."

"Did you look underneath her panties?"

"What kind of pervert do you think I am, Frank? With a corpse?"

I retold Pringely's story. Understandably, Rik had a lot of questions that I couldn't answer.

"This is terrible, Frank. An alien seducing customers at the Landfal. I could lose my job if this got out."

I was glad to see that Lane was keeping things in perspective.

"I take it this Peli isn't one of the working girls with whom you have an arrangement?"

"Geez, no, Frank. I wouldn't allow no alien hookers to work here."

"But you didn't know she wasn't human, did you?"

"Well, no. But she wasn't one of the regulars. I would have recognized her if she was. Why did she have to pick on the Landfal?"

"Maybe she's a guest," I suggested.

"A guest?" Rik asked incredulously. The Landfal doesn't cater to non-humans.

"That would explain what she was doing in the lobby bar."

"I don't know—"

"You could at least check."

Rik played some games with the keyboard on the desk. One of the video feeds on the wall screen was replaced with the registration images of current guests. He must have set up some sort of filter, because they were all women. It didn't take long until he froze on one. The caption read "Room 324, Peli Smythe."

I hadn't seen her from the front before. Rik had been right, she wasn't bad looking. True, her nose seemed just a bit too narrow and her green eyes were maybe just a shade too far apart, but neither was outside the range of normal human features. In the image she wasn't showing her teeth, hiding them with a pert little smile. She had blonde hair that had been cut in a "cute" style that framed her face and extended down just past her chin line. It was a face that would merit a second glance, but not because it was alien.

The registration card which Rik had brought up said that she had checked in three days earlier having arrived on a liner from Belize, a world I knew vaguely as being somewhere out on the fringes. Her occupation was listed as tourist. The room had been reserved for ten days, and she had paid for it with a credit stick issued by one of the major banks on Crockett. I knew from experience that those kind of credit sticks are hard to fake. In addition to the room charge, she had racked up a bill of 142.75 $C, mostly for room service. At hotel rates, either she was a light eater or she had been eating out for some of her meals.

"So what do we do now, Frank?"

"It seems like Ms. Smythe is still registered, Rik. Maybe we should go up to 324 and pay her a visit."

"Do you think that's smart?" Rik asked.

"I don't know. I suppose we could just wait around until she shows up dead again." I have to admit, I was kind of looking forward to meeting Peli Smythe.

"Good point," Rik conceded.

We rode the service elevator up to the third floor. Rik knocked a couple of times on the door of 324, but got no answer. Finally he used his passkey to let us in.

I think maybe we were both expecting to find her lying on the bed, dead again, but when we had entered, there was no one there. A quick check of the room showed a couple of suitcases of the sort used by starliner passengers. A number of dresses were hung in the closet, including the orange sleeveless number she had been wearing when we saw her get into the elevator. I took a quick peek at the labels. Most were from local Star City shops but a few were from Belize and a Crockett department store that has branches on a number of planets. There were quite a few pairs of shoes and several purses as well. Everything was of good quality but not from really exclusive labels. In short, it was about what you'd expect for a well-heeled woman traveling the stars for an extended period of time.

A look in the drawers of the dresser showed the usual assortment of women's unmentionables. I don't pretend to be an expert in those sort of things, but the panties seemed to have some custom padding in unusual places. The bras looked stock.

There wasn't much else in the room, no bottles of booze or anything like that. Housekeeping had evidently been in and tidied things up. There wasn't anything that I would have classified as a weapon, either. There was a reader sitting on the nightstand. A quick check of the index showed that it mostly contained novels of the type known as "romance" but which are really more about sex and seduction. There were a couple of travel guides for Crockett and Terra as well.

Nothing in the room provided me much insight as to who or what Ms. Smythe was or what she was up to.

"So what do we do now?" Rik asked yet again.

"Well, you could leave a note asking her to contact Security," I commented.

"Do you think that would work?" Rik asked hopefully.

"No. Do you?"

"I guess not."

"In that case, I don't think there's much point in my hanging around."

We headed down to the lobby. As we got off the elevator, I spotted Latimer and Rossetti talking to someone just outside the bar. Latimer is the lead homicide detective for the Star City security service. Rossetti is either his assistant or his partner depending on which one you ask.

Rik saw them, too. "I wonder what they're doing here?"

"We could always go ask," I suggested. I was curious to know myself, and I suspected their presence wasn't a coincidence.

I followed Rik over to where Latimer was interviewing a man. From the aggressive hounds-tooth check of his jacket, he looked to be an out-of-towner, which is anyone not from Star City, which probably meant he was a guest at the hotel. Though it was only the middle of the afternoon, it looked as if he had had a few and Latimer was having trouble getting coherent answers to his questions.

"Is there anything I can help you with, Sgt. Latimer?" Rik asked, trying to sound helpful.

Latimer looked like he was trying to think of a smart reply when he saw me. "What's he doing here?" he asked testily. Latimer is about as honest as a Star City cop can be and reasonably bright, which is more than I can say for his partner. He had some reason to be suspicious of my presence as we have a habit of meeting over dead bodies.

"Me? I was just shooting the breeze with my buddy Rik."

"Sure you were. You're hanging around wouldn't have anything to do with the dead woman in 702, would it?"

I had an odd feeling that I knew what he was referring to. "I don't have any idea what you're talking about, Latimer."

"So you don't know anything about the deceased blonde that Mr. Snarski here says he found in his room?"

"I know that we've met under some unfortunate circumstances before, Latimer, but that doesn't mean corpses pile up every time I'm around. Besides, I've never seen Mr. Snarski before in my life. Isn't that right, Mr. Snarski?"

He responded rather drunkenly with, "Whoareyou?"

"Between you and me, Latimer, Mr. Snarski here doesn't strike me as the most reliable witness."

"No one asked you, Sladek," Rossetti chimed in which earned him dirty looks from both me and Latimer.

"Still, if he says there's a dead body in his room maybe we should go up and check it out." Rik got a panicked look on his face at my suggestion.

"This is police business, Frank. No one has invited you to the party."

"It seems to me that you were questioning my involvement. I'm just trying to cooperate."

"Yeah, sure," Latimer said with a sigh, knowing that he'd been out maneuvered. "Well, we might as well check it out."

The five of us got into an elevator and headed up to the seventh floor. When we got out, Snarski turned the wrong way and Rossetti had to grab him and point him in the right direction.

Room 702 was down at the end of the corridor. Rik used his passkey to let us in, swinging the door open. I think he was afraid to look inside. He needn't have worried, though, the room was empty.

Latimer gave the room a quick once over while Rossetti deposited Mr. Snarski in a chair and went into the bathroom. When he came out he said, "No dead broad in there, either."

Latimer was looking like his patience was wearing thin. "Just where was this body, Mr. Snarski?"

"Right there in the bed," he answered, pointing. After a pause he asked, "What did you do with her?"

The bed looked rumpled, but then so did Mr. Snarski. There weren't any other signs that anyone else had been in the room.

"We didn't do anything with her. You know you can get in big trouble making false claims, Mr. Snarski."

"But she was there, I tell you. Lying in the bed, dead."

"Dead drunk, you mean," Rossetti commented, which got him another dirty look from Latimer.

"You don't have any idea what he's talking about, do you Lane?" Latimer asked.

"Sorry, Latimer," Rik replied. "I'm afraid Mr. Snarski must have been seeing things. Too many drinks."

"Yeah, either that, or he had a woman up here and she walked out on him. Come on, Rossetti, it's pretty obvious there's nothing for us here. Sorry to have caused you any trouble, Lane."

"Don't think anything of it, sergeant. Always happy to help out the police."

Latimer and Rossetti left. Rik and I stayed behind.

"Why don't you tell us what happened, Mr. Snarski?" I asked.

"I could use a drink."

I grabbed a bottle of brown from the mini-fridge and poured Snarski a weak one. I didn't want him to pass out before we got his story.

"Here you go," I said, handing him the glass.

"You're a real pal," Snarski said.

"Thanks. Now tell us what happened."

"Well, I was in the bar upstairs." I knew that the Landfal has a roof top bar, so his story was believable so far. "I was having a drink or two. Jus' got in this mornin'. Like I said, I was having a drink and this cute blonde sits down nex' to me. I bought her a drink and we got to talkin'."

"What was this blonde wearing?"

Snarski thought for a moment and then replied very proud of himself, "A dress, a green dress."

"Short? Long? Sleeveless?" I prompted.

"Short. Short sleeves I think. Real cute, though."

"Okay, what happened next, Mr. Snarski?"

"She suggested we go down to my room. So we did. It seemed like a good idea at the time."

"So how did she end up dead in your bed?"

"I don't know. I went into the bathroom and when I came out she was lying on the bed. She wasn't moving. I tried to wake her up but she wouldn't. She wasn't breathing, so I went down to the lobby and called the cops. Where'd she go?"

"That's a good question, Mr. Snarski," I said. I didn't think I was going to get much more out of him. Taking a quick look around the room, I noticed a billfold lying on the dresser. Inside, there were thirty three credits and twenty dollars Crockett in bills.

"How much cash did you have on you, Mr. Snarski?"

"I don't know. I guess a little less than three hundred in credits and a hundred and change in dollars."

"Looks like Ms. Smythe rolled Mr. Snarski here for a couple of hundred," I said to Rik. "And he didn't even have a good time."

"We've got to find her, Frank," Rik responded. He was sounding a little desperate. Personally, I was finding the whole business funny, but then it wasn't my job on the line.

"I don't think there's much more we can do here, Rik. Are you going to be okay, Mr. Snarski."

"Me? Sure. I'm fine. Just need another drink. Say, what happened to that cute little blonde? Oh, that's right. She's dead and gone." That fact didn't seem to bother Snarski much, but in the state he was in nothing was bothering him much.

We left him to sleep it off.

As we rode the elevator down to the lobby Rik commented, "I'm confused by this whole business, Frank. What's the deal with this dame? I guess I can accept the fact that she can fake being dead, but I don't understand why."

"My guess is that it's some kind of defense mechanism."

"I don't get you, Frank. It would seem to me that pretending to be a corpse wouldn't be much of a defense."

"I saw this video once when I was a kid in school. It was about animals on Terra. There was this one, it was called a possum I think, that didn't have claws or big teeth or anything like that. When it felt threatened it would just lay there pretending to be dead."

"I'd think that would be a sure way to get eaten."

"I think the idea i that predators like their food alive and kicking. With something that they didn't kill, they can't be sure what killed it. It might have died from poison or sickness or something like that, so it's just better to just give it a pass."

"Still seems pretty risky to me," Rik replied.

"Who knows what the planet she comes from is like or what quirks of evolution occurred."

"But this broad isn't an animal, Frank, she's a sapient being. It just seems like pretty odd behavior to me."

I have to admit that it sounded pretty odd to me, too, but then, having been born on Star City, neither Rik or I had ever had any exposure to wild animals. There is no wild on Star City. For that matter, there aren't many wild animals, either, except for a couple of cows and a goat at the zoo. What I did know was that the non-humans I'd run into had some pretty strange customs and habits. Maybe it did make sense on whatever planet this alien woman came from. I said as much to Rik.

"Maybe that's true, but it seems to be working for this dame. She's managed to make it to Star City. She's staying in a decent hotel. She's got a credit stick with a positive balance on it—"

"Yeah, that's better than a lot of the working girls."

Rik had a point. Ms. Smythe seemed to be doing alright for herself, and so far no one seemed to have gotten hurt.

When we got off at the lobby a quick look around showed that Latimer and Rossetti had left. That left Rik and me do deal with the problem on our own.

"So, Rik, what do you want to do about this business?"

"I don't know, Frank. I just want her out of the hotel before she gets me fired. I don't really care about anything else."

"What about the fact that she's rolled at least one of your guests for a couple of hundred? Who knows how many others she's pulled the same trick on."

Rik shook his head. "The way I figure it, Snarski and Pringely pretty much deserved what happened to them. They both were drunk, they let themselves get picked up in a bar by a strange broad, what else did they really expect. Pringely was getting his jollies before he panicked. So Snarski is out a few hundred. I'm guessing it isn't the first time. I don't see the harm. I just wish she'd do it in another hotel, that's all."

I sympathized with Rik's perspective. "So far no one's gotten really hurt, but will it stay that way?"

"I don't get you, Frank. You don't think this Peli chick would hurt anyone, do you?"

"Probably not," I conceded. "But Pringely and Snarski just shrieked like little girls and ran away when they thought they had a dead alien on their hands. How long until one of her tricks has a different reaction?"

"What do you mean?"

"Someone might hang around until she comes out of it and then decide they've been played for a sucker. They might try to handle the situation on their own."

Rik got the idea. "Oh."

"Yeah, you might have a real corpse on your hand."

"So what do we do, Frank?"

Somehow, this had become "our" problem rather than just Rik's. That was presuming a lot considering I wasn't getting paid. On the other hand, it was a pretty interesting situation.

"Well, we could spend the rest of the day chasing Ms. Smythe around the hotel—"

"You've got a better idea, don't you, Frank?"

"Ms. Smythe hasn't checked out of her room, yet. We know that she's been back at least once since Pringely to change her clothes. Maybe one of us should go up and wait for her."

"I've got to hang around the lobby, Frank. I'm still working," Rik said. I wasn't sure whether he was glad or disappointed that he wouldn't be the one staking out the room.

"Don't worry about it, Rik. Just let me into the room and I'll take care of it."

"Thanks, Frank. You're a real pal."

We went up to room 324 and Rik let me in with his passkey. He said he'd check in with me every couple of hours, and then he left.

There was a comfortable chair in the corner. I turned it so it was facing the door and sat down to wait. After half an hour I got bored, so I checked out the room being more thorough than I had been the first time. The suitcases were locked, but that didn't cause me much trouble. Not there was anything inside. Ms. Smythe had been very careful. There wasn't anything in her bags or closet that had originated anywhere outside of human space. There weren't any weapons, either, not even a knife. The only thing remotely suspicious was that she had quite a bit of cash, mostly in Crockett bills, stashed in a concealed compartment in one of the suitcases, and even that didn't really mean anything. Lots of people find it more convenient to carry cash when traveling.

An hour passed without Ms. Smythe showing up. As a detective, I've gotten pretty good at waiting without getting bored, but I was getting hungry, so I ordered dinner from room service. I billed it to the room; I didn't think Ms. Smythe would mind when I explained it to her.

The food came, a "meat" sandwich with fried stix. Having grown up poor on Star City my tastes are simple. I did wash it down with a bottle of beer imported from Crockett. When I was done, I didn't put the tray out to be picked up; I didn't want to tip off Ms. Smythe that I was in her room.

I tried reading one of the romance novels on the reader, but gave it up and settled for looking at the pictures in the Terran travel guide.

It was a little after 2000 when I heard the key inserted in the lock. The door opened and then Ms. Smythe saw me sitting in the corner. She dropped to the floor like a brick.

I shut the door after checking the corridor to make sure no one had seen, and then I picked her up and laid her out on the bed. I did a quick check for a pulse in her wrist and the veins in her neck. There wasn't one. There wasn't any respiration that I could detect, either. The skin seemed to be cooling off and taking on a waxy texture. When I opened her eyelids, there was no contraction of the pupils. I could see how she could have fooled Rik into thinking she was dead. I wondered if there were any detectable brain waves, but I didn't have a medical scanner, and I sure wasn't going to drag her off to the nearest autodoc to find out. I suppose I could have satisfied my curiosity about her anatomical differences, but I didn't. Instead I went back to my chair and waited.

About an hour later she started to stir on the bed. She sat up, saw me, and fainted dead again. I checked the pulse, just to make sure, but there was nothing.

After a half-hour she roused again, saw me, and went back to playing dead. I was starting to wonder if this pattern would just repeat itself indefinitely.

The third time she woke up I said, "We need to talk, Ms. Smythe."

That seemed to get her attention because she didn't slump back onto the bed. She was really quite attractive when you came right down to it. Not beautiful, maybe, or even pretty in the conventional way, but there was something—exotic—about her. Her eyes were an unusual shade of green, spaced just a little too far apart, and the irises and pupils were not quite round. Her nose was a little on the thin side, as well. It wasn't quite a human face, but it wasn't unhuman, either. As for the rest of her—well, without looking under the clingy green dress she was wearing, she looked all too human.

"Who are you?" she asked shakily.

"My name is Frank Sladek."

"Are you with the police?"

"Me. No, I'm a P.I., a private investigator. I'm here because Rik Lane, the hotel detective is a friend of mine, sort of."

"Oh."

"What's more important is who you are, Ms. Smythe."

"I don't know what you mean."

"Let's start with your name. It isn't really Smythe, is it?"

For a moment it seemed she was going to deny that fact, but then she just gave up. "No it isn't."

"What is it?"

She said something I'm not sure I could pronounce. I sure couldn't spell it.

"Okay. Let's just stick with Smythe for the moment. My next question is what are you?"

"I don't know what you mean."

"Look, Ms. Smythe. I know you aren't human, so there's no point in denying it."

"Just what is human?" She sounded genuinely puzzled. Under other circumstances, I might have felt sorry for her. What she looked like was a scared young woman.

"I'll keep it simple, then. You aren't descended from Terra."

"Do you mean Earth?"

"Yes."

"Alright. I'm not an Earthling or Earther or whatever you call yourselves."

"See, that wasn't so hard, was it. Just where are you from, Ms. Smythe?"

"I'm from a planet we call—" Again she said something I couldn't possibly spell. "It's in a star system outside human space. You wouldn't have heard of it."

"Probably not. Just how did you come to be here, Ms. Smythe? On Star City, I mean."

"It's a long story," she sighed. "I wouldn't want to bore you, Mr. Sladek."

"Oh, we've got plenty of time, Ms. Smythe. I don't think either one of us is going anywhere for awhile."

"Am I a prisoner, then?"

"No. You can walk out that door any time you want to, and I won't stop you. But I might say something to the police. I don't think you'd like that."

"Why are you doing this, Mr. Sladek?"

"The short answer is that you've been rolling drunks in this hotel and you could get my buddy Rik into trouble if you keep doing it."

"And the long answer?" She asked it in a way that made me understand why men would ask her up to their rooms.

"Let's just say I'm curious."

"Don't they say that curiosity killed the cat?"

"Maybe. But then, I'm not a cat. Look, Ms. Smythe, why don't you just tell me your story? If I like what I hear maybe I can help you out."

"How can you help me out?"

"We'll figure that out after I hear your story."

She looked at me, studying my face as if she could read something there. Usually, I've got a pretty good poker face, but I wasn't sure that was true. Finally she seemed to come to a decision.

"Very well, Mr. Sladek. As I said, I come from a planet outside human space. I suppose you'd think of us as primitive. We don't have space flight or really anything advanced technologically. Mostly we farm and fish. As far as I know, no other species has ever visited our planet before, but a human ship landed near my village. I'm not sure whether they were explorers or traders or even smugglers. In those days I didn't speak your language. I was just a young girl."

"How long ago was this?"

"Five, six years. I'm not really sure. It's so hard to keep track of days and years when you keep moving between planets. But getting back to my story, the ship landed and the crew came out. They looked so much like us and they acted so friendly and open handed that we saw no reason to fear them. They handed out such wonderful presents, too. The village held a big feast for the visitors. There was lots of eating and dancing and drinking. Everyone was having a good time—"

She sounded wistful as she recalled the events.

"There was one of the crew. He seemed very young and shy to me, almost as young as I was. We danced together for a long time and then we went out into the bushes. We weren't the only ones. The crew looked so much like us—The crewman and I snuggled for awhile. He taught me about kissing which we didn't do, but which I enjoyed. Then we—well he saw that I was different down there, but he didn't seem to mind."

"Not to be indelicate, Ms. Smythe, but exactly how are you different?"

She smiled at that. "Do you know what a marsupial is, Mr. Sladek? I think that is the right term. We are like that. I have a pouch—down there, and that is where our women bring our young to term. There are other differences, as well, but that's mostly in the details. Would you like to see?"

"That won't be necessary. I was just curious. Go on with your story."

"After that night, I continued to see the crewman when he wasn't busy. I learned that his name was Billy. I thought he was very nice and exotic and romantic. I'd never had a close male friend before, not of my own people. I thought I was in love. I think Billy was too.

"He started teaching me his language. He wanted me to go with him when the ship left. I wanted that, too. I thought how wonderful it would be to fly amongst the stars and to have all the amazing things the ship people had. Billy came up with a plan to sneak me onto the ship just before it left. So that's what we did.

"Of course, it wasn't as wonderful as I had imagined. I had to hide in a small space and Billy was busy with what he did on the ship and he couldn't spend much time with me. And then I was discovered.

"They took me to the captain. He wasn't so much angry as—well—disgusted. They locked me up in a little room and Billy didn't come to see me anymore. I was afraid of what they might do to me and all I wanted was to go home. Then the ship landed on some other planet and the put me off the ship on my own."

"That must have been rough," I said, meaning it. I didn't know how much of her story was true, but I had to admit it was a real tear jerker.

"It was. I didn't know much of the human language. There were all sorts of other species, too, strange beings that didn't look anything like us. I had no money, only the clothes that I wore. Billy's ship was gone. I survived the only way I could, by being nice to men. Gradually, I learned the language and how to act. Finally one of the men offered to take me on his ship.

"He was kind in his own way, but he—used me. He was a trader on a small ship. We went from star to star; I don't know how many or which ones. Eventually he got tired of me and left me off on one of these planets. He was decent about it, he gave me some money.

"After that, I tried to make myself look more human. Little things, like dyeing my hair blonde, it's naturally more greenish, and shaving a little of it here and there. I bought human clothes, too so I could pass. Things got easier for me, then. I could pass for human. I'd get money from men for—favors. One of them helped me get false identity documents. I traveled from planet to plant until I ended up here on Star City."

"Why didn't you just go home?" I asked.

I thought she was going to cry. "I would if I could. Except I don't have any idea where it is. There's no record of a species like mine, nothing about my planet in the databases. I think, now, that Billy's ship must have been smuggling or doing something else illegal. They never told anyone about my planet. And I had traveled so far before I got good at the language that I had no idea of where I'd been. I'd go home in a minute except I don't know where it is."

"That's tough, Ms. Smythe. I'd like to help you out, I really would, but I don't see how I can."

"Will you at least let me go?"

I took a moment to think. Her story certainly sounded plausible. I'd never heard of a species that so closely mimicked humans, and sooner or later, Star City being what it is, members of any alien species in contact with humans would at least pass through. If I accepted her story as true, then I had to sympathize with her plight. Not that I had any better idea of how to get her home than she did.

As to the way she made her living, well, she wasn't doing anything that hundreds of other Star City working girls weren't doing. If Snarski and Pringely had gotten themselves into a situation where they were compromised, that was their lookout not mine. If they hadn't run into Peli, they probably would have been targeted by someone human. And, when it came down to it, only Snarski was out any cash. I made a decision.

"Look, Ms. Smythe, like I said earlier, I'm not with the police. I'm not even working for the hotel. I was just trying to help out a friend who was in a jam. As far as I'm concerned, you can do whatever you want. Just as long as you don't do it in the Landfal, that is. I suggest you pack your bags and find some other accommodations. One thing Star City has is plenty of hotels."

In the brief moment when she flashed me a shy smile, I thought I saw too many teeth, but that might have been my imagination.

"Do you have any suggestions, Mr. Sladek?"

"You might want to avoid the Commodore. One of your previous encounters is staying there. I'd skip the Casino, the Rigel Royal, or any of the top tier hotels as well. They tend to have better security."

"Thanks for the advice."

I looked on as she began to pack her luggage. She didn't seem to mind my watching her. I didn't have any objections, either. It was amazing how convergent evolution worked to come up with an attractive form.

I was still watching when my comm went off. It was Rik Lane.

"What is it, Rik?"

"Frank, we've got a problem. Latimer and Rossetti are back in the lobby. There was another complaint about a body. Have you seen the girl?"

"I'm with her now, Rik. Does Latimer know which room she's in?"

"He's at the registration desk now. He'll probably figure it out pretty quick."

"Can you get away?"

"Yeah. No problem."

"Okay, this is what I want you to do. Come up to the room. I'll come down and try to stall Latimer. In the mean time I want you to stash Ms. Smythe somewhere, anywhere, an empty room preferably. Got that?"

"You sure about this, Frank?"

"You need to trust me on this one, Rik. Okay."

"Sure, whatever you say."

"Alright. I'm heading down now."

I turned to Ms. Smythe and said, "There's a little problem with the police down in the lobby. I'm going to take care of it. Finish packing. In a minute, Rik is going to be up to move you someplace safe."

She looked at me uncertainly for a second and then smiled. "Thanks, Mr. Sladek."

"Why don't you just call me Frank. All my friends do."

"Thanks, Frank."

I headed down to the lobby. Rik was getting off the elevator just as I got to them. He looked nervous as hell. I wondered whether it was such a bright idea for me to get involved, but I knew I had a much better chance of handling Latimer and Rossetti than he did.

As soon as I got off in the lobby, I ran into Latimer and Rossetti waiting for a car up.

"What are you doing here, Latimer? Looking for another vanishing corpse?"

"Get out of my way, Sladek. There's something funny going on in this hotel, and I mean to get to the bottom of it."

"You mean there really has been another vanishing body?" I asked trying to sound incredulous. "I was just kidding."

Latimer looked at me suspiciously, like he suspected that I knew more than I was letting on to. Of course, that was nothing new in our relationship.

"Just what do you know about this business, Frank?"

"Me? Nothing. I was just here helping Lane out with a security matter."

"Oh? What kind of security matter?"

"Nothing big. Just complaints of some of the housekeeping staff taking things from the guests."

"Anything to it?"

"Nah. If you ask me, it's just a case of some of the guests trying to get their bills knocked down by making a fake complaint."

"So it's got nothing to do with a working girl faking being dead to rob the john?"

"Is that what's been going on?" I asked innocently. "What's the deal with that?"

"That's what I'm trying to find out, Frank. We've had another report just like the earlier case with Snarski in 702. Same story. Guy goes into the bathroom and when he comes out the dame is lying dead on the bed. The guy panics, tries to get help, and when he comes back the broad is gone and so is some of his money."

"Gee. You'd think faking being dead would be pretty hard to do," I commented.

"You got to remember the victims have all been drinking. Look, this has been fun, Frank, but I have to go. We think we know which room the dame is staying in."

"Mind if I tag along?"

For a minute it looked like Latimer was going to refuse, but then he just shrugged. "Suit yourself, Frank."

The three of us, me, Latimer, and Rossetti rode up in the elevator together. To make it look good, I turned the wrong way when we got off.

"It's this way, Frank." The way Latimer said it made me wonder if I'd been too obvious.

Latimer had gotten the door code from the reception desk, so he went right in without knocking. The room was empty. Rik had been smart, and taken the room service tray with him.

"Doesn't look like anyone has been here, Latimer. No dame, no corpse."

"Can it, Frank."

"I'm hurt, Latimer. Usually you complain about there being too many corpses when I'm around."

"I'm going to ask you again, Frank. What do you know about this business?"

"I told you, I don't know anything, Latimer. It seems to me, though, that this broad has come up with a new dodge. I've never heard of a working girl playing dead to roll someone before. Pretty smart idea if you can pull it off."

"Yeah," Latimer said sourly.

"I don't know," Rossetti chimed in. "Plenty of women have played dead with me. I don't mind. At least they're not yapping."

As I said before, Latimer is the brains of the partnership. Rossetti isn't.

"What I want to know is how is she pulling it off?" Latimer asked. I presumed that he was addressing the question to me since he never asked Rossetti's opinion of anything if he could help it.

"I don't know. Maybe it's yoga or something. I heard about some monks that could control their breathing and even their body temperature. Maybe this woman picked up on how to do that. After all, the audience she has been trying to fool hasn't been in the sharpest condition."

Latimer thought about it for a moment. "You might be on to something there, Frank."

"Or, it might be some kind of drug that briefly suppresses the metabolism. Sort of like suspended animation. They were working on that for interstellar spaceflight before the tachyon drive was discovered."

Latimer just grunted, but I was pretty sure that Peli being an alien wasn't one of his working hypotheses., which was probably just as well for her.

"Well, it doesn't really matter how she does it as long as I can get my hands on her."

"Why the big concern, Latimer?" I asked. "What's it to you. After all, no real harm has been done. No one's died, have they?"

"No, but you know what the big boys are like. They don't want anything that will give Star City a bad name with travelers, and someone rolling hotel guests is just the sort of thing they worry about. I've had orders to clean this business up quickly and quietly."

I understood where Latimer was coming from. The "big boys" that Latimer was referring to were the real powers of Star City, the people that ran the big hotels, casinos, and other entertainments. The only reason for Star City to exist was to provide services for people in transit. Without travelers, there wouldn't be anyone to fleece, so anything that cut down on traffic through Star City affected the bottom line.

"Wish I could help you, Latimer, but I was just passing through."

"Yeah," Latimer commented, sounding unconvinced. "Let's get out of here, Rossetti."

I followed the two detectives down to the lobby where I said my good-byes and left through the main entrance. Out on the sidewalk, I called Rik.

"Where are you?"

"I'm up in Pringely's old room with the girl."

"Pringely's?"

"Well, I knew it was empty."

"Fair enough."

"Where are Latimer and Rossetti?"

"I left them in the lobby. I'm outside the hotel right now."

"Can you come up? I'm supposed to be on duty, and if I don't make an appearance in the lobby, someone might start asking questions."

"I'll be right up," I replied.

I went back into the hotel using a side entrance, one that let me get to the elevators without going through the lobby. I got off on the eighth floor and knocked on 817. Rik must have been waiting for me, because he opened up right away. Peli was sitting on the bed looking a little nervous.

"I've got to go, Frank," Rik said. "Will you be okay?"

"Me? Sure, I'll be fine."

I let Rik out of the room and locked the door behind him.

"How are you doing?" I asked Peli.

"I'm okay, I guess." I didn't know how quickly her species matures, but from the way she said it, it occurred to me that she really couldn't be much more than a young girl.

I went over to the mini-fridge. "Would you like something to drink?"

"Just a soda water. Alcohol gives me a headache."

"Me too." I pulled out a bottle of soda and handed it to her. I spotted a bottle of Crockett bourbon and poured it over a couple of cubes of ice, figuring that either Pringely or Rik would end up paying for it.

"What do we do now?" Peli asked.

"Right now we just sit tight and hope nothing happens."

I should have known that was tempting fate. My comm started buzzing. It was Rik.

"What's up?"

"We got a problem, Frank. Rossetti has parked himself in the lobby."

"Where's Latimer?"

"I'm not sure. I haven't seen him since I came down."

"Okay. Play it cool and don't try to attract attention. I'll try to think of something." I disconnected.

"What's wrong?" Peli asked.

"One of the two cops that was here is still down in the lobby. The problem is that I'm not sure where the other one, the smart one, is."

"Does that matter?"

"If there's one thing that Latimer is, it'ss tenacious. He's got his heart set on finding you and he's not going to rest until he does."

"What are we going to do?" Peli said with alarm.

"I think the time has come for us to get out of this joint."

I called Rik back.

"Frank, what's happening?"

"Is Rossetti still parked in the lobby?"

"Yeah. No sign of Latimer, though."

"Okay. Can you arrange for us to use the freight elevator? I want to get the girl out of the hotel without going through the lobby."

"Yeah, I can send it up with an override so that the door opens automatically when it reaches your floor."

"Good. Do it. We'll be waiting for it in a couple of minutes."
I hung up on Rik without waiting for an answer. To Peli I said,
"Good thing you're all packed because we're going." She looked
at me questioningly but didn't comment.

I picked up the bigger of her two bags and went to the door.
A quick peek down the hallway showed that it was empty. I
ushered Peli towards the service elevator at the rear of the
building. Rik had kept his part, the car was waiting for us with the
door open. We got inside, and I pushed the button for the
ground floor where the loading dock was. We descended. When
the doors opened, I stuck my head out. There was no one
hanging around in the freight bay. I grabbed Peli's hand and a
moment later we were walking down the sidewalk.

One good thing about Star City is it's public transportation
system, a network of free tram lines arranged so that you are
never more than a short walk from a station. Once on a tram,
you can get anywhere in a matter of minutes. I headed us for the
nearest one where we boarded the first circumferential tram.

I hadn't seen anyone tailing us, but I wasn't about to take any
chances. At the next station we transferred to a down line, rode
it for two kilometers and got off. We waited for the next tram to
stop. No one who got off showed any interest in us. We boarded
the circumferential after that one, rode one and a half times
around the city. I've been playing tram games since I was a kid,
but Peli was looking disoriented. We changed trams a few more
times and finally got off at the station nearest the Souk.

While we had been riding the trams, I'd been trying to think
of the best place to stow the girl. If Latimer was actively looking
for her, putting her up in another hotel was out of the question.
As soon as she registered, Latimer would have the information.
As far as I could see, that only left one alternative, my apartment.
The best way to get there from a tram is to go through the Souk,
the enclave where most of the non-humans on Star City live.

Now if you didn't know any better, you might think that the
Souk would be a wild and dangerous place entered at your own
peril. The fact is, nothing could be farther from the truth.
Mostly, it's a neighborhood of small mom and pop (or whatever

the relevant genders are) shops and restaurants. The beings tend to look after each other and no one wants any trouble. The most unruly elements are the human artists that live there because the rent is cheap, and they are mostly harmless.

Because I live so close and the walk through it on my way to and from the tram station, I'm pretty well known. A few people waved or called a greeting, most just didn't bother to pay attention. I found Peli's reaction interesting; she seemed surprised at the variety of species around her.

I live in an aging apartment building called the Aldeberon Arms just outside of New Minglewood. The building was intended for semi luxury apartments, but the proximity to New Minglewood has given the neighborhood a bad reputation and kept the rents down. New Minglewood really is a dangerous neighborhood, though all the residents are human. The other attraction of the building besides the low rents is that there is a decent bar called the Blue Moon just across the street.

For once the elevator in the Aldeberon was working, which was just as well. I was getting tired from schlepping a suitcase around, and I was sure the Peli was, too. We rode up to the fourth floor and home suite home.

Once inside, Peli hesitated in the entryway. I suppose I should have warned her. Hanging there facing the door is a rather disturbing portrait. It was given to me by an old girlfriend who is now a famous painter of alien landscapes on Crockett. I've been told that I could get upwards of thirty thousand dollars Crockett if I ever chose to sell it. The painting is supposed to be of me (it says so on the back) but it doesn't look quite human. I've never been sure if it was really meant as a gift or as revenge.

"It was painted by a woman I used to know. Her name is Lucinda and she's quite famous."

"She must have hated you—"

"No, she—it didn't work out—it's complicated." I couldn't explain what had happened because I didn't really understand it myself.

I steered Peli into the living room, which is a spacious room along the front of the building. It has some big windows and a small balcony overlooking the street below from which you can see the sign for the Blue Moon.

Peli stood there with wide eyes. "It's—"

"--not what you expected," I said, completing her sentence.

"I was going to say 'nice'."

I actually get that reaction a lot. The place isn't what people expect for a two-bit shamus. I've lived in the Aldeberon a long time, and over the years I've furnished it with a rather eclectic mix of furniture, most of which I've salvaged from the gutter. Many are nice pieces that are just a few decades out of fashion. There's a bookcase with a number of first editions, mostly by Marcus Fitzroy who's butt I saved once before he got famous. He sends me a signed copy of each new book as it comes out. I've even read a few of them. There's also a painting by Lucinda, the ex-girlfriend, hanging on the wall behind the sofa, one of her more beguiling landscapes. She hung it there shortly after we first met and didn't repossess it when she left. There's another in the bedroom that's even better, a nightscape of an alien beach with three moons in the sky.

"Make yourself at home," I said, waving a hand around the room. "No telling how long you're going to be here."

"Why am I here?"

"Because Latimer is looking for you. I'm hoping he won't think to look here."

"No. I mean why are you doing this? Why are you hiding me?"

"Look, it started out because Rik was in a jam and I was just helping him out. Then—well I guess I figured that you'd had a tough break and needed help, too. Or maybe it's just because I like the thought of putting one over on Latimer and Rossetti."

"Do you often do that?"

"Try to put one over on Latimer? Often enough, I guess."

"No, I mean help people?"

I thought about it for a minute.

"Oh, I guess I do it on occasion. Sometimes I even get paid for it."

"I think you're not as tough and cynical as you pretend, Mr. Sladek."

"Them's fightin' words, Ms. Smythe." That drew a smile from her. A brief smile.

"What's going to happen to me?" she asked, the smile vanishing.

"I don't think it's going to be safe for you to remain on Star City. Latimer can be pretty persistent. The people that run this place don't like waves, and I'm afraid that they'll see you as a big wave."

"What will happen if they catch me?" she asked.

"They tend to show people that upset them the door," I replied using a common euphemism.

"I see—"

"I don't think you do, Ms. Smythe. I meant that literally. They'll show you a door and push you through it. Only there won't be any air on the other side."

"Oh—" She looked as if her world was collapsing.

"Look, it's not as bad as all that. It's just that Star City, when you come right down to it isn't all that big a place. It would be too hard for someone like—someone like you to hide. What you need to do is get off this rock and go someplace like Crockett, someplace where you can lose yourself in the crowd. There are starliners leaving here every day. All you have to do is get on one of them. Once you're away from here, Latimer will forget all about you, and you'll be safe."

"Won't they be watching for me?" Peli objected.

"Oh, probably. But it will mostly be Latimer and Rossetti, and we can figure out a way to work around them. They will be playing this situation close to the vest, so I doubt that there will be a general alert out on you. All we need to do is book you passage and get you to the departure gate on time."

"Okay. If you think it best. How soon would I be leaving?"

"Let's see what's available."

I sat down at my terminal and checked departures. The good thing about the Star City to Crockett run was that there was plenty of traffic on it. Most days there was at least one liner scheduled for there, sometimes two or more. There was one leaving the next morning. It was an older ship, less luxurious then the newer models, but that meant it was less likely to be booked solid. It would also be cheaper. When I checked availability, I found that there were still second class staterooms available.

"How much do you have on your credit stick?"

She gave me a figure. It was enough to cover her passage and still leave her with a stake for when she reached Crockett.

"Okay, there's a liner leaving in about eighteen hours with second class cabins available. That means you won't have to share it with anyone. Do you want to go ahead?"

"Alright," she said uncertainly. "I'm trusting you, Mr. Sladek."

"You might as well start calling me Frank."

"Alright. And thank you, Frank."

I went through the process of booking the passage. There didn't seem to be any problem with Peli's credit stick. It looked like I'd been right about Latimer playing it close to his chest; he hadn't put a hold on the account.

"What do I do until the ship leaves?"

"Like I said, you might as well make yourself at home. You'll be staying until it's time to leave for the docking ring."

She looked around uncertainly, then smiled.

"Say, when was the last time you had something to eat?"

"This morning."

"Do you have any problem with what you can eat?"

"No, I can eat just about anything humans can."

"Good. I'll go out and get us dinner. Don't let anyone in until I get back. Just pretend you aren't here if anyone knocks at the door."

I slipped out. Out of habit, I took the stairs rather than the elevator. Now, there's a diner on the corner, but it caters to local tastes, which means that everything they serve comes out of a vat. Despite her claim, I wasn't sure that Peli would be able to stomach it. Fortunately, I was only a few blocks from the Souk, where I knew a place that had decent takeout. It was mostly vegetables and served over something which was almost like rice but wasn't. In any case, it was tasty enough, though a little oddly spiced.

It only took me ten minutes or so to walk there and less time for them to fill the order. The guy behind the counter was an alien who doesn't speak much Terran, but by pointing at the pictures on the back wall I didn't have any problem placing the order. Not knowing which items Peli would like, I got containers of four different dishes plus a couple of fried dumpling like things for good measure.

I hadn't paid much attention on the way to the Souk, but on the return trip, I had the feeling I was being followed. I paused a moment to look at a shop window, and in the reflection, I spotted my tail. It was Rossetti.

I didn't want him to get the idea I was trying to hide something, but I didn't like the idea of being followed, either. I waited for a side street and then turned the corner and stopped just out of sight. When Rossetti turned to follow I said:

"Fancy meeting you here, Rossetti."

"Can it, Sladek. Why'd you try to duck out on me?"

"Duck out? If I had wanted to shake you, Rossetti, I would have. I just stopped to say hello."

"Looks like you've got a lot of food there," Rossetti commented, nodding towards the bag of take out in my hand.

"This way I'll have leftovers. Saves me a trip. The gak-bek-mo isn't half bad reheated. Well, don't let me keep you from your business. You know where I live if you want anything."

I started walking again in the direction of my apartment leaving Rossetti standing on the street corner wondering whether to keep following me or drop it.

When I got home, I dropped the food on the table and took a quick peek out the window. Rossetti was across the street trying to look nonchalant.

Peli must have noticed me looking because she asked, "Is anything wrong?"

"Not really. It's just that Rossetti, one of the cops from the Landfal, is hanging around on the street trying not to be noticed.

If we're lucky, one of the drunks stumbling out of the Blue Moon will try to roll him."

"And if not?"

"I guess I'll just have to think of something. But let's not worry about Rossetti right now. Let's have dinner instead."

I got some plates and silverware out of the kitchen and laid out the place settings on the table. Peli watched me curiously. I guess she hadn't been waited on by a man lately.

Dinner was a quiet affair, though Peli dug into the take out with relish. We avoided the subject of her predicament. Instead, we mostly talked about her home world. I tried to get some idea of what it was like in hopes of helping her figure out where it was, but mostly what she told me was that it was "nice," and that she missed it a lot. I shouldn't have been surprised by this; teenagers aren't the most observant of beings, and she couldn't have been any older than that when she stowed away on the starship.

The conversation lagged after dinner, I was distracted glancing out the window to see if Rossetti was still there (he was), and reminiscing about her home had put Peli in a somber mood. After a while, I suggested that she should get some sleep and showed her the bedroom. She looked at me apprehensively, but I told her that I was going to sleep in a chair in the living room where I could keep an eye out the window. She gave me that curious smile of hers and then shut the bedroom door. I was just as glad that she did, I wasn't sure that I would have resisted if she had made an offer.

I made myself comfortable with a glass of brown over ice and some jive samba playing softly on the entertainment system so as not to disturb my guest. Rossetti was still standing watch on the street below when midnight came and went. That told me that Latimer was trying to keep the whole business quiet, which was good for us as it meant he wasn't going to bring in additional help. All we'd have to deal with would be the two of them, which would make things easier.

Latimer was an honest cop, which didn't mean that he wouldn't do favors for the men in the fancy suits that actually ran things. Mostly, he was interested in having things run smoothly, and if that meant running errands for the casino bosses, that was okay with him as long as it didn't actually break any laws, which, in any case, were pretty elastic on Star City. Somehow, someone must have gotten word of Peli's presence and told Latimer to handle it without going through official channels.

I must have fallen asleep shortly after midnight. When I woke up, it was 0700, and the music was still playing quietly in the background. I told it to stop. A quick glance out the window told me that Latimer had relieved Rossetti sometime during the night.

Peli must have heard me moving around, because she came out of the bedroom. She was wearing something demur, a skirt and sweater in muted colors, which only had a limited effect of reducing her exotic appeal.

"Is that man still out there?"

"No, he must have gone home. Latimer is there in his place."

"Oh—"

"Don't worry about it. This way I know where he is," I said, trying to sound more reassured than I was. "There's food in the kitchen if you want to make yourself some breakfast."

She must have been hungry, because she retreated to the kitchen where I heard her opening doors and banging pots. Somewhere along the way Peli had picked up human cooking because fifteen minutes later she emerged with a couple of plates of scrambled egg and toast, and I could smell coffee brewing in the kitchen. Okay, the eggs had come out of a vat and the flour for the toast had never been grain growing in a field, but it still smelled good to me.

Peli waited until I had finished before she popped the question. "What are we going to do?"

"Well, in a little over three hours you need to be at the boarding gate for your ship. I'll have to draw Latimer away to make that happen. That shouldn't be too hard."

"You have a plan?" she asked.

"Of course I have a plan," I replied. I did have a plan, too, though it mostly consisted of me walking out the front door and getting Latimer to follow me. "Let me make a call."

I dialed up Rik. He sounded nervous when he answered.

"What's going on, Frank? When I didn't hear from you I got worried that—you know—"

"I didn't call in case Latimer was listening in. He's not, because he's parked out on the street in front of my apartment. Can you get away this morning?"

"Sure. No problem."

"Good. I want you to come to my place around 0930. I'll be gone, but Peli will be here. I want you to escort her to gate 23 on the docking ring and make sure you're not followed. The last call for boarding is at 1100, so you should have plenty of time. Do you have all that?"

"Sure, Frank. Gate 23, 1100."

"Okay. Give me a call when she's safely on board."

"Uh, where will you be, Frank?" Rik asked uncertainly.

"Me? I'll be playing follow the leader with Latimer."

I hung up, hoping Rik would be able to pull off his part in the game. He was only a hotel dick, but he knew enough about tailing someone that he should be able to play the other part.

I smiled at Peli and said, "I better get cleaned up before I go."

I went into the bathroom to wash up and brush my teeth. I hadn't slept that well the night before, but a quick shave and I was looking fresh and perky. I changed clothes, picking a jacket with a pattern that was a little too loud just so Latimer wouldn't lose me by accident. A clashing shirt in orange completed the ensemble. I didn't bother to add a needle gun or a laser. I usually don't carry unless I have to, and I didn't want to give Latimer or Rossetti an excuse to shoot me, especially Rossetti, who would be happy for the opportunity.

When I came out of the bedroom I gave Peli her instructions. "Rik will be here in a few minutes. He'll take you to the docking ring and make sure you get on your ship okay. If anyone else comes to the door, pretend you're not here."

"What will you be doing, Frank?"

"Me? I'll be taking a stroll around Star City."

She reached up and planted a big kiss. I hadn't been expecting it, but I didn't put up a fight, either.

"When you get to Crockett, you might try and look up Lucinda."

"The woman who painted your portrait in the hallway?" she asked dubiously.

"Yeah. I think she would be interested in meeting you."

I gave her a smile and then left.

Outside on the sidewalk, Latimer was doing a better job of blending in than Rossetti had. He was playing with his comm, looking like a business type checking his messages. He didn't even look up when I came out of the Aldeberon Arms, but when I turned right at the corner I saw him move out after me.

I didn't bother to hurry, but I didn't slow down, either. I took the route through the Souk that I normally use to get to the nearest tram stop. Latimer knew me and the layout of the trams well enough that he would have been suspicious if I had done anything else. I timed my arrival at the stop so as to give Latimer just enough time to make the same tram as mine when it pulled out.

In my line of business, I've had a lot of experience at following people, and a fair amount of experience at trying to shake a tail, but trying to make sure Latimer didn't lose me was something new. On the other hand, I couldn't make it too easy, either. One thing I didn't want him to think was that I was leading him on a wild goose chase.

I was on an up tram headed to the end of Star City occupied by the top hotels and cultural attractions. I rode it all the way to the end of the line and then switched to a circumferential and rode that halfway around the city. Latimer was still with me, which was what I had hoped.

When I got off the tram, I started walking back towards the down end taking a zig-zag course. Periodically I made a show of pausing in front of shop windows, an old dodge that allows you to look in the reflection off the glass to see if someone is following without obviously turning your head. I wanted Latimer to think that I was worried about the possibility that someone was tailing me. I smiled at the detective's efforts to look nonchalant. The game we were playing was one in which I'd had a lot more practice recently than Latimer had.

After about ten minutes of this cat and mouse game I entered the TransGalactic building. TransGalactic operates much of the starliner traffic routed through Star City. The ground floor of their headquarters is given over to customer service operations. It's a big open room with agent counters, kiosks, storage lockers, and whatnot for purchasing tickets, collecting lost baggage, and filing complaints. At almost any time of day there are hundreds of people milling around, half of whom are lost and have no idea of where they are going.

All this makes it a great place to shake a tail, but Latimer would also have to consider the possibility that I had gone there on some legitimate errand. I spent several minutes at an information kiosk, long enough to make sure that Latimer had spotted me. When I spotted him out of the corner of my eye, I left the kiosk and headed over to one of the banks of storage lockers that TransGalactic supplies for passengers in transit to store luggage during short term layovers. In the past, I've found these lockers to be a great place to securely stash items that were too hot to carry around with me.

I went up to the kiosk for the lockers, transferred a credit from a credit stick, and got the code for one of the lockers. I dithered around until I was sure Latimer had me in sight and then I went to the locker and made a great show of opening the door, but I used my body to keep Latimer from seeing whether I had put something inside or taken something out. In reality, I had done neither, but I wanted Latimer to think that I had come to the TransGalactic building with some legitimate purpose.

Having confused Latimer enough, I exited the building on the other side from that which I had entered. A few blocks from TransGalactic there is a big open square which has a number of open-air cafés that make it a popular place with tourists. I stopped at one of them, grabbed a seat where Latimer would be sure to spot me, and ordered a cup of joe and a pastry, just to make it look like I was waiting to rendezvous with someone. With some satisfaction, I saw that Latimer had done the same at a different café that allowed him a clear view of my table.

I'd chose that particular café because the joe is pretty good. The pastries aren't bad, either. If I was going to sit around trying to fool Latimer, I thought I might as well enjoy myself. I finished the joe and ordered another one. It was a nice day, though on Star City the weather is always the same so it's always a nice day.

By the time I had eaten the pastry, it was getting to be 1030, and I was getting a little nervous wondering if Rik had had problems. I needn't have worried, as shortly after that my comm alerted me to an incoming call.

I answered it with, "Sladek here."

"It's Rik." It's funny how people always say who it is when the comm already gives the caller's ID, but they still do it.

"How's it going, Rik?" I asked. I couldn't be sure whether Latimer had a tap on me or not, so I was trying not to say anything incriminating.

"Oh, it's going just fine, Frank. I just wanted you to know that I put that package in the mail for you." Okay, it wasn't the most original of codes, but it was enough to provide us with legal cover if we needed it.

"That's great, Rik. Thanks. Look, I've got to get going, but I'll see you later and we can talk then."

"Sure, Frank. I've got to get back to work, anyhow. Bye."

After I disconnected, I finished my joe and got up. I left a decent tip for the waiter because I like to keep on their good sides. There's no telling when I might need to waste some time in a public place again.

I took a leisurely stroll towards the nearest tram stop. At this point, I didn't care if Latimer was still following me, but I had nothing to do and I was in a good mood. I caught a glimpse of Latimer getting up and fumbling for change before following me.

Just for the hell of it, I waited until the last second to board at the tram stop so that Latimer wouldn't have a chance to get on with me. As the tram pulled out, I gave him a wave like I hadn't seen him all day. He gave me a different gesture in acknowledgement.

I headed home, but instead of going up to the apartment, I decided to go across the street to the Blue Moon.

Daytime is my favorite time of day for the Blue Moon. It's quiet, it's dark, and it's cool. The only people in the joint was the kid tending bar, some old geezer at the end of the bar drinking something that glowed a faint blue, and myself. I ordered a double brown over ice with a splash of soda for good measure and waited.

It was about fifteen minutes later that the door opened and I saw Latimer silhouetted against the light outside. He didn't look like he was in a good mood. I got the bartender's attention and held up two fingers. He took the hint, and by the time Latimer slid onto the stool next to mine there were two fresh drinks sitting on the bar.

"What took you so long?" I said sliding one of the drinks over to him.

"I don't know what game you think you're playing, Frank—"

"I'm not playing any game, Latimer. I'm just sitting here drinking a drink. I suggest you do the same. You look like you could use one."

"Quit kidding around, Frank. Where's the girl or woman, or whatever she is?"

"She's out of your hair, Latimer. I did you a favor and saw that she got on a starliner bound for somewhere else. You can tell whoever it was that has been riding you that they don't have to worry anymore about Star City's reputation being sullied."

Latimer looked at me for a moment, trying to decide whether to believe me or not. "Are you giving it to me straight, Frank?"

"Straight as the brown in your glass there."

He thought about it and then took a sip of his drink. Like me, Latimer was born on Star City and is used to the taste.

"Tell me one thing, Frank. Was she really not human?"

"I didn't look for myself, but I believe that to be the case." I gave him a brief recounting of Peli's story up to and including her getting on the starliner to Crockett. I figured that it didn't really matter anymore. The liner should already have gone translight, so there'd be no way to contact it until it reached its destination.

"You believe her story?"

"No reason not to," I said before taking a pull on my drink.

"I guess she really did have it rough, then. You think she'll be okay on Crockett?"

"Probably. It will be a lot easier to blend into the crowd there. And who knows, she actually might find someone who can help her get home. That's all she really wants, you know."

Latimer looked at me, raised his glass and toasted, "To home." Latimer, like a lot of cops, can be surprisingly sentimental. The reality was, though, that for both of us, home was a hollowed out rock circling a star that never made it.

"So she really looked human enough to pass for an Earth girl?"

Several months later I received a package from Lucinda. It was a full sized print of a portrait she had made of Peli. It was just like Lucinda to send a physical image when she could just as easily have sent a data packet at much less cost. I have to say, it's a good likeness. Somehow, Lucinda managed to capture Peli's exotic nature without revealing the fact that she wasn't human. In the painting, at least, she looks happy.

THE BODY
OF AN
OLD FRIEND

THE BODY OF AN OLD FRIEND

There was a message on my comm from Lars Kendricks asking me to meet him at the Blue Moon for a drink. It was only a couple of hours after noon, but that had never stopped me before, neither Lars or I kept what you'd call regular hours. Lars was a spacer working on a contract freighter that didn't keep a fixed schedule, and me, well, I'm what some people call a private investigator. Of course people have called me a lot of other things, too.

Lars wasn't exactly a friend, but he'd saved my butt a few years earlier, and whenever circumstances landed him in town we made a point of having a drink or three together. The night we'd met, I'd been on the trail of a gang that had been lifting cargo that wasn't theirs from a warehouse at the lower end of Star City. I'd tracked them down to a spacer bar down near the ring where the freighters dock.

There were five of them and one of me, and things hadn't looked too good. Lars had just been a bystander having a quiet drink, but I guess he hadn't liked the odds, so he joined in. With him in the fight, it was the gang who were outnumbered. Three of them went down for the count, one managed to scurry out the back door and I ended up with the last one in a choke hold. With the information I got from him, I'd found the stuff that had been boosted, and offered to split the recovery fee with Lars. He'd turned it down, saying he had all the money he needed. I hadn't pressed him, but he had let me buy him a drink which began a tradition.

The Blue Moon is an old fashioned sort of saloon just across the street from the apartment building where I live. It's dark and quiet, at least in the afternoon, the kind of place where, if the police come asking around, no one knows your name. Lars was already there when I arrived, sitting at the bar drinking a double brown with a yellow chaser. That's what civilized people would call a shot of whiskey and a beer—if they were being generous. On Star City, it all comes out of the same vat at the down end, with artificial flavorings and color added to suit. Half the people on Star City never drink anything else and have no idea what the real thing tastes like. I do, but I grew up on the Star City on the fringe of New Minglewood, so I'm used to it.

Lars saw me come in, silhouetted in the doorway against the light outside. He nodded, picked up his drinks in one hand and a bag in the other and motioned towards one of the booths along the wall opposite the bar. Lars doesn't necessarily say much, which suits me fine. I caught the barkeep's eye, and held up two fingers. I come in enough that he knows what I drink, a double shot of brown poured over ice. That's another thing I like about the Blue Moon. All the important business had been conducted without a word being spoken.

It had been four or five months since the last time I'd seen Lars, but that wasn't unusual. He worked a small freighter that shifted cargo between all the places that aren't on the schedules of the big starliners. He hadn't changed any in that time, but then he never did. He was a big guy, having maybe ten centimeters and twenty kilos on me, all of it muscle, and except for the close cropped blonde hair could have passed for one of his Viking ancestors. He wore one of those jumpsuits spacers favor, but even without that, he had spacer written all over him, the pale skin, the gaze that seems to be looking into the distance even when he was staring at his beer, the way he moved as if he wasn't convinced that the gravity wasn't going to change on him at a moment's notice.

He waited until I sat down, then raised his glass and said, "Salud!" which for Lars was downright loquacious.

I muttered something in reply and asked, "How's it been?" or something equally inane.

Lars shrugged. He never talked much about what he'd been doing or where he'd been. I never really asked, either. Mostly when we got together we'd have a few drinks, maybe get something to eat, then go someplace to ogle females before going our separate ways until the next time. That seemed to suit both of us fine, which is maybe why we kept doing it.

This time, though, there seemed to be something on his mind.

"What's up?"

He looked at me with a look that seemed to be focused on a point several light-years past my head. He appeared to be thinking things over, debating whether he wanted to go through with something or not. Finally, he said, "Frank, I need to ask a favor of you."

I was surprised. Lars had always been the kind of guy who took care of his own business. He was more than willing to help out friends or even strangers, but he never expected any reciprocation.

"Sure, Lars. Who do you want killed?"

I'd said it as a joke, but Lars looked at me as if I was serious.

"Nothing like that, Frank. I've just got something I'd like you to keep for me for awhile. That's all."

"Do I need to know what it is?"

"Not particularly. Does it matter?"

"Not particularly." I meant that. As far as I knew, Lars had never been involved in anything illegal, which was more than could be said for myself. "What do you want me to do with it?"

"Just keep it safe for me until I ask for it back."

"That doesn't sound too hard. You do know they have things like safety deposit boxes in banks, don't you?"

"I'd rather not involve a bank. Or anyone else."

"Do you have this thing on you, or do we need to go pick it up?"

"I've got it right here." He reached into the bag he'd been carrying and pulled out a package. It was one of those foil bags that can seal and are supposed to be airtight in a vacuum. The package wasn't very big, maybe twenty by thirty centimeters and maybe three or four centimeters thick. There was a label on the front that just said "Lars Kendricks" in rather fussy looking block letters.

"That shouldn't be a problem. Anything special you want me to do with it?"

"No. Just keep it safe."

After that, we finished our drinks and walked across the street to my apartment. I stuffed the package into the safe I've got stashed in the back of my bedroom closet. Lars didn't seem concerned about the details. After that we got something to eat and a few more drinks. Once he'd turned over the package, Lars seemed to revert back to his old self. We made a good night of it and then parted, Lars to his ship, me back to my apartment.

I didn't see Lars for awhile after that, but that wasn't unusual, and I didn't think much about it. It had gotten to the point where I'd almost forgotten about the package in the back of my closet.

It was maybe six months later that I got a call from Latimer. Calls from Latimer are never good news. He's a detective on the Homicide Squad. I answered the call anyway.

"Sladek here."

"You know a guy named Lars Kendricks, Frank?"

"Why?"

"Maybe you'd better come down here." He gave me a location down city about as far as you can go without hitting vacuum.

"I'll be there as soon as I can, Latimer."

I tucked a needle gun in my pocket and left.

It took me maybe fifteen minutes taking the down city tram. There were a couple of uniformed cops blocking things off, but they must have been given orders about me, because they waved me right through. Latimer and his partner Rossetti were standing talking to a guy in a medical examiner's bunny suit. There was a body lying on the ground between them. Even from a distance I could tell it was Lars.

Latimer nodded as I approached and said, "We found your number in his comm. It was the only local one listed, He a friend of yours?"

"An acquaintance," I said.

Lars was lying face down on the pavement. I didn't have to be an M.

E. to know what had killed him. There was a burn mark from a laser in the middle of his back.

"What happened?"

"That's what we're trying to find out, Frank. How well did you know the guy?"

"Not all that well. He's a spacer—"

"We figured that out from his ID," Rossetti chimed in.

Latimer gave him a dirty look and said, "Go on, Frank."

"Like I said, he was a spacer. As far as I know he worked a contract freighter. He wasn't in town much, maybe once or twice a year. When he was, we'd go out for drinks, food, maybe chase some women. That was about the extent of our relationship."

"Know anyone that might have wanted to kill him?"

"No, but he never talked much about himself. Never talked much, period."

"I should be so lucky," Latimer said, giving his partner the eye. Latimer and his partner don't get along that well. He'd just as soon Rossetti never said anything. I don't blame him. Latimer is an OK guy for a cop; Rossetti is just a shade off from being a dirty one.

I eyed the bag that Lars had dropped. It looked as if it had been opened and someone had gone through it.

"Could it have been a robbery?"

"If it was, they weren't very good at their job. We found nearly two hundred dollars Crockett in his wallet."

"Find anything else?"

"Not much. His spacer papers, his wallet, and his comm. The bag doesn't seem to have anything in it except a change of clothes and a toothbrush. He was travelling light."

"Probably just planning to spend the night," I commented.

"He hadn't been in touch with you?"

"Not for months." Not since the time he'd left a package with me. I'd almost forgotten about the package. Was that what had gotten Lars killed?

"Look, Sladek," Rossetti piped in, "if you're holding anything back on us—"

"Can it, Rossetti. Can't you see the man's friend has just been killed?" Latimer isn't usually so concerned with people's feelings, but Rossetti had been getting on his nerves more than usual lately.

"Is there anything that you'd care to add, Frank? Anything that might help us?"

"Sorry, Latimer. I wish I did. I didn't know him all that well, but I liked Lars. As far as I know, almost everyone did. He was that kind of guy."

"Somebody didn't like him, Frank. Enough that they shot to kill."

"Yeah," I replied bitterly. "I don't have any idea who, Latimer. I really don't." I tried to sound convincing. I don't know if Latimer bought it, but he knew me well enough to know he wouldn't get anywhere by pushing me. Finally I asked, "Are you done with me?"

"Yeah. You can go. If you think of anything, let me know Frank. I mean it."

I didn't exactly rush home, but I didn't stop for the drink I wanted so badly, either. When I got to the apartment, I checked to make sure that the package was still in the safe at the back of my closet. It was. I pulled it out and stared at the plain surface of the bag. I could feel the outlines of a rectangular object inside about the size and shape of a book, though it seemed a little too heavy for that. I thought about opening it, but decided not to. At least not yet. It wasn't my business. Lars had left it with me for safekeeping. I'd honor his request for the time being. I put the package back in the safe on the bottom and covered it up with some papers.

"Mr. Sladek? This is Sovia Kendricks. I'm Lars' wife."

It was a few months after Lars had been killed that I received the call. I hadn't known that Lars had been married, but then that wasn't the kind of thing we'd talked about. Actually, we hadn't talked about much of anything other than whether to have another drink. Still, I was surprised. As a hand on a contract freighter Lars had led a pretty vagabond existence; no fixed schedule, no home port. If he had been married, he hadn't been particularly faithful. More than one of our drinking sessions had ended when he'd wandered off with a woman he'd just met. Still, there was no reason for me to doubt that he'd had a wife. Or two or three, for that matter. There's an old spacer saying about having a wife in every port. Maybe that had applied to Lars.

"Mr. Sladek?" The voice was warm and feminine, though with a hint of uneasiness.

"Sorry. I hadn't realized that Lars had been married."

"Oh," she said, sounding disappointed.

"Lars and I didn't talk about our personal lives much," I explained.

"I wonder if we could meet, Mr. Sladek? I tried to find your office in the directory, but there wasn't a listing, only a comm address."

"That's because I don't have a physical office. I would be unnecessary overhead. Usually I meet at the client's place of business or residence." I didn't mention that my unofficial office was a booth across the street at the Blue Moon.

"Where are you staying, Mrs. Kendricks?" I asked, though it felt strange.

"I'm staying at the Cosmos Hotel."

"I could meet you in the lobby. Say in half an hour."

"That would be fine Mr. Sladek."

"How will I know you?"

"I'll find you, Mr. Sladek. I'm sure that I will be able to recognize you from Lars' description."

Either Lars had been a lot more talkative at home, or Mrs. Kendricks was feeding me a line. It didn't really matter. Either way, I was sure the meeting would prove interesting.

The Cosmos is considered one of the top tier hotels. It's not quite the Casino, but it is a notch above the Rigel Royal, and maybe a tad pricey for the widow of a space hand, unless Lars had been making more money than I had realized.

The house dick spotted me as I entered the lobby, but had sense enough to look the other way when I waved him off. At one time or another, I've done work for most of the major hotels and I'm on speaking terms at least with the majority of their hotel detectives. I scanned the room looking for a face that matched the voice on the comm without luck. I was a few minutes early, so I took a seat where I could be seen and where I could keep an eye on most of the lobby.

I didn't have long to wait. A tall brunette stepped off the elevator looking around her. Her hair was pulled back into a bun that might have looked severe on many women, but had the opposite effect on her. She was dressed in a gray straight skirt and black high necked sweater over glossy, black, high heeled boots. The materials looked expensive, though the skirt was perhaps a little short for a woman so recently widowed, but people arrive from so many different planets that fashion standards on Star City are pretty flexible. If this was Lars' wife, he'd certainly had taste.

She spotted me almost immediately and strode purposely across the lobby towards where I was sitting. Now, by some accounts I'm not bad looking, but I also go out of my way not to look distinctive. The way she had zeroed in on me made me suspect that she'd seen my picture, though as far as I knew Lars had never taken an image of me.

"Mr. Sladek?"

"Mrs. Kendricks, I presume?" I said as I stood. "Please, have a seat."

She looked at the chair where I'd been sitting and its companion. "Is there someplace that we could go that would be a little more private?"

The reality is that there is almost no place more anonymous than the lobby of a major hotel, particularly in mid-afternoon when they tend to be the busiest. Out of habit, I'd picked a couple of chairs facing each other across a small table that was out of the line of traffic, but where I could easily spot anyone within earshot. But, if Mrs. Kendricks wanted to talk someplace else, I wasn't going to object.

"There's a lounge here, just off the lobby. It should be pretty quiet this time of day."

"Yes, that sounds better."

We moved to the lounge and took a booth off to the side. The only person besides the lone bartender was an older woman nursing something puce in a conical glass. Before I sat I asked, "Would you care for something to drink?"

"Yes, please. A glass of white wine, if they have it."

Now a place like the Cosmos has just about anything if you're willing to pay the price. Either Mrs. Kendricks didn't get out much or she was from some backwater star system. Somehow, I didn't think that either applied.

"Sweet or dry?" I asked.

"Dry," she answered without hesitation.

I went to the bar and ordered the wine and a double brown over ice for myself. The bartender raised an eyebrow at the latter. Only locals drink brown by choice. I didn't really care. I wasn't trying to impress the bartender. Or Mrs. Kendricks, either.

After I'd sat down, Mrs. Kendricks said, "I would have come here sooner, but you know what interstellar communications are like, Mr. Sladek."

I understood. The quickest way for information to flow between stars was by spaceship. Normal radio was limited to the speed of light, and so far no one has figured out a way to transmit information through tachyon space. This limited the spread of news. Depending on where she had been, it might well have taken a month or more for the news to reach her.

"Just where are you from, Mrs. Kendricks?"

"Please, call me Sovia, Mr. Sladek. From the way Lars talked about you, I feel we are old friends."

"You might as well call me Frank, then. But you haven't answered my question, Sovia."

"I doubt if you've heard of it, Frank. It's kind of off the beaten path, as it were."

"Try me. In my line of work I meet people from all over."

She mentioned a place, then. She was right, I hadn't heard of it. Maybe it didn't even exist.

"I'm afraid that you've come a long way for nothing, Sovia. The authorities disposed of the body several months ago. No one was aware that he had any family, I'm afraid. Not even the crew of the ship he'd been on."

"That's not why I came, Frank. I want to know what happened to Lars." She certainly sounded like an avenging widow. "I went to the police, but they weren't much help. All they had said was that your name had been in his comm. What did happen that night?"

"I'm not sure I can be of much help, Sovia. What I know of the case is pretty limited. Lars was shot in the back by a high powered laser. I know the detective that worked the case, a detective sergeant name of Latimer. He showed me the M.E.s report. The shot was probably fired from ten meters or more away. Robbery doesn't seem to have been a motive, because Lars still had nearly two hundred dollars Crockett in his wallet. The bag he'd been carrying had been opened, but nothing seemed to be missing. It just had a change of clothes in it."

"But what do you think happened, Frank?"

"Me? I don't know. It could have happened like the cops said. Maybe he was shot in the back by someone who wanted to rob him, but the killer was scared off before he could finish the job. Lars wasn't in the best part of Star City."

"But that's not what you think, is it Frank?"

"Like I said, I don't know. Lars didn't have any enemies as far as I know, but we didn't talk much about that kind of thing. It had been nearly half a year since I'd last spoken to him. A lot could have happened in that time—" I shrugged.

"I see—"

"What do you think happened, Sovia? After all, you were his wife—"

"You say that as if you have some doubt, Frank."

"I guess I'm just naturally suspicious. The first that I ever heard about Lars being married was when you called."

"I guess I can understand your doubts, Frank. Maybe this will settle them. I knew I might have to prove I was married to the authorities, so I brought it along."

She pulled a piece of paper out of her purse and unfolded it. It was an official looking document headed "Certificate of Marriage." The names Lars Kendricks and Sovia Karensky were printed along with the name of a Clerk of Courts for a municipality and continent that I'd never heard of on a planet that I didn't recognize. The date appeared to be in the local reckoning which meant it could be from twenty years ago or last week. There was an impressive looking hologram seal impressed on a circle of gold leaf, too. It might be real, but then again, I knew a dozen guys who could whip up the same sort of document in less than a half hour.

"I wasn't implying anything, Sovia. Which gets us back to my question, do you know any reason that someone might have killed Lars?"

"No, Frank. But I'm sure it wasn't a random criminal act."

"They rarely are, random, I mean. It's just that you don't always know the reason."

"You're a detective, aren't you, Frank? Well, I'd like to hire you."

"You'd be wasting your money. It's been three months since he died. I doubt if I could dig up anything the police didn't."

"I don't care, Frank. I want to find out who killed Lars."

"I don't come cheap, Sovia, even for the widows of friends."

"I've got some money, Frank. Lars had insurance. It was enough to get me here and some left over."

"My normal rates are a hundred twenty dollars Crockett a day plus expenses, but seeing as it's Lars, I'll knock that down to a hundred a day and expenses, but I'd still advise against it."

She reached into her purse and pulled out an envelope. She counted out ten crisp Crockett C-notes into a pile on the table.

"Here's a thousand dollars as an advance. That should cover at least a week, shouldn't it?"

"It'll do," I said, as picked up the money, folded the bills over and stuffed them into my jacket pocket. "Will you be staying here at the hotel?"

"Yes. For the time being, at least."

"Good, I'll keep in touch."

"You haven't finished your drink, Frank," she said, reaching her hand out to touch mine.

"Neither have you," I replied.

We stayed a while and talked about Lars, though it seemed that I ended up doing most of the talking. I left out the parts about the women he'd pick up, but I didn't get the impression that Sovia would have been surprised. Mostly I talked about myself, which I usually don't do. We had another round of drinks, but then people started to come into the bar, so we left. We parted in the lobby after I told her I'd be in touch in a few days.

On the way home it occurred to me that she hadn't asked about the package. For some reason, I hadn't mentioned it, either. Did she know about it?

Maybe it's my suspicious nature, or maybe it's just the business I'm in, but when I got back to my apartment I checked up on a few things. The passenger manifests of arriving and departing starliners are a matter of public record on Star City. It didn't take me long to verify that a Mrs. Kendricks had arrived several days earlier on a flight listing New Caledonia as its point of origin. I knew vaguely that New Caledonia was a planet out on the fringes of human space off in the direction away from the galactic center. It wasn't the place she had said she was from, but she could easily have made a connection there from someplace even more obscure. That part of her story, at least, seemed to check out.

The next thing I checked was the registration at the Cosmos. That kind of thing isn't a public record, but I'd done work for them in the past and had retained some access codes to their computer system. All of the information she had registered under matched what she had told me. As an added bonus, I discovered that she had deposited fifteen thousand dollars

Crockett with the hotel using a credit stick issued on the Bank of New Caledonia. That was a fairly common procedure to establish credit for someone planning on a long term stay. Fifteen grand was fairly serious cash, too.

It was getting late, but I wasn't feeling sleepy. I poured myself a couple of fingers of brown, added some ice, told the entertainment unit to play some jive samba, and then sat down with my comp to see what else I could find out.

Lars had arrived on a ship named The Lazy Lady, a contract freighter, a term that basically meant a ship that went anywhere that someone would pay them to go carrying anything that would fit in the hold. A quick check showed that he'd arrived as part of the crew of the same ship the time that he'd left the package with me. He was listed as second engineer, which on a ship that size was a description broad enough to mean just about anything. The arrival record gave the previous planetfall, but a ship like that might have been in dozens of different star systems in the time between when Lars had handed me the package and the time he'd been killed.

Interestingly, The Lazy Lady had departed less than eighteen hours after arrival, only a few hours after Lars' body had been found. Normally, a ship like that stayed in port long enough for the crew to have a night on the town and sleep it off in the morning. There was no way to tell if The Lazy Lady had been on a tight schedule or had just wanted to leave before the police started to ask embarrassing questions. The ship hadn't been back to Star City since.

I sat back in my chair, glass in hand, as the music played soft and slow in the background. There was nothing in the information that I'd found that in and of itself raised any suspicions. If Lars hadn't died, none of it would have seemed out of the norm. But the facts were that Lars had died, and that someone had killed him, and all I had to go on for a reason was that it might be connected to the package lying in the bottom of the safe in my closet. I closed my eyes and let the music lull me to sleep.

In the morning, I placed a call to Latimer. The detective sergeant was his normal cheerful self.

"What is it, Sladek? You usually only call to report dead bodies." This was only partially true, though it had happened often enough.

"Nothing as grim as that. I just called to see if you'd made any progress with the Kendricks' case."

"Not so you'd notice. No witnesses, no evidence other than the body. The ship he came in on pulled out before we could question anyone in the crew. But other than that, things are going about as you'd expect, which is nowhere. I know that you knew the guy, but why the interest, Frank?"

"There's been a development of sorts. I thought it might interest you."

"Oh?" Latimer said. "What kind of development?"

"A woman showed up. She claims to be Mrs. Kendricks."

"Any reason to believe she might be lying?"

"Not particularly. She showed me a marriage license."

"But--? What's the punch line, Frank?"

"I saw the license, but it's just a piece of paper from some municipality that I never heard of on a planet whose name I didn't recognize. There's no reason to think that it isn't legit. Some of those places the back of beyond have quaint notions of what constitutes an official record. It's just that Lars never mentioned having a wife anywhere. But then he was never much for conversation. As far as I know he might have had half a dozen wives on just as many planets."

"So what's this Mrs. Kendricks look like?"

"Tall, brunette, good figure."

"Was this Lars guy much of a lady's man, Frank?"

"He did alright when he wanted to."

"Good enough to land this woman? Particularly if she is from some god-forsaken ball of mud on the outer reaches?"

"It's certainly possible."

"I see. Is there any reason you can give me as to why I should go and question this woman?"

"No. I just thought you might want to know. I wouldn't want you to think I was concealing anything from you."

"You'd never do that, would you, Frank? It seems to me that it was a long way for this Mrs. Kendricks to come if she wasn't legitimate. That is, if she isn't trying to pull some kind of con. Is that what you're wondering about?"

"Maybe, though if she is pulling a con, I can't see what her angle is." I didn't feel the need to mention the package in the back of my closet.

"So this woman claiming to be Kendricks' wife looked you up. Any reason in particular, or just because you knew her husband?"

"She wants me to look into Lars' death. Do you have any objections?"

"Feel free, Frank. Knock yourself out. It's a three month old homicide going on four, of a non-resident with no clues and no active suspects. You know the way these things work. Let me know if you find anything useful. Otherwise, I've got plenty of cases keeping me busy."

The comm went dead. Latimer was never one for long good-byes.

There's one part of the job of being a detective that probably hasn't changed in a thousand years, and that's leg work. There comes a time in every case where, if you come up against a blank wall, you just have to go out and start asking questions until you either find some answers or stir things up enough that someone makes a move. I'd reached that point.

Not that it did me much good. I spent the rest of the day canvassing bars and diners at the down end of Star City where the spacers hang out from the ships that berth at the freight docking ring that sticks out of the ass end of the city. The trouble was, that the people in those kinds of places are a closed mouthed lot, especially with an outsider, which not being a spacer myself, I was. No one had known Lars, had ever heard of a ship called The Lazy Lady, or remembered anything about the night Lars had been killed. All I got were a lot of blank stares, even when I flashed around a double Crockett sawbuck. No one seemed to care that I was asking questions, but no one would admit to knowing anything, either.

Around 1600 I decided I could drink cheap brown in a place where I was more welcome and grabbed an up tram towards the Blue Moon. I didn't find any more answers from the ice melting in the brown liquor, but it didn't seem to matter. At least sitting on the bar stool, I got to rest my feet.

When the Blue Moon started to get noisy with the after work crowd, I grabbed a quick sandwich of vat grown meat at the diner on the corner. On a whim, I headed farther up town.

There's a little café across the street from the Cosmos that has a couple of tables and chairs out on the sidewalk. One was vacant, so I ordered a cup of joe and sat watching. I saw a lot of people coming and leaving the hotel, but none of them were Sovia Kendricks. After a bit, I ordered another cup of joe and some kind of cheesy pastry to mollify the waiter.

The crowd on the street became a little sparser as the evening progressed. With no Sovia in sight, I started to eye the passersby out of habit. One of the great things about Star City is that it attracts all kinds of people from all over human space. I tried to guess the planet of origin and occupation of random members of the crowd, knowing from experience that I'd be wrong about eighty percent of the time. The only place you can tell a left-handed neurosurgeon from Crockett from the way his brown shoes have worn down is in cheap detective stories.

The only thing that struck me as curious was that there was a man at the café at the other end of the block who seemed to be doing the same thing that I was. There was nothing particularly remarkable about him. He was average height, average weight, average looks, brownish hair, and dressed in a brown suit that looked neither shabby or too flashy. If I had had to peg his occupation, I would have said that he was a detective shadowing someone, but as he didn't seem to be taking any notice of me, I didn't give him another thought.

The waiter finally made it clear that he wanted to close up for the night. I dropped a Crockett five buck piece on the table as a tip and went home.

The next day I spent doing much the same thing as the previous, except that I worked some of the places that Lars and I hit during our drinking bouts. I had about the same luck, too. If anyone had seen the big spacer the night he'd been killed they either didn't remember or didn't feel like talking about it. Unless you're a masochist, you can only endure so many blank stares and shaking heads. It wasn't the first time I'd found myself hunting down a dead end, there isn't a detective alive that hasn't had the experience, but by the middle of the afternoon, I was wondering if it was time to give up on finding the man who'd killed Lars.

Late that afternoon, I got a call from Sovia.

"Have you found anything out, Frank?" she asked, after we'd exchanged greetings.

"It's a little early to expect much. After all, there isn't very much to go on. I talked to the detective on the case, a guy named Latimer. I know him and he's an okay guy most of the time. He says they haven't come up with any leads on the case, but then I'm not sure how hard they're really trying. A case of a dead spacer a few months old isn't exactly going to be a high priority."

"I realize that, Frank. I'm not criticizing you. I'm sure you're doing all you can. It's just that I've been holed up in this hotel since I got here, and I'm getting a little cabin fever. I don't know anyone on Star City, and I guess I called just to hear another human voice. Can you blame me?"

She sounded like a little girl. I had to smile at that. "No, it's quite alright, Sovia. I'm used to anxious clients, and you're the one paying the freight."

"Look, what I'm trying to say, Frank, is what would it take to get you to take me out to dinner or something just so I can get out of this hotel?"

"Is that all that's bugging you? I think I can manage something to help with the boredom. I know a place that serves a decent dinner. Can you be ready about 1900?"

"That would be great, Frank."

"Good. I'll pick you up in the lobby."

I had time to beat it back to my apartment, get cleaned up, and change into one of my more presentable suits. I pondered whether to pack anything. There didn't seem to be much need, but I compromised by slipping a needler into the pocket of my jacket. I gave a glance at myself in the mirror in the entry hall and decided I was acceptable.

I rode an up tram to the stop nearest the Cosmos, and walked the two blocks from there to the hotel. It was a nice night, but then on Star City they all are, and there were plenty of people roaming the street heading to dinner or a drink or just out for a stroll.

I was a few minutes early, and the house dick spotted me waiting in the lobby. He knew me well enough to know who I was.

"Should I be worried, Frank?"

"Nothing like that, Serge. I'm not here on business. I'm just here to take one of your guests out to dinner."

"No problem. I was just checking. Have a nice night."

Serge wandered off, but I could tell that he was watching me out of the corner of his eye. He must have gotten an eyeful when Sovia stepped off the elevator and walked over to where I was standing.

I barely recognized her. She'd let her hair hang loose. It was longer and thicker than I'd remembered from our first meeting. She'd ditched the skirt and sweater, too, for a body hugging sleeveless dress in a shade of red that is usually reserved for warning lights. The matching spikey heeled shoes raised her eyes so that they were level with my own.

"I hope I'm not overdressed, Frank. I figured that if I was going out for a night on the town, I might as well make the most of it."

"I don't see how anyone could accuse you of being overdressed, Sovia, not in that outfit."

"Why, Frank. It almost sounds like you're flirting."

"Let's get out of here before the house dick gets interested."

She chuckled at that and took my arm.

Once out on the sidewalk I said, "We can catch a down tram a couple of blocks over."

"Whatever you say, Frank. I'm just a country girl new to the big city."

I found that hard to believe. The rig she was wearing hadn't come out of any general store.

It didn't take long to get to the restaurant, just a couple of tram stops down city and then a transfer to a circumferential for a ride halfway around the city. I grew up on Star City and take the tram system for granted, but Sovia was impressed. The trams are free, frequent, and there isn't a place on Star City that is more than a kilometer or so from a stop. Out-of-towners, even from some of the big cities on Crockett or Earth always seem to marvel at them, though us locals just accept them.

The restaurant was a place called Roma Gardens. It wasn't a huge place, but the food was pretty good and not too expensive. Its biggest plus was that it offered dinner seating on the roof of the building.

I eat there often enough that the head waiter recognizes me. He's an older guy, and a brother of the man who owns the place, and he actually manages to sound pleased when a regular shows up.

"Two for dinner, Mr. Sladek?"

"Sure, Luigi. On the roof if you can manage it." I slipped a five credit coin to him when we shook hands.

"I believe one should be opening up in a few minutes. If you'd care to wait in the bar, I can come for you as soon as it's set up."

"That would be swell, Luigi."

We found ourselves a couple of seats at the bar.

"What'll you have to drink?" I asked. "White wine is it?"

"What do the locals drink, Frank? Maybe I'll try one of those."

"Locals mostly drink brown or clear depending on their preference. It all comes out of the same vat, so it doesn't really matter much. The only difference is what artificial flavorings get added. I can't say that I'd recommend it though. It's kind of an acquired taste."

"Maybe I'll just stick to wine, then."

I caught the bartender's eye and placed the order. I decided to splurge and ordered one of the cheaper Crockett whiskies over ice with a splash of soda.

The drinks had just arrived when Luigi came over, menus in hand, to tell us that our table was ready. The elevator at Roma Gardens is a real treat, an open cage of polished brass. It looks like it's been there for a couple of hundred years. Maybe it has, the restaurant has been run by the same family for four or five generations. Luigi waved us into the car with a flourish, then stepped inside and pressed the up button. There was a certain amount of clanking and other mechanical noises, but after a few moments we found ourselves deposited on the roof.

"I've got a nice table set up for you over in the corner, Mr. Sladek," Luigi announced.

The roof top of the Gardens isn't big, maybe ten by twenty meters, but some strategically placed potted plants provide a nice illusion of privacy. The best feature of the roof is the view upward. It was late enough that the glow tubes that run down the central spine of Star City had been dimmed for the night. That allowed us to see all the way across the hollow cylinder that is Star City to the far side, some three kilometers away, where the street lights and signs provided little twinkling dots of illumination.

I could see that the sight had taken Sovia by surprise, which was what I'd intended.

"I don't know if you appreciate how amazing the view is, Frank. I don't think I'll ever be able to get used to things just curving up the way they do. I guess I'm used to looking up and just seeing sky. That, and knowing that just a little ways below us is the emptiness of space."

"Oh, I think you'll be safe. There's at least half a kilometer of reinforced rock beneath our feet."

"You're making fun of me, Frank," Sovia protested.

"Well, I suspect that I'd have just as much trouble getting used to their not being anything overhead. Somehow, it just wouldn't seem right. The thought of all that emptiness up there with only gravity keeping you from floating away—"

"Now you are making fun of me. Haven't you ever been off of Star City? To some other planet?"

"Nope. Never have, and I probably never will."

We were saved from having to make more ridiculous small talk by the arrival of the waiter. The food at the Gardens is simple but good, how they manage to make it taste so fresh when anything that doesn't come out of a down city vat has to be brought in from at least a dozen light-years away is a family secret. I ordered a pasta with fennel sausage and peppers in a red sauce. I'm not sure what kind of beast a fennel is, but it tastes pretty good. Sovia had chicken with pesto which I gather is some kind of green thing. We washed it down with a bottle of red wine that did not come out of a vat, at least one on Star City. When the food came we pretty much stopped talking until we'd finished.

Sovia talked me into desert. While we waited, I asked a few questions.

"How'd you meet Lars, anyway? He never mentioned you."

She responded to the question with a hesitant, "oh," as if she was surprised at the fact.

"Lars never mentioned me? I know he told me all about you, Frank." I was starting to wonder if we were talking about the same Lars. The Lars I knew hadn't been talkative. But then I hadn't been a good looking woman, either.

"No. Lars never talked much about himself. Or his work. But getting back to how you two met—"

"That was simple enough. I was working at the spaceport. As a waitress. Lars came in one night, ordered a drink, then another. It was slow, so we got to talking. One thing led to another. Lars was a big handsome guy who seemed to have a steady supply of cash. Well, you get the idea." She almost sounded embarrassed by her story.

"He shipped out the next day, but he was back in a month. That's when he asked me to marry him. I said yes. I might have been a little drunk at the time."

"It must have been hard, with him being gone so much?"

"It wasn't so bad, really. I kept my job as a waitress, so that part of my life went on pretty much as it had been. Lars would come in for a day or two every month or so. I'd take off work, we'd party and—well other things, then he'd be gone again. But at least I had someone, something. It wasn't so easy for me when I was growing up, Frank. Lars brought some stability and security into my life. I don't regret marrying him at all. That's why I want to find out who killed him, Frank. Do you understand?"

"Sure, Sovia." I grew up on the streets of Star City, but I was saved from going into that story when the waiter brought the desert. It was served with little glasses of what looked like white wine but which had more of a kick.

By the time we had finished that, we were both feeling pretty good. I saw Sovia back to her hotel.

As I was walking out of the hotel lobby I caught a flash of a face that I thought I recognized. It looked a lot like the man in the brown suit that I had seen outside the hotel the day before. He was sitting off to the side of the lobby apparently studying the screen of a comp. It was possible that he was just a businessman catching up on correspondence, but I'd pulled similar stunts doing surveillance too many times not to think he might be doing the same.

Outside, I found a place where I'd be in the shadows and hung around to see if he came out. I waited there for ten minutes, but I didn't see him come out of the hotel. Whatever he was doing, it didn't look as though he was tailing me. I gave it up and took the down tram back to my apartment. On the way, I thought about Sovia's story. It had sounded plausible enough. Things certainly could have happened that way. I wanted to believe her.

I spent the next few days poking around trying to find out anything I could about the last time Lars had been on Star City. I didn't have much luck. I knew what time the Lazy Lady had docked, and the time that Lars had left the docking ring, and that was it. I hadn't been able to discover anything about what had happened to him between that time and when he'd been killed. During this time I didn't notice the man in the brown suit. And was thinking it had just been a coincidence.

Despite the lack of progress, I'd been too busy to see Sovia. I decided it was time to remedy that.

I made a call to Sovia to see if she was interested in another dinner. There was no answer. I placed a call to the Cosmos and had them ring through to her room, but there was no response. The reception desk was sorry, but they couldn't be of any help. They didn't know if Mrs. Kendricks was in the hotel or not.

It was several hours later that my comm rang. I answered it, hoping it was Sovia, but it was a man's voice that responded when I answered.

"Mr. Sladek?"

"Yes. Who is this?"

"We need to have a talk."

"Who is this?" I repeated.

"All in good time, Mr. Sladek. All in good time. If you are interested in seeing Mrs. Kendricks, you will come to room 521 of the Excelsior Hotel. You will come unarmed, and you will come alone. You will not tell anyone where you are going. Do I make myself clear, Mr. Sladek."

"Clear enough. When?"

"In one hour."

"I'll be there."

The connection broke.

I had no proof that whoever had made the call had Sovia, but somehow I didn't have any doubts on the subject. I also didn't know if any of this had anything to do with the package resting in my safe, but I wasn't going to bet against the fact.

I went to the closet in my bedroom, opened the safe, and pulled out the package from where I'd left it. The voice on the comm hadn't said anything about it, but I no longer felt safe leaving it there. I had to do something with it, and I had to do it quickly.

Slamming the safe door shut, I stood and checked the time. I had just about enough. I tucked the package into the back of my pants where it would be hidden by my jacket. On the way out, I dropped my needle gun on the stand in the hall.

The Excelsior was down city from my apartment. I took an up tram.

TransGalactic is the largest of the starliner companies. Their headquarters is on Star City, and the entire lower floor of their office building is given over to customer services. Among the services offered are storage lockers for people in transit with layovers too short to warrant a hotel stay. I walked up to the kiosk, transferred a credit from a credit stick and out popped a key card. It had the locker number, "C-347," displayed on its surface.

I went to the indicated bank of lockers, found the one with a matching number, and inserted the card. The door opened. I stuck the package inside and closed the door. Doing so activated the lock. The key card popped out of its slot, except that the number had disappeared, replaced only by the TransGalactic logo.

There was a postal kiosk at the other end of the hall. I went over, got a pre-paid envelope, and addressed it to an anonymous mailbox that I kept for just such a purpose. Stuffing the keycard inside, I slid the envelope into the kiosk's slot.

No one, including me, would be able to access the locker until the key card had made its way through the postal system. I'd just bought myself about twelve hours.

Star City, as the major transit point of human space, has plenty of hotels. The Casino is elegant, The Rigel Royal is respectable, and the Cosmos is fashionable. The Excelsior was none of these things. It offered cheap rooms with limited amenities a couple of kilometers down from top of the city.

I rode the elevator up to the fifth floor and found room 521. When I knocked, the door was opened by the man in the brown suit. That answered one question. He hadn't been tailing me, he'd been watching Sovia. He motioned me in without a word and shut the door. Once inside, he patted me down in a very professional manner. I didn't need to pat him down to know that he was carrying a laser pistol in a shoulder holster under his left armpit.

531 was a suite, which basically meant there was a sitting area two by three meters and an adjacent bedroom that was slightly bigger. There was a sofa in the sitting room. Sovia was sitting on it looking worried.

Facing her was a man I'd never seen before. There was nothing particularly remarkable about him. He looked to be about fifty and was cut from the same cloth as the man in the brown suit, except that he had short cropped blonde hair and blue eyes so pale as to be almost clear. They reminded me of ice cubes. It was clear that he was the one that was going to do all the talking.

"Mr. Sladek, I'll get right to the point. You have something that I want."

"And what would that be, Mr.—?"

"I don't think there is any need to get into names, Mr. Sladek."

"You'd seem to have the advantage on me then."

"Yes, I do. I'd keep that in mind, Mr. Sladek."

"Oh, I will. Trust me. Just what is it you want?"

"I believe that some time ago, a man named Kendricks left something with you for safe keeping."

"That's possible. It's been awhile since I saw Lars alive, and we were mostly drunk when together, but I suppose he might have left something behind."

"Don't play coy with me, Mr. Sladek. I know you have the item I'm interested in. I want you to bring it to me."

"Supposing that Lars did leave something with me. What do I get if I turn it over?"

"I would have thought that obvious, Mr. Sladek. If you bring me the package that was left with you I will allow you to leave and take Mrs. Kendricks here with you. If you don't-- Well, I'll leave that to your imagination. Suffice it to say that Mrs. Kendricks won't walk out of here alive. Not after my associate has finished with her. Do I make myself clear."

"Perfectly."

"Good."

"Do you agree, then, Mr. Sladek."

"Yes, in principle."

"Come, come, Mr. Sladek. Neither one of us can claim to be men of principle."

"What guarantee do I have that you'll let either one of us walk out of here alive."

"Absolutely none, Mr. Sladek."

"I don't have this 'package' on me. I've put it someplace safe. It will take me a little time to get it."

"You have exactly twelve hours, Mr. Sladek."

"I don't know if I can manage that."

"That would be unfortunate for the young lady."

"What does she have to say about all this?"

"Why don't you ask her?"

"Sovia?"

"Don't do it, Frank. You can't trust these men. Look what happened to Lars."

"What about that?"

"I don't expect you to believe me, Mr. Sladek, but neither myself or my associate had anything to do with Kendricks' death."

"I don't believe you. But I'll do it anyway. Do you want me to bring the package here?"

"Yes. And remember, within the next twelve hours."

After that admonishment I was allowed to leave. It was just after 2200. On the way back to my apartment, I considered my dilemma. Even if I was willing to turn over the package to the man with the cold, blue eyes, my own cleverness in protecting it had made that impossible. I had less than twelve hours to act, and the earliest I could hope to recover the key card to the locker would be noon of the next day. Any sort of attempt to rescue Sovia by violence would be risky. Neither the man with the blue eyes or the man in the brown suit had seemed the type that would panic or surrender easily.

That pretty much meant that my only option would be some sort of bluff or con. I could live with that.

I didn't know how much ice-blue eyes knew about what the package looked like. It didn't really matter. The foil bag that it had come in was common enough, I could pick one up on the way back to my apartment. The label would be easy enough to fake, as well. As to the contents, well, I'd have to work something out, but with luck they'd never get a chance to open the bag.

I stopped at an 24 hour convenience store a few blocks from my apartment to pick up the foil bag. On a whim, I picked up a second one on the theory that it might not hurt to have a decoy. In the same aisle they had adhesive labels that looked to be about the same size that Lars had used, so I took a package of them, too. I realized that I hadn't eaten, so I grabbed a sandwich from the cooler and dropped them on the check-out counter. It came to six and a half credits, most of which was the sandwich.

Back at my apartment, I laid the contents of my shopping trip on the kitchen table and got a bottle of yellow, what passes for beer on Star City, out of the refrigerator. I took a bite of the sandwich and then wished I hadn't. It tasted like cardboard. For a moment, I considered stuffing it in one of the foil bags, but unfortunately, it wasn't the right shape.

I got a pen, and tried to recreate Lars' writing on the labels. It took me several tries before I was satisfied with my efforts. I made a duplicate, and then looked around for something to stuff in the bags. There was an advertising directory on the counter, the kind that they give away free. It had about the right dimensions. I stuck it in one of the foil bags and looked it over. It looked to be about the right size and shape. I sealed the bag and slapped one of the labels on the outside.

I needed something for the second bag, but I only had the one directory. Nothing else in the kitchen had the right dimensions. Walking into the living room, I looked at my book shelf. I don't have a lot of books in print, though probably more than most people. Most of the ones I do are fairly valuable, particularly the Marcus Fitzroy signed first editions. I wasn't sure that I was willing to part with any of those, if only for sentimental reasons. Fortunately, I had a copy of Jack Feldman's one and only novel. Almost everyone who's anyone on Star City has a copy. Feldman gives them away freely; it's the only way he can get rid of them. Even if I lost my copy, Feldman would be sure to replace it in the remote possibility that I asked him to. I grabbed it out of the bookcase and returned to the kitchen. When I stuck it in the other bag, it looked to be a pretty good match for the directory.

It was just past midnight. By that time I was hungry enough to finish off the sandwich. Fortunately, I had the beer to wash it down with.

The first part of my plan was complete. I had a dummy package. What I didn't have was much of the rest of the plan. What plan I did have, involved distracting blue-eyes and brown suit during the exchange of the package and somehow getting the drop on them. I was counting on the fact that neither one of them was probably getting much sleep. If I brought the package to them at around 0400 they might not be that alert. I hoped.

I set the alarm on my comm for 0300 and tried to get some sleep in the chair in the living room.

When the alarm sounded three hours later I cursed at it before I remembered why I had set it. I started a pot of joe, hoping it might wake me up and then stared at the two bags on the table. I couldn't remember which had Feldman's book. It didn't really matter. I considered what to do with the spare package. The smart thing might be to just put it in the safe where the real one had been.

I went into the bedroom closet and opened the safe. Mostly I use the safe to store weapons. It's just too dangerous to leave things like that laying around. I don't really have that many, just a needle gun, and a few laser pistols, including a few that I've taken off various people that can't be traced to me. That's when I remembered a little toy I'd lifted from a grifter who I had been hired to catch cheating at cards. I had, and he'd tried to get the drop on me. He hadn't been quick enough.

He'd tried to do it with a little rig that he had had strapped to his wrist. It contained a small laser pistol on a spring that was supposed to pop it out into the wearer's hand when a button was pushed. It had popped out, alright, but he'd managed to drop it. The pistol wasn't much of weapon, 25 kJoule with a long recharge time, but the whole rig was thin enough to be almost undetectable under a jacket sleeve unless someone was looking for it. It was chancy, but it might be just the edge that I was looking for.

I strapped it onto my wrist and tried the action several times. I only dropped the laser once. I closed the safe, grabbed the fake package, and threw on my jacket. At the door, I checked to see if I could spot the holdout gun up my sleeve. I couldn't.

I was back in the lobby of the Excelsior at 0400. Except for the bored looking clerk at the registration desk, there was no one in sight. When I walked up to the desk he gave me the kind of look you'd expect to get when a not entirely reputable looking man with no baggage walks into a hotel at that hour of the morning. He wasn't any happier when I asked to see the hotel dick on duty. The fact that I showed him my investigator's license didn't improve his opinion, but he pressed a hidden button behind the desk.

A couple of minutes later a pudgy guy in his early sixties can huffing into view. He wasn't running or anything, just huffing. Over the years, I've come to know and be known by most of what passes for hotel security on Star City. I knew this one as an ex cop named Foster. That he was working the graveyard shift in a second class place like the Excelsior says something about Star City's pension system.

"We don't want no trouble, Sladek," he said as caught his breath.

"There shouldn't be any, Foster. That's why I asked to see you. I'm going to go up to room 521. I expect to be down in a few minutes along with a young lady. If you're interested, the lady will be coming willingly. She's a client of mine. As I said, I expect to be back down here in a few minutes and out of your hair, and that should be the end of it."

"If nothing is going to happen, why'd you want to see me?"

"Insurance. If I'm not down here in, oh say, half an hour I'd appreciate it if you'd call Latimer." As a former cop, I didn't have to explain to him who Latimer was. "Don't bother going up there yourself. Leave that to people on the public dime."

"So why shouldn't I just run you out of the hotel and save everyone some grief?"

"If you think you can do it, Foster, do it. Otherwise—"

I gave him my hard guy stare. It must have worked. Either that, or he was thinking about the breakfast that was waiting for him in a couple of hours.

"As I said, Frank, we don't want no trouble here."

"Good. Then we're in agreement. If I'm not down in a half-hour call Latimer. Don't let them shunt you off to Rossetti."

"Is that bum still on the force?"

"Yeah."

"Figures. Good luck, Sladek."

I'd be needing it. I headed over the elevators and rode up to the fifth floor.

The man in the brown suit opened the door when I knocked, except that he'd taken off his jacket. It looked like he might have been trying to nap. The shoulder holster he wore had a Kunstler stuck into it. He patted me down like he'd done earlier, but he missed the holdout rig.

Sovia was still sitting on the sofa. When she saw me she flashed me a tense little smile. Blue-eyes was sitting across from her in a chair, a small laser pistol resting on the table next to him.

"So you've returned, Mr. Sladek, and with the package. Very wise."

"Let's get this over with. I give you the package and the woman and I leave. That's what we agreed to."

"I don't see that you're in any position to quibble about terms, Mr. Sladek, but that's the way it will happen—If the package is what it is supposed to be."

"It's what Lars left with me. That's all I know. I never opened it."

"Your lack of curiosity astounds me, Mr. Sladek. I'd have expected a man in your profession to have been tempted as soon as it passed into your hands."

"Lars was a pal of mine."

"Ah. Honor amongst—Well that's neither here nor there, is it, Mr. Sladek. Hand me the package." He stood up with his hand out.

I handed it over. In the process of doing so, I maneuvered so that I was no longer between blue-eyes and brown suit, but was at the apex of a triangle where I wouldn't be in a crossfire.

Blue-eyes looked at the package in his hand, weighing it and feeling the outline of the contents. Satisfied, he reached into his pocket and produced a small folding-knife. Brown-suit looked on hungrily, one eye on the package and one eye on me.

There wasn't going to be a better time. I brought up my left hand to the right sleeve of my jacket. By some miracle, I didn't drop the tiny pistol when it popped out.

"Hold it."

Blue-eyes stared at me, or rather the laser pointed at a point between his eyes. Brown-suit started to reach for his own pistol, but hesitated, trying to judge the odds. He knew that no matter how fast he was, I'd be able to get one of them.

Blue-eyes replied, "Mr. Sladek, you may be able to hit one of us, but I doubt that that toy you hold in your hand would recycle fast enough to enable you to shoot both of us before the other could respond."

"That's probably true, but, if it makes a difference, the one I'm going to shoot is you."

"Boss?" brown-suit questioned.

"I think we had better assume Mr. Sladek is a man of his word."

"I think I can take him, boss."

"Do you really want to chance it?" I answered. Sovia looked on with wide eyes.

"Let's not do anything foolish, Mr. Sladek," blue-eyes said.

"That's fine by me. Now, using only the tips of the fingers of your left hand, I want you to push that pistol lying next to you off the table on the side away from you."

"Mr. Sladek—"

"Do it," I interrupted.

"Sovia, I want you to stand where you won't be between me and this guy--

" I said pointing at brown-suit with the laser in my hand. "I want you to pull out the pistol and hand it to me. Can you do that?"

"Sure, Frank."

Sovia was as good as her word. I transferred the small laser to my left hand. I felt better with the heavier Kunstler in my gun hand.

"OK. Now I want you to go get the package, Sovia. Be careful not to get between me and either of these two gentlemen."

"Mr. Sladek," blue-eyes said, "can't we come to some arrangement? I admit that you seem to have gotten the drop on us, but that is only a temporary situation at best. Now I'm prepared to make a deal for the package. I can give you ten thousand dollars Crockett right here and right now if you leave the package with me."

"It's tempting, but I don't think so. Not right now. Perhaps later we might talk money, but I think you might have to talk a little louder. For the moment, all I'm concerned about is taking Mrs. Kendricks back to her hotel."

"You're making a mistake, Mr. Sladek—"

"Quite probably. But then it wouldn't be the first time. Sovia, get the package."

She snatched up the package, squeezing it with her red-nailed fingers, and then moved so that she was between me and the door.

"OK. Here's the deal. We're going to back out through the door and get on the elevator. If either of you pops your head out into the hallway before we get on, I'll put a nice little hole in it. Do I make myself clear?"

"Perfectly, Mr. Sladek."

"Good. Sovia, open the door. See if anyone is in the hallway."

She did as I asked. "No one is there, Frank."

I backed out into the hallway and pulled the door shut after me. Still holding onto the handle, I commanded, "Go press the down button."

She ran to the elevator and did as I asked. I was still holding onto the door handle, but there weren't any attempts to open it from the other side. It seemed like an eternity, but it was probably only a few moments until the elevator door opened. I backed my way to the elevator, got in, and said "Lobby." The doors closed and we began to descend.

I slipped the little pistol back into the rig and dropped the Kunstler into my jacket pocket. It made a noticeable bulge, but that couldn't be helped.

"Give me the package, Sovia."

"Is this what Lars left with you, Frank?"

"Yeah," I lied. I'm not sure why.

Down in the lobby, Foster was leaning on the reception desk chatting with the desk clerk. Both were staring in the direction of the elevator. I waved in their direction and ushered Sovia out of the hotel.

Outside, we headed down city towards the next circumferential tram line. I figured that if blue-eyes and brown-suit tried to follow us, they'd be less likely to take that direction. Once we'd gone a block, I slowed us down to a normal walking pace.

"Thanks, Frank. I thought those two were going to kill me. I wasn't sure what was happening. Was it the package that they wanted? Was that why Lars was killed?"

"Maybe. I don't know for sure. I'm not even sure that they had anything to do with Lars' death. All I know is that they had you. How'd that happen, anyway?"

"I was bored. I went out to do a little window shopping. Just to get some air and get outside. I didn't even realize they were there until the shorter one stuck a pistol in my ribs. The other

one came up on the other side. There was nothing I could do."
She was starting to show the signs of hysteria.

"It's alright, now, Sovia. I'm with you. You're safe. At least for now, but it might be better if you didn't go back to the Cosmos tonight."

"What are you suggesting, Frank?"

"I've got an apartment. It's not far from here. We can be there in ten minutes."

The hysteria was gone, replaced with something else. I'm not sure what, but I wasn't going to object. "Frank, are you propositioning me."

"I can sleep on the couch, if you'd like."

"We'll see."

We got back to my apartment without incident. As we entered, Sovia started as she saw the painting that hangs in the entry hall.

"Whoever gave you that must have had it in for you," she commented.

The picture in question is one of the few portraits Lucinda has ever done. It's a full-length image of a not quite human figure. Lucinda is an artist on Crockett well-known enough to go by one name. She was also a former lover.

"It's supposed to be my portrait. It was a parting gift from an ex-girlfriend."

"She must really have hated you."

"Not really. She just got to know me too well. Hence the painting. Can I get you a drink?"

"I could really use one, Frank."

I ushered Sovia into the living room, and then went into the kitchen to fix the drinks. When I came back I noticed that Sovia had dropped the package on a coffee table and looked around in that way women do when they see where a man lives for the first time.

"This isn't quite what I expected. It's—"

"Tasteful?"

"I'm not sure that's the right word, but it doesn't look like a bachelor lives here."

I've lived in the apartment for a number of years, mostly because the rent is cheap and there's a decent bar across the street. The building had originally been built as luxury apartments, but that had been in the early days of Star City when New Minglewood was supposed to be a large park instead of the lawless slum that it has become. That was several centuries ago. From the balcony, you can just see the fringes of New Minglewood over the top of the building holding the Blue Moon.

The apartment itself is quite large by Star City standards, with a bedroom, bath, living room, kitchen and separate dining area. Over the years I've managed to furnish it with a certain amount of the style that interior designers label "eclectic." Most of the pieces are cast-offs I've salvaged from the gutter, but I've been selective, and most are quality if a bit worn. There's not much in the way of decoration except for a large landscape in oranges and reds that hangs over the sofa. It's another, more typical, Lucinda, the kind that made her famous, and rich, after she left for Crockett.

"Now that picture I like," Sovia said. "It's a lot more cheerful. You should get something by that artist for your hall." I didn't bother to correct her.

I called out to the entertainment system to play something quiet. It knows my taste pretty well and played a soft jive samba. It also took the initiative to dim the lights.

"Are you trying to seduce me, Frank?"

"I just thought we could both use something to relax by."

I perched on the arm of the sofa and sipped my drink while I watched Sovia continue to prowl the apartment. Her movements were lithe like a caged tiger, or at least what I imagine a tiger looks or moves like. Having never been off Star City I've never actually seen one in person, or any other animal much larger than a rat, for that matter.

"If you're interested, there's another painting by the same artist over the bed." That one is a seascape in blues and greens whose most prominent feature are the three moons hanging in the sky. Lucinda never told me whether it is of a real or imagined scene. It's always hard to tell with her work.

"I'd like that, Frank," Sovia said as she drained her drink and set the glass down.

In the end, I didn't spend the night on the sofa.

In the morning, Sovia woke first. She was laying propped up on one elbow as if studying me.

"You're awake," she said.

I looked at the clock on the nightstand. It said 0940. We'd slept late, but then it had been a busy night.

"That's obvious." For a moment I thought she was going to hit me with a pillow.

"Frank?"

"Yes?"

"What do you know about that package? That is what this whole business is about, isn't it?"

"As far as I can tell. Unless there's something you're not telling me. But as far as the package goes, Lars didn't tell me what was in it. He just asked me to hold it for him. He never mentioned it to you?"

"No, but then, whenever he was around we had other things to talk about."

She gave me a look, then, and it wasn't bedroom eyes. "You never looked inside, Frank? Even after he was killed?"

"No. I thought about it, but somehow it didn't seem to be any of my business."

"You're an unusual man, Frank Sladek."

"I've been told that before, though usually not in such polite terms."

She smiled at that.

"I can fix us breakfast, if you'd like," I said.

"Is it okay if I take a shower first? I think I could use one."

"It's fine by me."

She got up and went into the bathroom. She took her time at it. I could hear the water running in the shower as I lay in the bed. After she came out, I went in for a quick shower myself.

When I came out of the bathroom, Sovia was gone. So was the package that had been sitting on the coffee table.

In a way, it was just as well that Sovia had left, I only had enough egg mix for one serving. As I fried up some breakfast sausages, I wondered if Sovia had grabbed the package just because it was of value, or if she really knew what it contained. I wasn't sure if I was comfortable with either answer.

After breakfast I tried to call her, but the call was rejected because her comm was "out of service." Another call to the Cosmos revealed that Mrs. Kendricks had checked out that morning without leaving a forwarding address. For good measure, I called the Excelsior. Not surprisingly, it turned out that the two gentlemen who had been in room 531 had also checked out without leaving word. I did manage to talk the desk clerk into giving me their names, a Boris Cumberland and an Ian Nathan from Nordholm, though I had doubts as to whether either the names or their planet of origin were real.

I wasn't sure where all this left me. I was pretty sure that I was now without a client, though that might change when Sovia opened the package and discovered either the directory or Feldman's book. I wasn't any nearer to discovering who had killed Lars, either. Blue-eyes had denied having anything to do with that. I was inclined to believe him as he'd had no real reason to lie. All that told me was that there were more players in the game than I had thought, though I still wasn't clear what that game was, other than that it had something to do with the package that Lars had left with me.

For the moment, the package was sitting in a locker in the lobby of the TransGalactic building, which, considering everything, might be the safest place for it. The key was working its way through the postal system, but would probably show up at the blind address sometime later in the day. I wasn't in any great hurry to pick it up.

What I was in a hurry for was a drink. I glanced at the clock. It was early yet, still before noon, but then I've never operated on the clock. I headed across the street to the Blue Moon, but not before strapping a shoulder holster with a laser pistol on beneath my jacket and tucking a needle gun into my waist band in the small of my back.

If the Blue Moon is quiet in the early afternoon, it's even deader in the late morning after the crowd coming off the night shift drinks up their breakfast and stumbles home. I had the place to myself except for the bartender and I grabbed my usual stool in the middle of the bar. The barkeep grunted an interrogatory and I grunted a response which got me a tumbler of brown over ice. My status as a regular does result in a certain efficiency of communications.

After the first sip, I was in no rush to finish the drink. I had a lot of thinking to do and all afternoon to do it in. I had a feeling it was going to be a three drink, maybe even a four drink problem.

I had just about finished the first of those drinks when the front door opened. I turned to see a stocky figure silhouetted against the light outside. I didn't recognize the shape, but as it appeared to pose no immediate threat, I turned back to the contemplation of the ice melting in the glass in front of me.

The newcomer took a stool close to me. This violated the etiquette of the Blue Moon and most good bars, where normally, given a nearly empty bar, the polite thing to have done would have been to have sat at one end of the bar or the other, as far as possible from any previous occupants.

I looked at the slightly distorted image in the mirror behind the bar. It bore a resemblance to a carrion crow, a sharp beaked face dressed conservatively all in black except for a sliver of white at the neck that broadened to a small square just over the Adam's apple. I recognized the face from a previous case as one Father Pagani, an agent of the Curia of the Reconstituted Catholic Church.

The good father ignored me and engaged in a muted conversation with the bartender. After a moment or two, the bartender turned and retrieved a rather dusty bottle for the highest shelf behind the bar. From the father's choice, it appeared that the Church was doing well for itself. Two fingers of the amber liquid were poured into one of the special glasses the Blue Moon reserves for only the best liquors.

The padre took an appreciative sniff before asking "I trust you remember me, Mr. Sladek?"

"Well enough. I thought you had gone back to Earth."

"As you know, my work takes me hither and yon. I indeed have been back to the Holy See in Las Vegas, but I have returned on a new mission."

"I'm sorry to hear that, father." Earlier, I alluded to the fact that Pagani was an agent for the Curia, what I left out was that he also acted as muscle and occasional hit man whenever the Church required a bit of dirty work.

"I bear you no grudge, Mr. Sladek, and I trust you harbor no ill-will against me. I was only acting in a professional capacity. Please, join me in a drink. Bartender, another of what I'm having for my friend here." The bartender knew me well enough not to draw any conclusions when I accepted the snifter. The Blue Moon is my unofficial office and I've had drinks with any number of unsavory characters.

"Perhaps it would be better if we continued our conversation in one of the booths."

I shrugged, picked up my drink and went over to one of the booths along the wall opposite the bar. Not that the change of venue was necessary, the place was empty except for Pagani and myself, and the bartender knew enough to keep out of earshot.

Without any preamble, Pagani said, "I believe you knew a man by the name of Lars Kendricks." It was not framed as a question.

"I've had a drink or two with him over the years. He's dead now."

"Yes. I heard. How unfortunate for him. May his soul rest in peace."

"I'm not sure that Lars had a soul, father."

"Oh, we all have souls, Mr. Sladek. Even you."

"If you say so, father. Me, I have my doubts. Why the interest in Lars? He never struck me as being the religious type."

"Perhaps not. I never met the man, myself."

"You didn't answer my question."

"I see you are as blunt as ever. Very well, then, I'll get to the point. Rumors are that your friend Kendricks came into possession of a certain item of, shall we say, historical interest. My superiors have charged me with recovering said item. As you know from our last encounter, Mr. Sladek, much of my vocation consists of restoring the patrimony of the Holy Church."

"And this item once belonged to the Church?"

"Not exactly," Pagani equivocated, "but the Church is interested in its recovery for political reasons."

"I would have thought that politics would be of little concern to the Church."

"I don't believe that you are that naïve, Mr. Sladek. The Church exists in a secular universe, and politics are a way of furthering its interests."

"OK. I'll buy that. Getting back to this item. Just what are we talking about?"

"Oh, it's a book. A diary, in fact. Not particularly large. About so big—" he measured out dimensions in the air with his hands. The dimensions matched those that I had felt in the bag Lars had left me.

"Oddly, enough, padre, you aren't the first to approach me about this item that Lars was supposed to have had. Why just last night I was discussing the matter with some gentlemen at the Excelsior Hotel. They seemed to have acquired the notion that Lars had left it with me."

"Yes, I am aware of your encounter, Mr. Sladek. Boris and Natasha. I'm pleased that you survived intact."

"Boris and Natasha?"

"Not their real names, of course. It's a code name we in the Curia's intelligence bureau use for them. They are, in fact agents of the Interplanetary Confederation, rather dangerous ones, I might add."

The Confederation was a rather loose political grouping of fringe planets of a particularly militaristic and expansionist leaning. Nordholm was one of the members. Someone had described them to me as fascists. I looked up the term later. It seemed to fit.

"Just what is their interest in this—item? I wouldn't think they'd have much in common with the Church. Or am I wrong?"

Pagani took a sip from his glass and looked across the table at me as if judging how many of his cards he should reveal.

"Just how well do you know your history, Mr. Sladek?" he asked finally.

"I admit that there are some gaps in my knowledge. After all, history happened so long ago. I tend to live in the present."

"A common enough, attitude, Mr. Sladek, but a mistaken one. The past has a lot of influence on the present. The reverse is also true. The way the past is interpreted depends on the politics of the moment."

"And this is leading up to--?"

"You are aware, of course, of the somewhat chaotic conditions that followed the struggle for independence initiated by Crockett and some of the other, at the time, colonial worlds? Conditions that I might mention caused the dissolution of the original Church."

"I've got some vague notions of that period, yes."

"It took some time for things to recover. Some planets, such as Crockett, recovered fairly quickly and have become quite prosperous worlds with a distinctly democratic bent. For others, the recovery took much longer, and the political situation was resolved along other lines. Among those systems are numbered those of the Confederation. They took much longer to achieve stability and then only under the leadership of a man named Jonas Kent. Are you familiar with the name."

"I've heard it. Frankly, I never thought he was a real person."

"Oh, he existed, Mr. Sladek. But you are right in one aspect, he has assumed an almost mythic place in the philosophy that underpins the Confederation, where he is almost worshipped as a god."

"I gather the Church sees this as competition?"

"Actually, it is somewhat the other way around, Mr. Sladek. The Church is seen as an opposing force by the planets of the Confederation and the exercise of religious freedom is denied."

"I never took much interest in religion, but my understanding is that religious freedom is mostly taken to mean only the freedom to believe what the advocate believes."

"You do take the cynical view of things, don't you, Mr. Sladek?"

"I've been accused of that. But what does all this have to do with this item or diary or whatever it is?"

"The diary is one that was kept by Jonas Kent at the peak of the struggle to found the Confederation."

"OK. I can see why the Confederation might want to get their hands on it, but what is the Church's interest?"

"You don't understand, Mr. Sladek. In this diary, Kent kept a record not of his public pronouncements, but of his innermost thoughts, and those thoughts often ran counter to his more public statements. If the diary were to be made public, to be published, it would shake the very foundation of myths that the Confederation was built on."

"If you know this, what does it matter if the diary is recovered or not?"

"Because, Mr. Sladek, so far, this is only rumor. The person who found the diary wrote a description of what he'd found, but shortly thereafter he was killed and the diary disappeared again."

"How convenient," I remarked.

"Yes. For the Confederation. Which is why they are so eager to recover the diary so that they can destroy it and suppress the contents forever."

"OK. I can understand that part of it. What is the Church's interest in all this?"

"As I said, the whole Confederation is based on the myths surrounding Kent. If those myths would prove to be false it might very well cause the downfall of the Confederation, thus providing an opportunity for the Church to fill the void. At the very least, it might weaken them enough so that they would be forced to grant concessions to the Church."

"Sounds like you're playing a dangerous game, padre. It seems to me that all religions are based on myths, and if you call one set of myths into question, why not all?"

"You are the cynic, Mr. Sladek. We of the Church are bolstered by our faith that what we believe in is true."

There was a flicker of fanaticism in Pagani's eyes.

"I appreciate the history lesson, father, but I'm not sure what all this has to do with me."

"Come now, Mr. Sladek. You were friends with Lars Kendricks. We have reason to believe that somehow he came into possession of the diary. What would be more natural than to think that you might have some knowledge of its whereabouts. Or that you might even be in possession of the diary, itself. I'm obviously not the only one who this thought has occurred to, as witness your escapades of last night. I know that Boris and Natasha kidnapped Mrs. Kendricks in hopes of exchanging her for the diary. Fortunately, you were clever enough to outwit them. But you were observed and you did have the diary—"

"Or a reasonable facsimile. What was in the bag that I took to the Excelsior was just a city directory. Or Feldman's book. I'm not sure which. I made up two fake packages just in case."

The padre smiled. "I must remember not to underestimate you, Mr. Sladek."

"In any event, I don't have the fake. Mrs. Kendricks walked off with it this morning."

"You mentioned two fakes, I believe."

"Yeah. The other is in the safe in my apartment."

"And the real diary?"

"I've never seen it, and it's not in my possession." Both of these statements were technically true, which is the secret of selling a lie.

"A pity, Mr. Sladek. The Curia would be willing to pay a great deal of money for the recovery of the diary."

"That's good to know, padre. I'll keep it in mind. But my real concern is to find who killed Lars. You wouldn't happen to have any insight on that, would you?"

"No, Mr. Sladek, I'm sorry to say I don't. And if you were perhaps thinking that I had anything to do with his death, I was on Earth at the Curia in Las Vegas. You can check on that, as I'm sure you will."

"Oh, I think that you can count on it. Well, thanks for the drink, father. It's been enlightening."

"As you wish, Mr. Sladek. One thing more, though. A word of caution. I wouldn't go trusting Mrs. Kendricks too far. I think there is more to her than is obvious."

"From the way she left this morning I think I've seen the last of Mrs. Kendricks."

Of course I was wrong about that.

A couple of days passed. During that period Sovia didn't turn up. Neither did blue-eyes and brown suit, or as Father Pagani had called them, Boris and Natasha. I was a little surprised about that, as I would have thought they'd have made some attempt to recover the package, which they probably thought was hidden somewhere in my apartment.

I made no move of my own to retrieve the real package from the locker at the TransGalactic building, reasoning that that was probably the safest place for it. As I knew what was inside the bag, at least if I believed Pagani, there was no real reason for me to lay my hands on it.

I was starting to think that the whole business had blown over, when things got hot again.

I was crossing the street in front of my apartment intending to get an early start on the day's drinking at the Blue Moon when a police cruiser pulled up to block my path. Inside was Latimer.

"Get in." It wasn't a request. One of the rear doors popped open. I got in. The door shut.

The back seats of police cruisers aren't designed for comfort. The seats are hard with hooks sticking out to attach shackles, and the space is cramped. The doors don't have handles. There's a clear plastic partition two centimeters thick between the rear compartment and the driver. Needless to say, the windows don't roll down, either. At least Latimer hadn't slapped restraints on me.

It wasn't the first time that I'd enjoyed a ride in the back seat of Latimer's car; I knew it wasn't likely to be my last. Latimer wasn't saying anything, but after a minute or two I knew that we weren't headed to that squat blot on the architecture of Star City that is police headquarters.

Finally I asked, "Hey, Latimer, where are we going?"

Latimer just grunted. I guessed he was in one of his moods.

We drove down city for maybe a kilometer into a neighborhood mostly given over to short term rentals. We pulled up at one of these. There were a couple of more cruisers parked out front and a meat wagon from the Medical Examiner's office was backed up to the front door. That could only mean one thing, that there was a body inside that hadn't expired from natural causes. I still wasn't sure what connection Latimer thought there was to me.

The door popped open again. I took the hint and got out and waited on the sidewalk for Latimer. There wasn't any point in running. Besides, I was getting curious. As far as I could remember, I'd never been to that particular building before, though in that part of Star City they all tend to look alike.

Latimer joined me. He'd made no effort to park the cruiser where it wouldn't block traffic, but then, on Star City there never is much traffic.

Latimer grunted, "Fourth floor." There are times when the detective sergeant could be incredibly terse.

We took the stairs for the simple reason that there wasn't an elevator. We were both huffing by the time we reached it. Latimer didn't have to tell me the apartment, there was enough activity going on to figure that out.

The apartment was typical enough, a small bedroom off to one side, a bathroom next to it, the rest of the unit given over to a combination sitting, dining, and kitchen area. It looked like it probably came furnished, if one could call the beat up sofa, arm-chair, and flimsy table furniture. Not great, but livable if you only had to put up with it for a month or two. I'd grown up living in far worse, and look how I turned out.

There was a forensic team doing what they do at crime scenes. Rossetti was sipping joe from a styro cup and staring out the window. He barely looked up when he saw us.

The M.E.'s crew had gotten the body into a bag and onto a gurney and were about to wheel it out when we stepped inside. I didn't envy them the chore of getting the body down three flights of stairs. You'd think there would be a better way, but there isn't.

"Hold up," Latimer ordered. He unsealed the bag and pulled it open to reveal the face.

He asked, "Know him?"

I looked, but I didn't know him from Adam. "Should I?" I replied.

"I thought you might. Your name and number is in the address list on his comm." Latimer gave a wave to the M.E. technicians telling them they could move the body out. "Just so you know, he was shot in the heart with a laser at close range. Bled out almost immediately."

"I've never seen him before in my life," I said. I think Latimer believed me. Maybe because it was true. "Any idea who he is?"

Latimer grunted. "His I.D. says his name is Rell Simplad. From New Nova Scotia."

I tried to remember where New Nova Scotia was, but failed. "Why do I get the feeling you don't believe it?"

"Maybe because there's no record of a Rell Simplad ever entering Star City, and certainly not from New Nova Scotia. There isn't any such a place. I checked."

That explained why I couldn't remember where it was. In the previous millennia, humanity had spread out to so many planets, no one could keep track of them all. It appeared that "Rell" had been counting on that fact.

"Sounds like you've got a mystery on your hands, Latimer."

"I don't need any jokes out of you, Frank. I've got a dead body on my hands and my feet hurt. Any idea why your name is in his address list?"

"It pays to advertise?" I could see Latimer wasn't in a joking mood. "Seriously, not a clue, Latimer. I've never seen the guy before. I've never received any calls from a Rell Simplad, either. You can check."

"I already have," Latimer said with a tired shake of his head. "I'm going to ask you again, Frank, any idea why he had your name? Any case you're working on?"

"The only thing I've worked on lately is the Lars Kendricks case for his widow, and that arrangement is over."

Latimer raised an eyebrow at that.

"Where is the widow Kendricks?"

"I don't really know. Like I said, she indicated my services were no longer required. She only paid me for a couple of days, anyhow."

"And you don't think there's any connection?"

"Not that I know of. At least Sovia never mentioned anyone else being involved."

"And no one else has approached you about Kendricks?" I got the feeling that Latimer knew more than he was letting on. I decided it was time to drop him a crumb.

"There was one guy. You remember that black crow from the Reconstituted Catholic Church?"

"Pagani?"

"Yeah, that's him. Well, he's back. He came up to me in the Blue Moon a few days ago. Asking questions. He seemed to think that Lars might have been trying to peddle something. He spun me a story about a diary that Jonas Kent was supposed to have kept. I didn't know whether to believe him or not."

"And you didn't think of mentioning this to me?" Latimer asked with some irritation.

I shrugged. "It didn't seem important."

"You got anything else you don't think important that you want to tell me?"

"Pagani mentioned that there were two other guys looking for this diary. The names are Cumberland and Nathan or something like that. Might be working for the Confederation."

"Great, that's all I need. A couple of birds working for the Confederation and an agent of the Vatican. Any other tidbits up your sleeve, Frank?"

"That's about it, Latimer."

"And this 'diary?' I don't suppose you know anything about that?"

"I've never seen it in my life. It probably doesn't even exist. You know how stories like that get spread around."

"Yeah, by private dicks playing their own game," the sergeant said cynically.

"That hurt, Latimer," I replied with mock anguish.

"Getting back to Kendricks' widow. Funny thing, Frank. She checked out of her hotel, but there's no record of her taking passage on a starliner or registering at another hotel. Know anything about that?"

"Maybe she's staying with friends?"

"Like you, Frank?"

"She's not staying with me," I said, maybe a shade too quickly.

"Like that, is it," Latimer said, shaking his head. "There wouldn't have been anything between you and the widow Kendricks, would there?"

"Our arrangement was purely business, and as I said, the arrangement is over. I doubt I'll ever see Mrs. Kendricks again."

I'd said that twice, but even I was starting not to believe it.

"Look, Frank. Whether this damn diary exists or not, it looks like somebody already has gotten themselves killed over it. Two people, if you count Lars. It would make my life simpler if no one else got killed. If you know of anything or if you find out anything, I want you to let me know. You got that, Frank?"

"Sure thing, Latimer. If there's anything I think you need to know, I'll be in touch."

"Why don't I believe you, Frank?"

"Can I go now?"

It looked like Latimer was going to respond, but instead he just said, "Get the hell out of here."

That incident gave me a lot to think about. If the body in the apartment was tied in with Kendricks' package, then someone was willing to go to great lengths to retrieve it. The question was who. The field already seemed loaded with players; Boris and Natasha, Pagani, probably Sovia. The dead guy had been a player, too, just one who had not been very good at the game. Someone had killed Rell Simplad, either to put him out of the game or in an attempt to get information. Pagani was quite capable of killing someone if he had to, but he hadn't struck me as a cold-blooded murderer. I didn't know enough about Cumberland and Nathan to rule them out, especially Nathan, but neither one of them had struck me as being as efficient at the job as whoever had done the killing. As for Sovia, I had to admit that I didn't want to think about her as a killer. So what did that leave me with? It seemed like there might be another party looking for the package, one that was more ruthless than the others. I didn't find the idea particularly comforting.

It was a couple of days after that that my apartment was broken into. It was a professional job done with a minimum of fuss and damage. I only realized it myself when I noticed that one of the little tell-tales I leave around the apartment had been disturbed.

I did a quick recon of the place. Nothing was missing, nothing was out of place, but someone had gone over the apartment quickly and thoroughly. I could tell by the little things, the carefully ordered books in the bookshelves were out of alignment, one of the paintings on the wall wasn't quite level, the spacing of my shirts on their hangars in the bedroom closet wasn't quite as I'd left them.

I opened the safe in the back of the closet. All the weapons were there as well as the stash of ready cash that I kept in case I needed it in a hurry. What was missing was the second dummy package that I'd made up. I asked myself, what kind of burglar takes a plain envelope and leaves nearly two grand in small denomination Crockett currency? I was afraid I knew the answer;

someone who knew what they were looking for and had a good idea of where it was.

They had also known their business. Now, I admit that the security on the Aldeberon Arms isn't what it should be. The building is almost two hundred years old and maintenance has been a little lax the last century or so. My apartment was a different matter. I'd replaced the locks on the front door with ones that, if not state of the art, were certainly good enough to discourage the casual break-in artist. The safe, too, was pretty good quality, not impregnable, but capable of defeating anyone not an expert. Yet both the door and the safe had been penetrated handily without leaving so much as a scratch. I knew most of the quality break-in men on Star City, at least by reputation, and it didn't look like the work of any of them.

Whoever had pulled the job had had a pretty good idea of my habits. I'd gone down to the diner on the corner for some lunch and then stopped across the street to the Blue Moon for a quick one before returning. I'd been out of the apartment for maybe a hour and a half. Not exactly a lot of time for that kind of caper, especially mid-afternoon when the chances of running into someone were high.

I had one more thing to check. I've got a camera that runs constantly taking images once a second and storing them on a memory stick. It's concealed in a nick-knack hanging on the wall, and it's equipped with one of those fish-eye type lenses so that it pretty much covers everything in the living-room and front hall.

I popped the memory stick and plugged it into the entertainment system. What I saw didn't reassure me. I forwarded through until I found the time where the front door opened. A few frames later, I saw the door shut. The images hadn't shown anyone entering. I kept watching as the system played the next few minutes of images. It was like watching a ghost or an invisible man. I could see books being pulled out of the shelves and pushed back in, but there wasn't any hand doing it. Instead, what I saw was like a ripple moving across the room. Whoever had broken in had worn a distorter, a piece of high-end tech designed specifically to confuse imager optics. They are expensive and not readily available. Most planets restrict their usage to the military and law-enforcement. Star City tends to be looser in such matters, but it was still not something your average burglar was likely to have.

I watched through the whole image sequence until the door opened and shut itself again. It had all happened in under five minutes. The invisible thief had known the layout of my apartment, probably not that hard to find out, and had had a good idea of where the likely hiding places might be. I don't invite that many people up to my apartment, but enough people had been there that someone enterprising might ferret out that information. There were other ways to find those things out, too; if you have enough resources. The problem was, it didn't fit the profile of any of the known suspects. Pagani, from what I knew of him, played a lone hand, relying more on bluffs and cash than direct action. It hadn't appeared that Boris and Natasha had been overly endowed with resources, certainly not the kind that I'd just witnessed. If they had, they wouldn't have tried anything as crude as snatching Sovia and using her as leverage. I wasn't even sure that Sovia was a player in the game, at least not more than the opportunistic type. Sure, she'd walked out with one of the dummy packages, but it had just been laying on the table, a temptation to great to resist.

The only conclusion I could draw was that there was another person, or persons, involved, one with skills and resources that the other players didn't have, and one who was both capable and ruthless.

It wasn't a cheering thought. I debated informing Latimer, but decided to hold off, at least for the moment. Latimer was a complication I didn't need. He was too likely to start asking embarrassing questions at the most inconvenient times.

As I went about my business the next few days I kept having this feeling that I was being shadowed, but if I was, they were good, as I wasn't able to spot them. Nathan, the man in the brown suit, went in for that kind of thing, but I knew what he looked like, and I was certain it wasn't him. Pagani, in his black outfit, should have been easy to spot, if he had been tailing me. As for Sovia, she was hard to miss. That meant the most likely suspect was the unknown party, the one who had killed Rell Simplad.

I didn't like the idea of an unknown player in the game. The hairs on the back of my neck seemed to stick up at the slightest provocation. I took to going armed any time I stepped out of the apartment, something I didn't normally do without a reason, but the weight of the laser in a shoulder holster was somehow comforting.

Latimer checked back with me a couple of times, which was out of character for the police detective. We both had more questions than answers, but neither one of us was able to satisfy the other with any useful information.

Things dragged on until I got the call from Sovia.

"Frank? This is Sovia. I need your help. I'm in trouble."

It wasn't exactly what I had been expecting to hear, but then it wasn't exactly a surprise, either.

"What kind of trouble?" I didn't bother to ask what kind of help she needed. I had a pretty good idea as to what that would entail.

"I'm being followed. Frank, I'm afraid." It's always hard to read someone's emotional state over a comm, but there was an edge to her voice that indicated she might be telling the truth.

"Who is it? The two guys that kidnapped you?"

"Yes, I think so. At least I think I've spotted the skinny guy. The one who was wearing the brown suit. He's been following me for the last three hours, at least. Can you come get me?"

At that point, I didn't really feel that I owed Sovia anything. After all, she had robbed me, but I had a feeling that if I kept her in play, it might lead me to whoever had killed Lars. Besides, I've always been a sucker for a desperate woman.

"Where are you?"

"I'm in Founder's Square."

That was good. Founder's Square was a large plaza at the up end of the city. It was close to some of the big hotels and a favorite with tourists. At that time of the day, it was early afternoon, there would be lots of traffic and people hanging out.

"That's good. Park yourself someplace conspicuous near the tram stop and I'll come pick you up. I should be there in under twenty minutes. Can you do that?"

"Sure, Frank. If that's what you think is best. But hurry."

"I'm leaving now."

I checked the charge on my laser pistol and stuck it back in the shoulder holster. I also had a rig holding a needle gun in the small of my back. It's uncomfortable, but hard to spot under a jacket. I realized that I might be overreacting. Cumberland and Nathan weren't likely to want gunplay in a place as public as Founder's Square, but I didn't want to take any chances.

From my apartment I took a brisk walk through the Souk to the nearest tram stop. The up line from there ran up to the square. When the tram arrived, I waited until the last moment to board to see if anyone else got on. They didn't. The tram was almost empty, just a couple of tourists and a guy dressed as a maintenance worker. From the Souk to Founder's Square is about two kilometers. With stops, it takes about ten minutes.

As the tram pulled up to the stop, I scanned the square, more from habit than hope that I could see anything. Founder's Square is actually rectangular, about eighty by a hundred meters. There are benches, a handful of statues of people no one remembers and a sprinkling of food carts. In the early afternoon on a typical day there might be as many as a thousand people just standing around or walking across the empty space. That day was typical. You could tell the out-of-towners, because they were the ones staring up at the spar that runs down the central axis of Star City and beyond it to the far side of the cylinder that I call home. I'm told that there isn't another view quite like it in human space. It's all I've ever known. Frankly, I find the thought of looking up into a blue sky that extended forever kind of frightening.

It didn't take me long to spot Sovia. She was wearing a gray skirt and a red high-necked sweater and knee length black boots and was sitting with her legs crossed on a bench not far from the tram stop.   She was eating a meat tube sandwich, which reminded me that I hadn't eaten since breakfast.

I didn't approach her right away, but kind of circled around the bench looking to see if I could spot Boris or Natasha. The one problem with a crowd is that it's too easy for someone to hide without being obvious about it. At least I was sure that if either of them was in the square they weren't within twenty meters of where Sovia was sitting.

After I had completed my circuit, I walked up to the bench from the front. Sovia played it cool when she saw me, making it look as if we were friends meeting by appointment. Acting casually, she handed me a paper-wrapped bundle, another meat-tube sandwich. For that, I could almost forget the fact that she'd stolen the fake package from my apartment. I unwrapped it and took a bite.

After I had swallowed I asked, "Where's the man in the brown suit?"

She took a last bite of her own sandwich and then gesturing with the wrapper answered, "Over there, about thirty meters by the drink cart."

She was handling the whole situation like a professional. I should have wondered about her handling things so smoothly, but at the time I was more concerned with the matter at hand.

"OK. I see him.   Have you spotted the other one? Cumberland?"

"No." That didn't necessarily mean anything. Cumberland could be hidden behind a food cart, or he could be somewhere on the other side of the plaza. He might even be watching us from one of the buildings that surround the square. It didn't really matter, if he wasn't close by, he wouldn't be able to move fast enough to follow us when we made our move.

"In a couple of minutes, we're going to get up and walk over to the tram stop. Make it look casual, as if we're in no hurry. Oh, be sure to toss your wrapper in one of the waste receptacles. Littering is frowned upon."

"Which tram are we going to take?"

Founder's Square is one of the places where a circumferential line meets one of the four up/down lines. The timing is arranged so that stops on both lines overlap for a minute or so making it easy to make connections. Most locals never give it much thought, but at one time someone gave a lot of consideration to the workings of the tram system.

"I haven't decided yet. We'll wait to see what Mr. Brown-Suit does."

"Whatever you say, Frank." I appreciated the fact that she wasn't second guessing me, but I should have recognized that as another sign that she wasn't an amateur.

We sauntered over to the tram stop which occupied one corner of the square. Brown-suit was moving, too, not quickly enough to draw attention to himself, but headed toward the stop.

Flashing lights indicated that a tram was approaching. There were about two-dozen people waiting. We took a place on the platform. So did Nathan. I caught his eye as he stood there. I think he was surprised that I'd spotted him.

The circumferential pulled to a stop. Etiquette dictates that boarders wait until everyone who wants to disembarks, which suited my plan. The lights started flashing for the approaching down line. Brown-suit had figured out what I was planning and started to look a little nervous.

The two trams were stopped, and people started to cross from one to the other as they made connections. Almost everyone had gotten onboard when the lights started to flash signaling departure. Brown-suit was looking at me trying to figure which way I was going to jump. Just as the buzzer sounded, I grabbed Sovia's hand and dragged her onto the circumferential.

We slid into one of the seats. Out of the corner of my eye I caught brown-suit jumping onto the tail end of the tram. He almost didn't make it. Sovia looked at me quizzically.

"Don't get settled. We're getting off in two stops." Two stops ahead was where the circumferential intersected another of the up/down lines.

We stayed put for the intermediate stop. When we pulled into the intersecting stop, I motioned to Sovia to keep her seat. We waited while other passengers got off and new passengers boarded, then just as the buzzer sounded I stood up and pulled Sovia to the exit.

Across the aisle from us were a couple that looked like they came from Crockett. I don't know if they overheard us, but the man looked at us as if he thought we were crazy.

The tram had just started moving as we stepped off. As it pulled away, I saw brown-suit staring out the tram window at us. I couldn't resist the opportunity and waved.

"What now?" Sovia asked.

"We grab the next down tram and then we go for a ride."

She gave me a look of uncertainty.

"Brown-suit will have figured out that we are trying to lose him. It won't take him more than ten minutes or so to get back here. The up-line only goes for another half a kilometer, so he'll know that we'll take the down line."

"Then wouldn't make sense to take the up-line?"

"Trust me, I know what I'm doing. I've been playing this game since I was a kid, Sovia."

The down tram came and we got on. It was nearly empty, and we had a compartment to ourselves.

"OK. You know what you're doing. What do we do next?"

"Sit back and catch our breath. Then we ride the tram for a while and see if we're being followed. If we are, we try to lose him."

Sovia started to say something but thought better of it.

"Do you have a weapon?" I asked.

She opened her purse to show a laser pistol. It was a small one, 25 kiloJoule. Not much in the way of stopping power, and it probably had a long cycle time, as well, but it would be good enough for close range work which was all we were likely to run into.

We rode the down tram six kilometers, about as far as you can go and still stay in a half-way respectable part of the city. The stop where we got off wasn't in a fancy plaza. Instead, it was just a platform along one side of a street. On the other side of the street were a number of small shops, the kind that cater to the needs of the working class types that lived in the neighborhood, most of who worked in the hotels and restaurants up at the top end of the city.

I ushered Sovia around a corner to a spot where I could keep an eye on the platform. Then we waited. The next tram halted at the stop a few minutes later. There was no man in a brown suit. We waited for the next tram. He didn't get off, but I thought I saw his thin face through the window of one of the cars. I didn't think that he had spotted us, but he was still on our trail. Sooner or later he'd realize he'd gone too far down city and start to double back.

We caught the next up tram and took it to the next circumferential which we rode halfway around the city, then hopped on another up tram and rode that two kilometers up. I could see that Sovia was starting to wonder if I was a bit crazy.

"See that kid over there," I said, indicating a boy who might have been anywhere from thirteen to a young looking twenty. "He's doing the same thing that we are."

"Which is?"

"Trying to lose a tail. I don't know what he's done, maybe stole something, picked somebody's pocket, wrote something nasty on a shop window. Maybe no one is really after him and he's just doing it for fun. But he's trying to lose whoever might be following him."

As if to confirm my point, at the next intersection with a circumferential he got off. As we pulled out we could see him get aboard the circumferential tram.

"You seem to know a lot about it," Sovia said.

"When I was his age, I was doing the same thing. I ran messages for a minor league gambling operation. Later I was a bag man. Either case, it didn't pay to be followed."

"You grew up around here?"

"No, not here. My neighborhood was rougher, just this side of New Minglewood, both physically and metaphorically."

I could tell that she was puzzled by my reference.

"New Minglewood is the slum of Star City. It's where the crooks, the unemployables, the grifters hang out."

"Yet you use words like metaphysical."

"I've learned a lot since then. That's how you survive; by being smarter than the next guy."

"How—why did you become a detective?"

"I figured out pretty fast that people who were doing what I was doing, that were maybe a year or two older than me, didn't last long. They either got themselves killed, died of an overdose of something or other, or ended up being jettisoned out one of the waste chutes. I started getting a reputation for being able to find stuff, things, people. I found myself working the other side of the law, the good side. It doesn't pay as well, but your chances of collecting are better. Eventually I even got a license."

Our conversation might have continued, but I decided it was time to change trams. We did that for another hour or so until even I had to check the station numbers to figure out where we are. Brown-suit was nowhere to be seen. I wasn't as sure about the other one, the one that I had sensed but not seen following me the last few days.

"So what do we do now, Frank?" Sovia said. I could see that she was getting tired. So was I. And hungry.

"We find someplace to hole up for a bit. We can't go back to my apartment. Cumberland and Nathan know that you're with me. That will be the first place they'll look."

"But if we check into a hotel, won't they be able to find us?"

"Yeah. If we check into a hotel. But there are plenty of places that rent out short term that don't produce a record. That's kind of why I got off at this stop."

The neighborhood we were in had a lot of transients, people new to Star City, people changing jobs, people just needing a new place to stay. My plan was to walk the streets until we spotted a vacancy and then rent a room for a week.

It didn't take long to find a place. The landlady was a little suspicious at first. Sovia was dressed a little too upscale for the neighborhood. Me, well I can fit in anywhere. I managed to assuage her suspicions by paying in advance in Crockett dollars and adding a double saw-buck as a "security deposit." She handed over the key to an apartment on the third floor, and that was the last we saw of her.

The place wasn't bad, actually. There was a bed tucked away in an alcove, a worn sofa, a table and a couple of chairs to eat on, and a two burner cook-top to prepare meals on. Behind a flimsy door was a bathroom with a shower. It was all surprisingly clean, as well.

"Make yourself at home," I said as I locked the door.

Sovia plopped down on the sofa, crossing her legs and looking beautiful in the backlight that came from the only window.

"I want to thank you, Frank. I'm sure that Cumberland and Nathan would have kidnapped me again, if it wasn't for you."

"Probably. If not them—well there are other players in the game."

"Oh?"

"Yeah, there's a black crow of a priest named Pagani. He spun me a story about what he thinks is in the package. There was another guy, as well, but he's dead now. The thing is I don't think either Pagani or Boris and Natasha, excuse me, Cumberland and Nathan, are responsible. That means there's at least one other party after Lars' package."

"About the package, Frank. Do you have it?"

"I thought you had it, Sovia. You grabbed it from my apartment before you left, didn't you?"

"Maybe I did, Frank. After all, as Lars' wife, it's rightfully mine, isn't it?"

"Maybe. You could have asked, though."

Sovia turned her big brown eyes on me. "I guess I wasn't thinking, Frank. Lars told me that he was onto something that would make us rich. You don't know how much I wanted that. It doesn't matter, though, does it. The package was a dummy. But you knew that, didn't you, Frank?" she asked accusingly.

"Maybe," I agreed. "What did you find when you opened it?"

"A ten year old city directory. Unless Lars thought there was something in it that was worth a lot. But there wasn't, was there?"

"You were the lucky one. You might have gotten a copy of Feldman's book." I could see she didn't get the joke, but I didn't see the point in explaining it.

"You've got the package, the real one, don't you, Frank?"

"No. As a matter of fact, I don't," I answered. In a way, I was telling the truth. I'd never bothered to pick up the key from the mail-drop where I'd had it delivered and the package was still sitting in the TransGalactic lobby. I figured it would be safer that way. I'd left word to hang onto the letter with the key until I called for it. "But I can get my hands on it, if I need it."

"Whatever you think best, Frank," Sovia said. We both knew that she didn't mean it, but it sounded good.

"Look. I'm going to go out for a bit, get us some food and stuff. Is there anything you need?"

"No. I'm fine, Frank."

"Will you still be here when I come back?"

"I'll be here."

There was a little grocery on the corner. I picked up a few items that could be cooked on the little stove in the apartment, enough so that we wouldn't have to leave for a few days if we didn't want to. I added a bottle of brown and one of a cheap white wine, as well.

Across the street was a store that sold candy, magazines, and other small non-perishables. One of the things they sold were "burner" comms. I don't have any idea where the name comes from, but the deal is that people in transit on Star City for more than a day or so can buy a short term comm unit, one that is only functional for a week or two. If they're smart, when they're about to depart, they sell it to one of the buyers waiting at the departure gate. They get five credits and the buyer gets a unit that can't be traced to the next purchaser that it is sold to. It's a long established racket on Star City. The one I picked up was only good for three more days, but then I wouldn't be keeping it that long.

I'd turned off my own comm when I'd left my apartment so that my position couldn't be followed. Any calls for me would be held in a storage facility until retrieved.

Before going back to Sovia, I checked to see if there were any messages. The only one worth playing was from Latimer:

"Frank, there's something I think you need to know. I ran a check on that woman who claims to be Lars Kendriks' wife. I'm still waiting on word about that. But I did find out something curious. I also checked her arrival records. Nothing surprising there; her arrival matches what she's claimed. But the computer did a cross reference as a matter of routine. There was a woman matching her biometrics exactly that was present on Star City at the time Kendricks was killed. She left the next day. The name and identity don't match, of course, but according to the biometrics, it's the same woman. I'm not sure what it means, but I thought you'd want to know. I've tried to get a hold of you, but you're off the grid. Give me a call when you get this."

I turned the comm off and went back to Sovia.

She was still there when I got back to the apartment. I hadn't been sure of that. We had a dinner of warmed up meat stew washed down with the cheap wine. We didn't talk much over the meal, though I had a feeling we both had plenty to say. Afterwards, Sovia laid down in the narrow bed. I sat up drinking brown with a splash of water while I thought over what Latimer had said in his voice message. By the time the bottle was half empty, I still hadn't reached any decision. I gave it up and joined Sovia in the bed. She didn't object.

Sovia was awake and sitting up in bed when I woke up in the morning. She was looking at me intently, but I couldn't read her expression.

"Why didn't you tell me you'd been to Star City before?" I asked, trying to sound casual.

"I don't know what you mean, Frank," was her reply.

"You were here, on Star City, at the time that Lars was killed. You weren't using your own name or identity, but it was you. Either that, or you've got a twin sister somewhere."

She looked as if she was going to deny it, then realized that that wasn't going to work.

"How did you find out?"

"In case you've forgotten, I am a detective." I didn't see any need to go into the details of my relationship with Latimer.

"I see. You've been checking up on me."

"Wouldn't you? If you were in my place, I mean. You come breezing in claiming to be Lars' wife that I didn't know he had. I asked around. I know a lot of people. They got back to me."

"Alright. I admit it, I was here. What of it?" I couldn't be sure if her defensiveness was real or just an act. I couldn't be sure of anything about her.

"Maybe nothing. What's your story?"

She looked around as if trying to find an escape route. Instead, she saw the bottle of brown and poured a couple of fingers worth into the glass I'd been using the night before. She drank about half of it straight in one gulp. She didn't even wince.

"I was here because Lars had sent me a ticket. He said he was on the verge of a big deal that would make him—us—rich. I didn't know what it was all about. Not at the time. All I knew was that I wanted out of where I was and Lars seemed to promise a way to provide that. He was supposed to meet me when I arrived, but he never did. I found a hotel room and waited. After a day I found out he was dead. I was running out of money, I didn't know anyone, I wasn't sure why Lars had been killed. For all I knew, I might be next. I bought a ticket back home, and left."

"And you didn't have any idea what this big deal that Lars was working on was?"

"No. Lars never talked much about business. He never talked much about anything that mattered, except how he was looking for the big score, the big deal that would set him up for life. He always had big plans. That's what had attracted me to him. The fact that he had plans, real plans. Not like the losers back on the one space port planet where I came from. Lars had been places. I knew that."

"So how did you find out? About the package, I mean?"

"A couple months ago a man came around. Asking questions about Lars. He was interested in a package that Lars had, he said. He asked me if I knew where it was. He was willing to pay good money for the package or information that would lead to it."

"What did you tell him?"

"The problem was, I didn't know anything, so I made up a story. The only thing I knew about Star City and Lars was that he'd mentioned your name a few times, about how the two of you would go out drinking whenever he was docked there. So I made up a story about how Lars had given you the package for safe keeping."

"Just like that?"

"Yeah. Just like that. I wanted the money he was offering. Lying seemed the only way to get it."

"So you sold this guy a line and took his money. What then?"

"I got to thinking. Maybe my story was close to the truth. Lars had told me that you were some kind of private detective or something. He'd thought that that was a big joke. But he always made you sound like you were someone who knew his way around both sides of the law. I thought maybe that if Lars thought he was in trouble, he might turn to you, maybe leave this package with you for safe keeping. That's pretty much what happened, isn't it?"

The reality was that it pretty much was. The question was had she known that or had she just been guessing.

"So you got your money. Why did you come to Star City?"

"As I said, I got to thinking. This guy had given me a lot of money for my story. A thousand dollars Crockett. If he was willing to pay that much, this package that he was looking for must be worth a lot more than that. A whole lot more. More than a waitress could ever hope to make. I had the thousand dollars and a little more, besides. I decided to take a chance and come here. I thought that if I could find the package and sell it, I'd be set for life, or at least for a long time."

"Or end up dead," I reminded her. "That's what happened to Lars."

"Yeah, well living the way I was living wasn't much better. I decided to take a chance. So I came here and looked you up, figuring that you would lead me to the package."

I reached for the bottle of brown. There wasn't another glass available, so I took a swig straight from the bottle. There were just enough details to Sovia's story that it just might be the truth, or some version approximating it. Or, it might be a complete invention, the kind of story that would sucker a guy like me in. At the time, I had no way of deciding which. I wasn't sure that it mattered. The whole business was coming to a head, whatever part Sovia was playing.

"This guy, the guy that paid you the grand in Crockett, what did he look like?"

"I don't know. He was just a guy. I'd never seen him before. Medium build, a little above medium height, not bad looking. A little bit like you, Frank." The last part came out in a bedroom voice, or at least what women like Sovia think of as one. The important thing that it didn't sound a bit like Father Pagani. It didn't sound like either Boris or Natasha, either, which just meant there was another faction involved, though I'd been pretty sure of that already.

"Look, Frank. You said you could get your hands on the package. Is that the truth. If it is, then we can go get it, sell it, and split the money between us."

"If I'm the only one who knows where the package is, why can't I just sell it on my own and keep all the profits?"

"Because you're not that kind of guy, Frank. You wouldn't cheat Lars' widow out of something that really belongs to her. But I'm willing to cut you in, because I need someone who can play it straight and who will protect me. What do you say, Frank? Do we have a deal?" She sounded desperate. Her offer was tempting. Potentially, it was a lot of money, even split two ways, and her tone implied that she was offering herself as part of the deal if I wanted her.

"There's one problem, Sovia. I know where the package is, and I can pick it up whenever I want. But I don't know where to sell it. It's not like we can just run an add 'Package for sale, best offer. Previously owned by Lars Kendricks,' and wait for someone to contact us."

"I know someone who will buy it. Or at least I have an address to contact. The guy who paid me the money left it with me."

"Here on Star City?"

"Yes."

I thought it over.

"You know there are other parties that might want in on the act."

"But do they have the money to back it up?" Sovia countered.

"Maybe, maybe not. But I'm not sure how they'll take to being cut out."

"Once we turn over the package, it's someone else's worry, Frank. The sooner we get rid of it the better."

"I have to agree with you on that," I responded. I noticed that she had said "we," though we hadn't come to an agreement. I decided to let it slide.

"What do you say, Frank? Do we have a deal."

I tossed her the comm. "Make a call to that address you've got. See what they say. Don't worry, they won't be able to trace the call on that unit."

She started dialing.

I hadn't bothered to try and overhear the conversation Sovia had made. I knew that if there was a double-cross in the works, I wouldn't pick up on the fact by anything that was said over the phone. What she told me when she was done was that she had arranged a meeting in three hours. The person on the other end had agreed to pay a hundred thousand Crockett which Sovia and I would split evenly between us. The meeting itself was to take place in a hotel room at the Excelsior. For no good reason, the Excelsior seemed to be the epicenter of this whole business, a theme that kept popping up. I wondered if Boris and Natasha were back in residence.

"Are you okay with this deal, Frank?" Sovia asked, when she had explained it to me.

"Sure, Sovia. Whatever you are comfortable with," I replied, trying to sound sincere. I'm not sure either one of us bought it, but it was what it was. "Just one thing, how far do you trust this guy? Is he really going to hand over a hundred G's for the package?"

"I trust him, Frank." But I could hear the doubt in her voice. "Can we go get the package now?"

"We've got plenty of time. It will only take us an hour to retrieve the package and make it to the Excelsior."

"Whatever you say, Frank."

We'd finished the wine the previous night, but there was still about half a bottle of the brown. I found a second glass in the bathroom, used a towel to wipe it off, and then poured a couple of fingers of liquid into each glass before handing one to Sovia.

"Here's to a hundred thousand dollars Crockett, Frank," she said before tossing half of it down.

I made my own toast. "Here's to Lars."

She looked at me with those big eyes of hers wide in surprise, but she finished the rest of the brown. I took a sip of mine, and then set the glass to the side. I didn't feel like drinking any more at the moment.

After that we waited a couple of hours. Sovia sat on the edge of the narrow bed where we'd spent the night. I sat in a chair staring out the window. There wasn't much to see, only another grimy building much like the one we were in.

When the time had passed, I asked, "Are you ready?"

"I'm ready as I'll ever be, I guess, Frank."

Sandy's is a small store front in a non-descript part of town, not good, not bad, just there. It sells candy, legal recreational pharmaceuticals, lottery tickets and all the other little items people can't seem to do without. The owner, whose name was not Sandy, but George, also acts as a postal drop of convenience.

For a small fee, he'd hold things sent to his address with no questions asked until the recipient chose to retrieve them. It was a very useful service for a certain class of people.

From the apartment, it was only a short tram ride to Sandy's. George was behind the counter when I walked in with Sovia following me. George paid more attention to Sovia than to me, but then he'd seen my mug before, and there weren't that many women as good looking as Sovia that frequented his shop.

"Got anything for me?" I asked casually, as if I wasn't sure there'd be anything or not.

"Let me check," George said and then disappeared into the back room. He returned a few moments later with the envelope I'd sent myself. "Just this," he said as he placed it on the counter. I dropped a Crockett fin next to it. George looked up at me. The normal charge for a letter was a buck.

"For luck," I said as I picked up the envelope.

Outside, Sovia said, "That's not the package."

"No it isn't," I responded. "This thing has already cost a couple of lives. Do you think I'd trust it to a place like that?" She looked confused. "We'd better get moving if we're going to make our appointment."

We took another tram up to the TransGalactic building. It was the middle of the day and the lobby was crowded which suited me just fine. I pretended to be getting my bearings as I scanned the crowd, but I didn't recognize any of the faces.

I walked over to the machine by the bank of lockers and stuck the card in the slot. The display flashed the amount I owed on the locker. I inserted a credit stick to pay the fee, and the card popped out, the locker number C-347 now displayed prominently on the front. I took the card over to the locker, stuck it in and the door popped open. The package was still inside. I pulled it out. On the way out of the building, I tossed the card into the hopper next to the machine, freeing C-347 for the next customer.

"Do you mean the package has been sitting there in a locker the whole time?" Sovia asked, incredulously.

"Can you think of a safer place? It's been guarded by the whole force of TransGalactic security. Can't get much better than that."

"You continue to surprise me, Frank."

"I'm not an amateur, Sovia."

Twenty minutes later we were in the lobby of the Excelsior waiting for an elevator. I hadn't recognized the clerk at the desk, which meant that he hadn't recognized me either, which was just as well.

The room where we were to make the exchange was on the seventh floor. I knocked and opened the door. It looked much the same as the one Cumberland and Nathan had used, except for the fact that there was a man inside holding a laser pointed at my chest. He used the pistol to motion me inside. I noted that he hadn't pointed it at Sovia.

I didn't recognize the man with the laser, but Sovia seemed to. I guess I wasn't surprised by that. Sovia was smart enough, but this whole business had had the fingerprints of someone more experienced and ruthless behind it.

"I take it that this means that you don't have a hundred grand for me?"

"Very perceptive of you, Sladek. Why don't you remove that pistol from your holster and toss it on the bed. Do it carefully, if you want to live a little longer."

I didn't see any point in disobeying. I didn't recognize the make, but it was a large laser, 65 KiloJoule at least. I reached in with the thumb and forefinger of my left hand and pulled out the pistol by the barrel, pitching it over onto the bed. The man with the pistol picked it up and placed it on the table behind him.

"Now hand the package to Sovia."

At least I knew now they were on a first name basis. I handed the package to Sovia who moved off to the side once she had it.

"Open it."

Sovia said, "Can't we just get out of here, Carl? We've got what we came for."

"I want to make sure that it's the real thing, Sovia. Sladek has played games with the diary before."

"I'm sure it's the real thing this time."

"Open it," the man with the pistol commanded.

"Whatever you say, Carl." Sovia reached into her purse and pulled out a tiny knife which she used to slit the outside film of the package. Inside, was a small book bound in what looked like leather. It had a small clasp that kept it closed.

"Look, Carl. It's the real diary just like I said. Now let's get out of here."

"We can't. Not until I take care of Sladek. He knows too much, now. He knows that we killed Kendricks and Dietweiler."

I didn't know who Dietweiler was. I figured he must have been the dead man that Latimer had showed me.

"Hasn't there been enough killing, Carl?"

The look in Carl's eye said that he didn't agree. From where he stood there was maybe a sixty degree angle between Sovia and me. I could see that he was trying to decide which of us to kill first.

That moment of indecision is what got him. His laser was swinging towards me, and I could see his finger tightening on the trigger. Then there was a look of complete surprise on his face before he slumped to the carpeted floor. I looked over at Sovia who had a tiny laser in her hand, the kind that they sell to women for security, the one she'd showed me earlier.

I'd thought it likely that she had had some kind of weapon on her, likely enough that I hadn't bothered to check. Now the laser was pointed at me. With a little pistol like that I couldn't be sure what the recycle time was before it was ready, but as the seconds ticked away the likely hood of it being recharged increased.

"Tell me, Sovia, which one of you was it that killed Lars? You, or Carl here?"

"Does it make a difference, Frank?"

"I suppose not, but I'd like to know all the same. I figure I owe Lars that much."

"As long as you're so eager to know, Frank, it was me. The idea was Carl's, but I was the one that pulled the trigger."

"And Lars was just a poor sap in the way."

"You really didn't know Lars very well, did you Frank. He was as much of a schemer as Carl was. How do you think he got the diary? He didn't just find it, you know."

"Oh, I had no illusions about Lars. He'd said enough over the years when we were having drinks together that I knew he'd been up to some shady things in the past."

"You don't know the half of it, Frank. Lars had a way of using people. I wasn't the only 'wife' that he had. He used me. When you think about it, he used you, too. He could have gotten you killed by handing you the diary for safe keeping. He nearly did."

"Yeah, I suppose. But I'm a big boy, and I knew there were risks. So what now, Sovia?"

"Now. Now I walk out of here with the diary. That's what happens. And if you are smart, you won't come after me."

"No one has ever accused me of being smart, Sovia."

"That's too bad, Frank. I kind of liked you. You're the only honest man I've ever met. It's too bad we couldn't have met under different—"

"—circumstances," I said. I had my needle gun in my hand pointed at her chest. "Yeah, I could have wished that too, except I don't think it would have worked out."

"You're probably right, Frank. Okay, we've both got guns and we're both willing to use them. Why can't we just call it a draw? Let me walk out of here, Frank."

"I don't think I can do that, Sovia. You killed Lars. He may have been a crook and a cheat, I won't deny it. But he was a friend of sorts. That counts for something."

"You know he wouldn't have done the same for you, don't you, Frank?"

"No, I suppose not. But then I never asked him to."

Her eyes betrayed her. I knew she was going to shoot, so I shot first. The needles caught her in the chest, tearing into her heart. I hadn't had the heart to shoot her in the head, though it was a surer shot with a needle gun. Her pistol had fired wide, missing me by a meter.

I was standing over her body when Pagani came in. He had a laser in his hand, but when he took in the scene, he didn't look as though he was going to use it.

"Behold the wages of sin."

"I suppose you're here for the diary?"

"What else. You have no objection, Mr. Sladek?"

"It's just a book to me. You weren't the one that killed Lars Kendricks."

"An interesting viewpoint, Frank. Somehow, very moral."

He walked over to where Sovia had dropped the diary and picked it up. I noticed, with that part of my mind that deals with survival, that the aim of his pistol didn't waver from me.

He fumbled with the catch of the book for a moment, then got it opened. He thumbed through a few pages at first, and then more until he had rifled through the whole volume. Then he began to laugh. Not broadly, but a little chuckle as if he were entertained by some private joke.

"You'll find this amusing, Mr. Sladek," he said, and then reading the expression on my face continued, "or perhaps not. But take a look for yourself."

He handed the diary over to me. I pocketed the needle gun. There didn't seem much point for it anymore. I leafed through the pages of the diary. They were blank. All of them. If Jonas Kent had ever written a diary, this wasn't it.

I handed the diary back to Father Pagani.

"I suppose you're disappointed?"

"Maybe, maybe not. I've learned to take these things philosophically. While the Church would have liked to have possession of the real diary, perhaps this sham will do as well."

"I'm not sure I follow you, Father," I said, confused and drained.

"As far as anyone knows, Lars Kendricks had the real diary. Now they will think that it's in the possession of the Curia. For the Church's purposes, that will serve as well. It will give us a point of leverage to use for the greater good. There's only one problem, though. Two people, at least know the truth, you and me, Mr. Sladek. I know I won't tell but you—"

"I'm not a political animal, Pagani."

"No, that's true. But I need to ensure your silence on the subject."

I looked at the man in black. He still held his pistol on me, but he didn't seem ready to shoot."

"You're the one with the gun."

"Oh, I wasn't thinking of anything as crude as that, Mr. Sladek. After all, the Church does consider killing a sin."

"I'll remember that. Just what are you proposing?"

"What if I were to offer you five thousand dollars Crockett for your silence? Would you take it? Just on the contents of the diary, not any of the peripheral matters."

"Just like that? I promise not to say that the diary was blank and you give me five grand? You'd trust me?"

"Why not, Mr. Sladek. I know enough about you to know that you're a man of honor. After all, you tracked down the killer of your friend."

I looked down at the body of Sovia. I hadn't loved her. I hadn't even really liked her, but I had shot her just the same.

"It's agreed then?" Pagani asked.

"It's agreed."

"Good. I'll be off then. It would be better if I wasn't involved in this," he waved has hand around the room. "You might do well to do the same yourself, but I will leave that to you to decide."

With that, he walked out of the room. I waited half an hour for him to get clear before calling Latimer. The next day I discovered that five thousand dollars had been deposited to my account.

AUTHOR'S AFTERWORD

Unlike the first two Star City collections, I wrote the novellas in Three Body Problems around a common thread, how Frank Sladek handles himself in the situation of being confronted with an inconvenient body. It's not a particularly new idea in hard-boiled detective fiction, but I think placing it in the context of science fiction makes for some interesting results.

Other than that common thread, the three stories don't have a lot in common. They were written over the span of more than two years as I worked on a number of other projects. One is serious, one is comic, and one falls somewhere in between. I'll let you judge which is which. The only thing they really share is Sladek's unique way of dealing with problems.

A number of reoccurring characters from the previous Star City collections make appearances, including the mysterious Lucinda. Partly, this is because I am lazy, but I also think makes Star City seem more like a real place.

For those readers who are interested, I wrote An Old Friend first, followed by The Corpse with Four Arms, and finished with The Corpse That Wasn't, not that it really matters. Each story is complete unto itself.

As with the other books, Three Body Problems is probably best read at night with a glass of brown on the rocks in the reader's hand and some jive samba playing softly in the background.

SPECIAL PREVIEW!

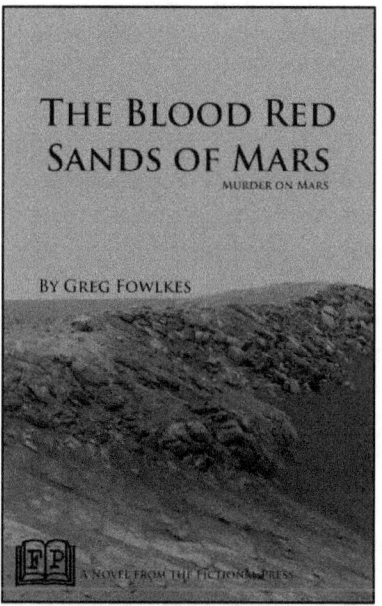

THE BLOOD RED
SANDS OF MARS
By Greg Fowlkes

Book One from the Murder on Mars Series

Now available from The Fictional Press
www.TheFictionalPress.com

THE BLOOD RED SANDS OF MARS

The wind was blowing again against the west wall of the hut. He could hear the grains of sand abrading the thin aluminum skin that protected him from the outside. Through the window, half frosted from the continuous onslaught of sand and dust, he could see clouds of dust obscuring the sky. The sky was a pastel pink, a color no sky had any right to be. The wind, despite its 120 kph. velocity, made only a thin howl as it blew over the half buried cylinder of the hut.

McKernan lay on his cot trying not to admit that he was awake. It was a losing battle. After a few minutes he surrendered and glanced over at the clock sitting on the crate next to his bed. The dim red digits of the LED display read 7:58. It was too early to get up, too late to go back to sleep. He rolled over, shivering at the cold. The temperature couldn't have been more than ten degrees Celsius inside the hut. For the twentieth time he thought to himself that he would have to fix the heater before winter—if he could get the parts. Either that, or put in more insulation—if he could find that. The cold finally forced the decision to get up.

Standing, he felt the cold plastic floor beneath his bare feet. With his foot he fished the worn and patched pants from beneath the cot and pulled them on. He dug underneath his pillow and came up with a switchblade knife that he stuck in his pocket before drawing on the turtleneck sweater that had lain next to his pants. The cold feel of the cloth did nothing to dispel the cold from his body. From the crate he picked up a shoulder holster with a small automatic pistol and put it on. McKernan drew the weapon, worked the slide once, and after examining it perfunctorily, placed it back in the holster. Satisfied, he pulled on a worn pair of leather boots and placed another knife in a sheathe between his skin and the boot top.

Dressed, he went over to the shelf that served as counter and table. He put a pan of beans onto the heating unit and got a soysteak from the small refrigerator that held up one end of the shelf. The steak went into the frying pan on the other heating element. An egg would have been nice, but at the current price of three dollars apiece it was an extravagance that he would have to put off for a while.

As the food cooked he drew a liter of water from the spigot in the corner of the hut and watered the plants in the garden under the window. The carrots and tomatoes were doing nicely. He smiled briefly because it would be good to have fresh vegetables for a change. The big, leafy oxygen plants were doing well, too. He would be able to cut down on his oxygen ration this month and save some money.

He took the beans off the heating element and replaced them with the coffee pot. The beans were still half cold, but he wasn't in the mood to hassle with them. He only had the two heating elements, and he didn't want to have to wait for his coffee. He forced down the beans and then wolfed down the steak. It almost tasted like real beef, but then maybe his memories were fading. As usual, the coffee tasted terrible and tepid, too. The air pressure in the hut was too low for water to boil properly.

He finished his meal and scraped the remnants of food into the pressure vessel that served as a compost heap. The gauge on its neighbor showed that he had almost half a tank of methane. He'd be able to sell that soon and use the money for something useful, like a still. Completing his rounds, the gauges on the life support systems showed that everything was still working at keeping him alive. He went back to the pots and scrubbed them clean with sand. That, at least, was plentiful and cheap.

He checked his watch against the clock. It was time to get going. Pulling on his jacket he went to the airlock at the corridor end of the hut. After checking the gauge to make sure that there was pressure on the other side, he undogged the latches and stepped through. Closing the door behind him, he repeated the process with the outer hatch, latching both doors behind him. The outer door he locked with a heavy padlock.

He had entered a low tubular corridor made of the same aluminum foil and plastic foam construction as the hut. The walls, however, were even thinner, and no pretense was made of heating it. He could see his breath condensing in front of him as he began to walk down its length. It was a hell of a way to live, he reflected, not for the first time. But then, it had been hell living in L.A. where he'd been born, with brown air, rats, a chronic shortage of water, and overcrowded tenements. He had made his choice, but sometimes it seemed as though life was a continual shiver.

The corridor was pierced at regular intervals by hatches identical to his own. The huts behind the hatches were identical, too, except for the modifications the owners had made to make them more livable. This part of the city was old, dating back a couple of decades to the first days of the settlement when it had been part of a scientific base. The scientists had departed, at least from that corridor, and been replaced by those who had the money to buy or rent the huts from the Trust Authority. Maintenance was pretty much left up to the residents.

Along the sides and overhead ran the pipes and conduits that pumped in the gases, liquids, and power necessary for sustaining life. The whole system looked as jury rigged and fragile as it actually was, though surprisingly few people died whenever the system failed. Martians were a cautious lot. One didn't talk much about injuries. Accidents on Mars didn't leave many.

A hundred meters down the tube he came to an airlock. Going through the same ritual that he had used on his front door, he went through to another length of corridor indistinguishable from the one he had just left. Continuing on, he passed through two more airlocks until he entered a corridor that sloped downward. The hatches were farther apart, and larger. Signs overhead indicated the businesses or functions that were carried out behind them. The air was warmer because the corridor was buried beneath the sand which provided insulation. At the end of the tunnel was a larger airlock set into a wall of fused silica bricks, the first substantial piece of construction he had met that morning.

Passing through the portal was like entering another world, which in a way he had. This was the public Mars, the planet seen by the corporation men and the officials of the Trust Authority. It was also the planet seen by tourists, the brave new colony, man's first outpost on another planet. The tourists didn't really care to see the hut town. They were part of the same world as the corporation men and the government types. It still took a great deal of money or power to reach Mars.

The difference was more than one of degree. For one thing, the temperature was a comfortable twenty. For another, the walls were flat and met the floors and ceilings at right angles, unlike the inflated skins of the huts and corridors. With a little imagination it could almost be an enclosed shopping mall on earth, though the presence of fused silica blocks was more prevalent than any architect would allow.

The most important difference, however, was the sight of people scurrying along. He hadn't met anyone in the outer corridors. People rarely lingered there because of the cold. Now, McKernan could see at least twenty people and it was still fairly early. No airlocks interrupted this corridor. Extending for two hundred meters in either direction, it was twenty meters wide and ten high, the largest enclosed volume on the planet. Arrayed along its length were the offices and store fronts of the corporations that owned Mars, as well as the more prosperous saloons and bordellos.

One day the Trust Authority promised that the whole city would be like that, with apartments and condominiums for the ordinary workers, but neither the Authority nor the corporations had yet come up with the money. For the moment all that existed was the one street of a few blocks.

McKernan headed towards the Authority's offices which dominated one end of the mall, but turned aside at the last moment when he noticed that a small, dark doorway was open. He knew that he should resist the temptation, but he was not in a very disciplined mood. He went through the doorway into the darkness beyond.

Finnegan's was the only real, honest bar on Mars. There were any number of saloons and even a cocktail lounge in the Mars Sheraton, but only one quiet, dark place where a man could drink in peace. McKernan felt the need for some of that peace at the moment.

He sat down on one of the stools before the only mahogany bar on Mars. Finnegan, himself, was behind the bar, though in fact he almost always was, no matter what the hour. The bartender looked up and greeted the newcomer, "Good morning, Constable. Beer or whiskey?"

"It's too early for beer. It's too early for whiskey, but give me a shot, anyway."

Finnegan poured out a shot glass of amber liquid and placed it before McKernan and then stood back polishing a glass while he studied the man opposite him.

McKernan knocked back half the glass before he spoke. When he did, there was a bitter edge to his voice. "Sometimes I wonder if it's worth it, Finnegan. I could be back on a planet fit for human life."

"Could you, now, Constable?" Finnegan said, putting down the glass and picking up another in equally gleaming condition. "If mother earth was such a bed of roses, why are you here?"

He breathed on the glass and examined it against the light for a moment, then looked at McKernan with the same intentness. "You're here because you're not the sort to live off the dole or to spend your life with another man being your boss. Instead you'll spend your life trying to make this planet a fit place to live and retire in twenty years with a nice pension. Now drink up and get to work, laddy."

"Yeah, sure. Sorry to burden you with my problems. Early morning depression, I guess. See you." He finished off the shot and left five dollars in Authority script on the bar.

The bite of the whiskey so early in the morning didn't really help his disposition, but it did give him enough courage to make it to the office. The morning ritual at Finnegan's was becoming too much of a habit. His three years on Mars were beginning to show.

The jail wasn't in the brick part of the Authority building, but in the complex of pneumatic architecture that sprawled behind it. The huts were old—older than his own—but dated back to the days when governments had not begrudged a few billions for exploration, back before space had to show a profit. For that reason, they were sound and well insulated, though a bit tacky looking.

The jail consisted of two huts joined together, one for offices, the other for the two makeshift cells and storage. Ferris was the only one there when he walked in, a young kid, younger than he had been himself when he had come to Mars. He was still impressed enough with his responsibilities and had not yet been worn down by the grim realities to take his job in any way but seriously.

Ferris greeted him with a solemn, "Good morning, sir," with a stress on the sir. As a three year veteran of Mars, Ferris looked on his boss with more than a touch of awe.

"Anything exciting happen overnight?" McKernan didn't really expect much. A few fights in the saloon district, a knifing maybe if things got out of hand. Petty thievery, or perhaps not so petty. He looked at Ferris and saw a flash of excitement in his eyes that the younger man was trying hard to suppress in order to match the hard bitten image he had of his superior.

"Yes, sir. We've got a murder on our hands."

"Another knifing down at Thelma's?" he asked, naming an infamous saloon and bordello that figured in a quarter of all the police reports.

"No. A prospector was found out on his claim yesterday, over on the far side of Olympus Mons. He was shot, Inspector."

That was bad, McKernan thought. People on Mars weren't supposed to have guns. With the thin skins of most buildings and a hostile atmosphere outside that would support life exactly as long as you could hold your breath, they were dangerous, and not just to the targets. The Authority had made them illegal and the corporations had been more than willing to agree. They weren't easy to get—not something that could be picked up casually or made, like a knife. Even without the details it sounded like the work of a real criminal and not just a squabble over a claim or a woman.

"Okay. Let me have the report. I'll take a look at it."

He took the folder from Ferris who looked a bit crestfallen. He probably expects me to go rush off to the outside and track down the murderer like an Indian scout, McKernan thought. He'd learn in time. Mars was a big planet and a dangerous one, but because of its nature there were also very few places that a man could run to and none where he could hide indefinitely.

He was leafing through the report when he came to his door. For the thousandth time he read, "Inspector Erik McKernan, Chief Constable." Mother would have been proud, he thought sardonically. She had hated the L.A. cops like all the other residents of the barrio. He went through the door into the little cubicle that was his real home. There, sitting at his desk, he began to read the report, sketchy though it was, to look for some explanations.

The Blood Red Sands of Mars is available now from The Fictional Press. Find it on TheFictionalPress.com, or buy it on Amazon.com!

BOOKS BY GREG FOWLKES

From the Wizard at Law Series:
The Laws of Magic
Trial by Magic

From the Murder on Mars Series:
Blood Red Sands of Mars
A Death at Station Alpha
A Corpse in Hut Town
Murder at the Mars Club

From the Fictional Detective Series:
The Fictional Detective
A Fictional Detective Trifecta

Star City Stories: Space Opera Noir Featuring Frank Sladek

The Uncorrupted Corpse

Tequila Visions

Cargo From Paradise

Ice Viking

FROM THE WIZARD AT LAW SERIES BY GREG FOWLKES

THE LAWS OF MAGIC

Egil Njalsson was an aspiring lawyer. A lawyer with a difference. Not only had he passed the bar, but he had an undergraduate degree from the most prestigious school of magic in the country, the California Institute of Thaumaturgy. Needless to say his caseload and clients tended to the unusual. Like witches; or vampires. And the opposition, well they were likely to be demons. But Egil Njalsson had sworn an oath to uphold the law of the land, and... *The Laws of Magic*!

TRIAL BY MAGIC

Egil Njalsson is just another practicing attorney. Except, that is, for the occasional unusual client. Such as the ghost who retained his services using e-mail. Or the wolf who has been cursed by an Indian shaman to turn into a human during the full moon. Or the Leprechaun who is facing the loss of his saloon. Even when the clients are human, they have unusual problems like the Creole chef accused of making a rival a zombie or the scientist accused of transmuting a man into a statue of silicon. Yet somehow, Egil manages to resolve all his client's problems whether legal or magical. Of course it helps that he is a wizard as well as a lawyer.

Trial by Magic includes five new tales from the same world as *The Laws of Magic*.

FROM THE MURDER ON MARS SERIES BY GREG FOWLKES

BLOOD REDS SANDS OF MARS

On Mars the wind was rising. The grains of sand could be heard abrading the thin aluminum skin that was the only protection against the outside. On the far side of Olympus Mons a prospector lies dead in the sand. Inspector Erik McKernan, head of the handful of men that make up the small Martian police force must find the killer while threading the maze of corporate and international politics that govern the planet, and he must do it while trying to survive . . .*The Blood Red Sands of Mars!*

A DEATH AT STATION ALPHA

Station Alpha, a remote Martian research facility isolated by a planet wide dust storm. When one of the scientists is found murdered, it falls to Inspector McKernan to determine which of the remaining twelve people at the station wielded the fatal weapon. But, as the crime was committed in a locked laboratory with no possible access and all the suspects would seem to have unbreakable alibis, it will take all his skills as a detective to solve the puzzle of *A Death at Station Alpha*. Thirty years in the making, the long awaited sequel to *The Blood Red Sands of Mars*.

A CORPSE IN HUT TOWN

Hut Town is the remnants of the original Martian settlement; a collection of inflatable buildings abandoned by the Trust Authority and the mining corporations and now occupied by those catering to the baser needs of miners and construction workers in for a spree. But when a corpse is found in one of the service tunnels, Chief Inspector McKernan is called in.

He has plenty of questions. Who's body is it? How did they die? How did they get to Mars in the first place, and why weren't they missed? And the most important one on the Inspector's mind— are there any more bodies down there?

MURDER AT THE MARS CLUB

The Mars Club was the sanctuary of the rich and powerful on Mars, so when one of the members is found dead, Chief Inspector is called in to solve the case as discretely as possible. Will the solution of the case prove to be the one man he'd least like to implicate?

FROM THE FICTIONAL DETECTIVE SERIES BY GREG FOWLKES

THE FICTIONAL DETECTIVE

Mystery writer Ezekial O. Handler has been killed in a suspicious car crash. Private detective Frank Slade has been hired by Handler's beautiful girlfriend to investigate. Handler, seemingly with a premonition of his death, has left a trail of clues. Can Slade discover the murderer, or will he instead uncover a secret that will shake his existence to the core?

A FICTIONAL DETECTIVE TRIFECTA

The Fictional Detective has gotten out of the Private Investigator game. Instead, he's trying to write hard-boiled masterpieces such as *Death Buys a Condo*. But despite the fact that the door of his office now says WRITER, some of his clients haven't gotten the word. And a strange lot of clients they are. A man that only contacts him during séances because, well, he's dead; a female impersonator who has inherited a house that's just a little too haunted for the market, and a small time gambler who's trying to end an affair with Lady Luck.

Three All New Novellas featuring the Fictional Detective!

The Fictional Press
www.TheFictionalPress.com

The Fictional Press is a small, independent press specializing in the publication of fictional works by emerging authors. If you are interested in bringing your fictional works to life in print as well as electronically, contact us! We can help!

Find out more at www.thefictionalpress.com.

www.ingramcontent.com/pod-product-compliance
Lightning Source LLC
Chambersburg PA
CBHW070113030726
47506CB00002B/727